"I wouldn't do that if I
from behind them.

The man whirled around. Siobhan turned as well. For
a moment she couldn't see anything through the thick
mist, then a tall silhouette appeared through the white.
She could see nothing of his features, but something
about him chilled Siobhan to the bone.

The young rider slowly stood up and faced the figure
as it walked into the light. Siobhan clamped a hand over
her mouth to stop herself from crying out.

It was Euan, the Fey Prince. And he wasn't wearing
a glamour. She saw his true face, just as the man was
seeing his true face.

In the Serpent's Coils

By Venom's Sweet Sting

Between Golden Jaws

Maiden of the Wolf

Queen of the Masquerade

Oracle of the Morrigan

The Marsh King's Daughter
March 2009

Snake Dancer
May 2009

Redemption
November 2009

Ouroborus Undone
Spring 2010

HALLOWMERE ®

Volume Six

Oracle of the Morrigan

TIFFANY TRENT & PAUL CRILLEY

MIRRORSTONE

Hallowmere®
Oracle of the Morrigan

Cover design by Trish Yochum
Cover Art © Roy McMahon/image100/Corbis
First Printing: Sept. 2008

Library of Congress Cataloging-in-Publication Data is on file

9 8 7 6 5 4 3 2 1

ISBN: 978-0-7869-4974-8
620-21779740-001-EN

U.S., CANADA,
ASIA, PACIFIC, & LATIN AMERICA
Wizards of the Coast, Inc.
P.O. Box 707
Renton, WA 98057-0707
+1-800-324-6496

EUROPEAN HEADQUARTERS
Hasbro UK Ltd
Caswell Way
Newport, Gwent NP9 0YH
GREAT BRITAIN
Save this address for your records.

Visit our Web site at www.mirrorstonebooks.com

To Caroline,
Bella, and Caleb

-P.C.

PROLOGUE

To Frater Josephus from Pater Iamblicus, sincere greetings.

My Son:

Long has it been since you have graced these halls, but word nonetheless reaches me from the hands of our friends who watch over you. Doubtless you have heard that a strange power moves among the Fey. Elaphe does not yet understand the nature of it, but he cautions us all to be wary. He asks that you come to us and aid us in being watchful for this.

Children have been born on the border, children with Gifts. We do not know what this means. They are not as other children, not even like the children born between mortal and Fey. But there is hope that perhaps these children will reveal this power to us and what it means for those of us who hope to live in peace alongside the Fey.

I hesitate to say it, but if we could but find one with the Sight, perhaps such a child could lift the veil over this darkness that our friend senses but cannot see. Such a child could show us the way. I pray that God will forgive me for resorting to such heathen ways, but it is all we seem to have left. Come speedily, my son, and lend us the vigor of your youth.

Yours in Christ,

Iamblicus

~ ONE ~

SIOBHAN TRIED TO BREATHE IN, BUT HER FACE WAS PRESSED hard into the ground. It smelled of peat, of damp earth. She shifted slightly, wondering where she was, and heard a sudden noise off to her left, the rustling of something moving through leaves.

She clenched her fingers in soggy mulch, then slowly turned her face to the side, blinking rapidly to dislodge small clumps of mud from her eyelashes. Weak light filtered into her vision, a wet, gray light that bespoke the faint beginnings of a new day.

The noise drew closer, and on top of the rustling she heard snuffling, like an animal nosing through the undergrowth. She couldn't help but imagine the worst Unhallowed Fey she'd seen in her life, all spider legs and pincers, far worse than any wolf she might meet in the woods. Lying as still as possible, Siobhan prayed that whatever it was would stay well away from her. But her wet clothing chilled her, and her teeth started to chatter.

What had happened? The last thing she remembered was Corrine and Mara gathering them all in a circle, then all her friends fading into nothingness. And something else—Rory, breaking into the circle and grabbing Christina, dragging her off into another rath. Siobhan's breath caught in her throat. What would become of Christina? Would Father Joe go after her? Surely they couldn't just leave her. Not after all they'd been through.

Something moved against her cheek, wriggling like a cold finger. Siobhan stifled a cry and leaped to her feet, frantically brushing away leaves and dirt. An earthworm wriggled around on the leaves, then found a gap and burrowed back into the earth.

The snuffling had stopped as soon as she had moved. She paused, looking around to make sure she wasn't about to be attacked.

She was in a forest. The weak, gray light of dawn filtered through the branches of almost-bare trees. Her frightened breath clouded the air before her. She couldn't see any living creature. Just thick underbrush and lots of sycamore trees. Maybe she'd frightened the creature off.

But then her gaze stopped by the trunk of one of the trees, where a large bush grew up from between its gnarled roots.

Something stared at her from behind the bush.

She couldn't see what it was, just the glint in its eyes as it watched her. She shifted her weight in case she needed to run. A twig snapped, a loud crack that silenced the chirrups and tweets that had filled the early morning. The creature started, then turned and vanished into the trees, an orange-brown blur that darted through the undergrowth. Siobhan sighed, suddenly feeling lighter.

It was only a fox.

She looked around again, studying her surroundings more carefully this time. Trees closed in on her at all sides. She walked forward, the wet grass clinging uncomfortably to her legs. It looked like she was deep in the heart of the woods. But where were these woods? Father Joe hadn't been specific on how the spell would work that would send her and the other girls off to find the rathstone. Siobhan could be anywhere in any of the Unhallowed raths.

But no. She looked around in the dim light, studying the trees—lots of sycamore, but others as well. Yew and oak. It was all familiar to her. She was still in Scotland.

At least that's something, she thought as she set off.

She walked rapidly in an attempt to chase off the chill. She wasn't really sure what direction would take her to civilization, so she just picked one and started walking.

As the day gradually lightened, a morning mist appeared and slowly twined its way around the boles of the trees. It grew so thick that it soon covered her feet from the ankles down. She glanced over her shoulder and saw she was leaving swirls and eddies in the white blanket as she walked. The animal life in these woods was rich—birds sang when she walked quietly enough, and she saw signs of other small creatures—rabbit prints and even a deer or two.

After half of an hour of walking, Siobhan noticed that

the ground started to slope upward. She climbed the rise and found herself standing atop a bank that dropped down to a half-frozen stream.

She wanted to leave the shelter of the trees, but something told her to stay hidden. She wasn't sure what it was. A feeling in her stomach, a twinge of unease that called for her attention.

It wasn't the Sight. That felt different—more like someone slapping her in the face. This was something more mundane—a hunch. She dropped down to her knees, wincing at the cold, and shuffled forward until she pressed between the exposed roots of an oak tree. She surveyed the hollow below her, but she couldn't see anything out of the ordinary.

A second later a horse exploded into view on the opposite bank. It neighed loudly, breath steaming into the air, then slid noisily down the slope until it hit the water with a loud splash, cracking the frail ice beneath its hooves. Siobhan gasped, staring at the huge beast as it tossed its head and fought the reins that its rider held firmly. The horse neighed again, an action that caused the rider to lean forward.

"Quiet," the rider whispered angrily. "I'll not have you ruining this!"

The horse subsided with a snort of irritation, expelling twin clouds from its nostrils. Steam rose from its heaving flanks. This horse had been ridden hard.

She switched her attention to the rider. At first she thought he was huge, but after a moment realized this was because of the layers of clothing he wore. She could see dull tartan leggings wound about with dark fur for added warmth. A huge pelt of matted fur hung over his shoulders, hanging down his back and covering the horse's croup. His hair was long, hanging in sweaty disarray down to his shoulders. As he looked around, obviously searching for something, Siobhan realized with some surprise that he was quite young. Certainly not over eighteen.

From downstream came the sounds of splashing. The young man yanked the horse around and dug his heels in, sending the creature directly toward Siobhan's hiding place. She ducked down as the horse pulled itself up the bank, its front hooves landing not an arm's length from her face. She tried to push herself deeper into the hollow formed by the tree's roots, but she was already pressed right up against the bark.

The rider leaned over and gently patted the horse's neck. "Hush, Keir," he whispered. "Hold your tongue."

His calming words had the desired effect, as the horse stopped its stamping and finally lowered its head to tear at the wet grass. The rider peered upstream, where the sound of splashing was growing louder.

Siobhan craned her neck, resting her chin on a cold root. From this position she could see all the way to the bend in the river.

So she was perfectly placed to see the Fey as they came into view.

First came a woman sitting straight-backed atop her horse. She was breathtakingly beautiful, with long, golden hair bound in a thick braid that fell down to the small of her back. Her face was as white as newly-fallen snow, her amber eyes like a winter sun setting over a lake of ice.

Behind this woman marched four creatures that had Siobhan trembling with fear. Her first sight saw them as they looked to the world: tall, elegant, humanlike creatures sitting proudly atop mud-spattered chargers. But her Second Sight . . . her Second Sight saw them for what they truly were.

The first in the line was a huge, shambling creature with no head. It was the size of two men standing one atop the other. At the creature's side loped a green-tinged dog the size of a calf. Behind this monster strode a skeletally thin man. Or at least so Siobhan first thought. As she watched, his body stretched and he fell over into the water. When the splashes died down a gray horse ran where the man had been. It galloped down the stream a few steps, then it stopped suddenly and shrunk back in on itself, and the man stood there once again. He peered around at the riverbanks as if trying to catch sight of prey, then he walked on.

Taking up the rear was a creature with the broad shoulders of a human warrior but the head of a wolf. Light glinted on his sharp teeth.

Siobhan stifled a cry of fear and pushed herself back into the roots of the tree. She squeezed her eyes shut, trying to cut off the Sight, trying to fight off the sensory battering she knew was about to sweep over her mind and erase all sense of who she was.

Not now, she told herself. She opened her eyes again, thinking that if she could focus on something real, something tangible, then she would be able to stop the attack. But the ground pitched and swayed before her, even though she was absolutely still. Bile rose up in her throat, and she snapped her eyes shut again.

She kept seeing glimpses of the creatures, images that flashed past her mind's eye faster and faster until she could focus on nothing else. She could smell the rancid animal stench of the man-horse. He was coated in salty sweat that left a white mark down his back and legs. She could taste rotting meat in the mouth of the wolf creature. It had recently eaten a rabbit that had been far into decay. Her stomach heaved. Maggots had writhed in the rabbit's skin, but that didn't bother the wolf creature. It had eaten the rabbit, then had devoured every last wriggling maggot.

The huge, lumbering creature with no head had no thoughts, just a sense of hatred, an unspecified anger that seeped through its body like a poison. Siobhan tried to shy away from it, but the taint entered her and she could feel what it was like to hate everything in the world, to want to reach out to every living thing and simply crush away its life.

The only spark of compassion in its being was for the vicious dog that walked by its side. The dog acted as the creature's eyes, hunting for it, bringing back prey that was still alive, so the huge monster could finish the job of murder.

Stop. Please. Oh God, please make it stop.

She couldn't let the madness take her again. Not now. She would be discovered before she'd even had a chance to look for the stone. She couldn't let the others down, not after she'd finally said she'd help. She just couldn't.

And then she noticed something she hadn't ever seen before. A tiny patch of blackness. A gap in the whirlwind of sensory information. The hole was calm, a small dot of nothingness. A quiet shelter in a raging thunderstorm. Siobhan instinctively focused on it, and the patch of darkness grew bigger.

She wasn't sure if it was her desperation that had created it, or if it had always been there, but she wasn't about to complain. She gazed into the blackness, letting it grow with her attention and totally envelop her mind. It swallowed everything, all the alien sensations in her head, bringing silence to her thoughts in a way that made her think she had gone deaf.

But she hadn't. The noises of the forest still surrounded her. But her mind was quiet, the Sight subdued. That was the difference. She focused on the dark patch and concentrated on sealing it up again, trapping all the horrific feelings and emotions on the inside. It was difficult to do. It felt like something was straining to get out, that whatever she had put in there would not remain locked up forever.

So be it. At least for the moment, she would have peace, peace that she had never been able to feel before this moment. She wondered what had changed that allowed her to do this. She had never been able to hide the Sight away like this before. Had Father Joe done something to her before Corrine and Mara sent her here?

Siobhan opened her tightly closed eyes and glanced up

at the rider. He hadn't noticed her. His whole attention was taken up by the Fey.

For the first time she noticed the huge sword that was strapped to the side of his horse. Was he planning on attacking them? On his own? That was madness. There was no way he would be able to defeat them.

The rider carefully slid off the saddle and lowered himself to the ground. He was so close that Siobhan could almost reach out and touch him. He crept forward until he was at the lip of the rise, frowning.

The Fey drew level with their hiding place and stopped. The group of fairies didn't move; just stood stock-still. They were waiting for something.

The man crawled slowly backward and reached up to unfasten his sword.

"I wouldn't do that if I were you," said a low voice from behind them.

The man whirled around. Siobhan turned as well. For a moment she couldn't see anything through the thick mist, then a tall silhouette appeared through the white. She could see nothing of his features, but something about him chilled Siobhan to the bone.

The young rider slowly stood up and faced the figure as it walked into the light. Siobhan clamped a hand over her mouth to stop herself from crying out.

It was Euan, the Fey Prince. And he wasn't wearing a glamour. She saw his true face, just as the man was seeing his true face.

Except he looked utterly different from the diminished Fey Prince she had last seen. Here he stood tall and powerful. Every movement of his body told of barely restrained, primal energy. It was like watching nature take shape before her very eyes. He was . . . *vibrant*, dangerous. Beautiful and cruel. All the things nature could be. But there was something . . . inhuman about him. His face was longer, thinner, the proportions and angles ever so slightly off. It was hard for Siobhan to put her finger on what was so different about him compared to a human. It was as though someone had tried to put together a human after seeing someone briefly and at a great distance. All the pieces were there—they just didn't add up.

But it was his eyes that drew her attention and held it. They were dark, but they crackled with raw energy. Siobhan got the impression that those eyes could see into her soul, could see into her deepest heart.

As Siobhan watched Euan, she became aware of a slight movement in the woods around her. She looked around, half-expecting more of the Fey to step out of the mist.

But then she realized what it was—the branches of the trees were turning toward him. The effect was subtle, but she was sure it was there. The forest turned ever so slightly in Euan's direction, attracted to his energy like a magnet to metal. Even the scraggly grass that poked through the fallen leaves reached out to him.

Siobhan didn't understand what was going on. Why did Euan look so different? Where had he gotten the power he suddenly radiated? It was as if the Euan she had seen before and the Euan standing before her now were two different people.

The young man standing next to her sidestepped

forward. Siobhan tensed, readying herself to flee during the fight that was about to follow. But then the man did something that astounded Siobhan.

He laughed.

"Damn you, Euan. I thought I had your worthless hide this time."

And to Siobhan's utter amazement, the Fey Prince smiled and grasped the man's arm in a gesture of comradeship.

"Bad luck, Conal. You led us a merry chase, but you've a long way to go before you can trick one of the Fey."

"Aye, I can see that." The young man shook his head, bemused.

Siobhan looked from one to the other, not understanding what was happening. Why were they talking as if they were friends? Shouldn't they be fighting each other? Weren't they enemies?

But a second later all such thoughts fell from her head, because the Fey Prince turned slightly and stared directly into her eyes.

"And who is your friend?" he asked.

The rider turned in surprise and spotted Siobhan for the first time. She scrambled to her feet and tried to dart around them, but Euan was too fast. He lunged to the side and grabbed her arm. She cried out in fear.

"No, no, my pretty. Where are you going in such a hurry?"

He grabbed her other arm and lifted her off her feet. She kicked and squirmed but his grip was iron-tight; she couldn't move an inch. The Fey Prince cocked his head to the side and smiled, showing gleaming white teeth as he drew her close.

"Enough of that, Euan. You're scaring her half to death."

Euan frowned, still staring at Siobhan. Then he shrugged and dropped her to the ground. She caught herself and darted behind a nearby tree, desperate to put something solid between herself and Euan.

"Here," said the young man. Conal, the Prince had said his name was. He stepped in front of her, blocking Euan from sight. He crouched down. "Are you all right?"

Siobhan forced herself to look into his eyes. They were gray, deep set. He looked truly concerned. She opened her mouth, but only a frightened whimper came out.

"Leave her, Conal," said Euan. "Can't you see she's witless?"

Conal frowned. "No," he said softly, so that only Siobhan could hear. "Not witless. There's intelligence there." Louder, he said, "How did you come here, lass? Your clothing is fair strange."

Siobhan frowned. She had to concentrate on Conal's words to understand them. His accent was so broad, it was almost impossible to make out what he was saying. But she understood enough to realize she needed a story. Her mind raced furiously, trying to come up with something at least half believable.

"Uh . . . my mistress. She . . . she left me here."

"Left you here? Why would she do that?"

"My master. He was . . . he was making eyes at me. His wife thought I encouraged him. But I didn't, I swear it. He was fat and ugly. And . . . and he always fell asleep over his drink and drooled on the table."

"Sounds like you humans right enough," said Euan with a laugh.

Conal ignored him. "And?" he prodded.

"My mistress said we were traveling to visit her sister, but when we got to the forest, she threw me out the cart and left me here."

Conal stared at her thoughtfully. After a few moments he said, "What's your name, girl?"

"Siobhan."

"Siobhan. You're from Eire, yes?"

Siobhan nodded. "Yes."

"Conal," said Euan in a bored voice. "Can we go now? We've a feast to attend this afternoon and I need to get cleaned up."

Conal looked at Siobhan again, then he seemed to reach a decision. He stood up and held out a gloved hand to her. Siobhan stared at it blankly, then up to the tall Scotsman.

"I can't leave you here on your own, girl. People have been disappearing in these woods." Conal squinted up at the sky. "Besides, if you stay, you'll freeze your arse off. There's bad weather coming."

Siobhan hesitated, then took his hand and let him pull her to her feet. She glanced at Euan as she stood. The Fey Prince was watching her with a frown. But it was not one of anger. More of puzzlement. Almost as if he recognized Siobhan but couldn't figure out why.

"Picking up more strays, Conal?" he asked suddenly.

"Will you let this one warm your bed?"

Siobhan flushed with embarrassment.

"Don't mind him," said Conal. "We're of the opinion he and his people are half-animal. Unfortunately, that half happens to be the back end."

Euan laughed. "I'll see you back there, Conal." He walked past them both to the top of the rise that led down to the stream. He winked at Siobhan as he passed. "And you as well, my pretty."

Siobhan shivered and shrank back behind Conal. "Away with you, Euan," he said, and this time his voice had changed. There was steel in it.

Euan laughed and disappeared over the rise. Siobhan could hear him splashing through the water. She crept forward to get a better look. He was talking to the woman who had led the other creatures along the river, and seeing them standing side by side made Siobhan realize that she actually looked a lot like Euan—she had that same almost-human appearance, as if they had glimpsed people from a distance and tried to copy what they had seen from an imperfect memory. But there was something else different about her—for some reason her glamour and her real face had switched, and she looked more like Euan as Siobhan knew him before than the Euan she was looking at now.

As Siobhan tried to puzzle out what that might mean, the woman glanced up. They locked eyes, and Siobhan found herself unable to look away. It felt as though she was trying to see Siobhan's very soul.

"You coming?" said Conal.

Siobhan blinked, and the spell was broken. The woman turned away, and Euan led his companions off down the stream. Siobhan watched them go, waiting until they were finally out of sight before breathing a small sigh of relief.

Siobhan gripped her arms tightly around Conal's waist as his horse cantered through the sodden forest. The morning was cold and gray; the mist had thickened into a deep fog, shrouding the trees and casting the surroundings into a half-seen spirit world. Conal had given her his huge cloak, but water still managed to drip from the branches and slide down her neck. It felt like a finger of ice was caressing her spine every time one hit.

"No need to squeeze so hard," he said, turning his face to the side so she could hear him. "You're not going to fall."

Siobhan flushed with embarrassment and loosened her grip. "Sorry," she mumbled.

They traveled on for another few minutes.

"Uh . . . Conal," she said apologetically. "Sorry, but—"

Conal turned in the saddle, glancing over his shoulder at her. "Do you apologize for everything? You're allowed to speak, you know."

Siobhan flushed and lowered her head, staring at the ground passing beneath Keir's hooves. Conal shifted uncomfortably.

"Here," he said. "I'm sorry. I didnae mean anything by it. Just that you don't have to ask permission to speak."

Siobhan didn't look up.

"Come on now," he said gently. "What were you going to ask?"

Siobhan hesitated. Then she looked up again to see him staring at her. *He has nice eyes,* she thought absently.

"I was wondering . . . That person. Euan. What is he?"

Conal frowned, then understanding shone from his face. "Ah, I see. You *are* new around here." He shrugged. "They're the Fey, lass. You must know about them."

Siobhan thought carefully about what to say next. Yes, she knew about them. But to her knowledge, they'd never actually lived side by side with humans like this before. What kind of rath had Nephri's spell thrown her into? Were the humans here the Fey's slaves? But it didn't seem so.

"I've heard of them," she said cautiously. "Back home we call them the Gentry."

Conal chuckled. "Aye, they like that kind of thing. Makes them feel important."

"But I've never actually seen them before. I thought they . . . hid away from humans."

He nodded. "They do. Usually. I don't know why it's different here. Truth to tell, I've never really thought about it. This is the way it's always been."

"And . . . they're nice to you? The one that was here. Euan—"

Conal laughed. "Aye, he's a one, that Euan. You shouldn't mind him, though. He's a bit rough around the edges, but honorable."

Honorable? Siobhan stared at the back of Conal's head in amazement. She decided she would keep her opinions about the matter strictly to herself for the moment.

The next few hours of travel were something of a peaceful interlude for Siobhan. After all the trouble she'd been involved in, it was nice to pretend that her biggest concern was whether or not it would rain before they reached their destination. Conal kept up a steady stream of conversation as they rode. Half of it she didn't understand. He spoke so fast that it was sometimes hard to follow his accent. But after the first few times when she responded to him with a "Really?" or a "Mmm," when he had, in fact, asked her a question, he slowed his speech down to make sure she could understand.

He said he was the son of the local laird, which meant that his father ruled over the local village and was answerable only to the king.

"We have an Irish family working at the house, actually," he said. "They have a daughter a year or two younger than us. Nice girl."

Siobhan smiled to herself. Either he was being polite, or she looked one or two years older than she actually was. Either way, she wasn't about to correct him.

The sun made brief appearances as the morning wore on, casting weak beams of light down through the clouds and gradually burning away the fog. The forest emerged from its shroud glittering and gleaming in the new light. Birds sang their appreciation to one another.

Sometime before noon, Conal shifted on his horse.

"We'll be at the village soon," he said.

His words woke Siobhan out of her lull, bringing her thoughts back to her task, a task she still thought beyond her capabilities. How was she even supposed to begin looking for the rathstone? The enormity of the task daunted her. It could be anywhere, and she was on her own with no one to turn to for help.

First things first, she told herself. She needed to find out more about where she was. Then she could start thinking about the search.

Conal guided Keir out of the thinning woods and onto a roughly made road. The forest receded behind them as they traveled, the landscape opening up to reveal gentle, heather-covered hills that sprawled away into the distance to join up with a line of distant mountains.

After making their way along the road for a while, Conal guided Keir off the road and up a low hill. He urged the horse up through the thick heather and reined him in when they reached the summit, turning to the side so Siobhan could get a better view of what lay beyond.

A valley opened up beneath them, and nestled in the heart of this valley was a village. It was protected on two sides by the rocky hills and on the third by a river ending in a massive body of water. The fourth side was given over to extensive farmland. Smoke drifted lazily into the sky from the numerous huts and houses. In the center of the village was an empty grass square and facing directly onto this square was a small, neat stone church with a single spire. At the far end of the village, on a small hill of its own that allowed it to overlook its surroundings, was a walled piece of land. Inside the walls was a house much bigger than any of the others in the village. Siobhan actually wondered if it could be classed as a castle, as it looked like the walls were fortified enough to withstand attacks from outside.

"That's my father's house," said Conal, noting the direction of her gaze. "And this is Ballach, my village."

Siobhan gazed around the peaceful setting. She could see people tending crops out in the farms. Women and children walked around the small streets of the village, pausing to talk, or in the case of the children, running off to play with friends. It was all very peaceful.

"It's beautiful," she whispered.

Conal looked at her strangely. "You think so?"

"Don't you?"

"Well . . . aye. But that's because it's my village."

Siobhan shrugged. "I've never had a place like this to call home. To me it's beautiful."

Conal smiled. "Fair enough."

Siobhan looked over the lake again and frowned. "What are those?" she asked, pointing to a series of strange islands out on the water. There appeared to be remnants of wood and stone structures dotting the masses.

"Crannogs," said Conal. "Our ancestors built them and used to live on them. The loch protected them from attack."

"Which loch is that?" Siobhan asked. The answer could confirm her suspicions. This land looked very familiar, though she thought she was seeing it from a different angle.

"Why, that's Loch Tay. Ballach sits right on the Taymouth," he said. She had been right. She was still close to the same loch that Sir James's estate stood near, though farther east. Did the spell work and send her to another version of Scotland? Or was something even more complicated going on?

Conal turned. "Come on. Best be on our way. Don't want to be late."

Siobhan reluctantly tore her gaze away from the village. "Late for what?"

Conal grinned, and Siobhan saw a bit of the wolf in that grin, a bit of the troublemaker. "For the festivities, of course."

~ Two ~

At first Siobhan thought Conal was just taking the road around the outside of the village to enter the valley closer to the laird's castle. But then he guided Keir off the road and headed toward a dark line of distant fir trees.

"Where are we going?" she asked.

"I told you. To the festivities."

"But where——?"

And then Siobhan remembered. The Fey Prince had said something about a feast today. She had thought he meant some kind of event at Conal's village, but now the true meaning of his words hit her like a shower of icy water. She was being taken into the heart of her enemies.

Her heart thudded painfully at the thought, her throat clenching up in fear. She couldn't go there.

She wouldn't. That was all there was to it.

Siobhan looked around. If she didn't go with Conal, what were her options? It was far into the afternoon, and they were already some distance past the village. If she abandoned Conal, abandoned the one person who had shown her the slightest bit of kindness, what would happen? She couldn't protect herself from the Fey, and she knew nothing about surviving in the wild. And she was under no illusion that this part of Scotland—or whatever Fey approximation of Scotland this was—was anything but wild. The nights would be freezing, filled with all kinds of predators.

No, she could not survive on her own. What then? What else could she do?

Stay with Conal and hope she could rely on him should anything happen? It was not a comforting thought, but it was the best she could come up with.

As they crested a rise in the moors, Siobhan saw that the line of fir trees turned out to be the beginning of a huge forest that stretched into the hazy distance. She couldn't see how they could possibly get through it before dark.

Conal didn't seem overly worried though. He gave Keir the reins, allowing the horse to plod sedately through the woods.

Siobhan was not anywhere near as comfortable with her surroundings. The forest was a chill place, filled with shadows and strange noises. The trees were like skeletons, twisted bones rising up against the stark gray clouds. The floor was strewn with mildewed branches, fallen beneath the weight of ice and snow, and soggy brown leaves filled every hollow and depression. Siobhan looked about, searching for the slightest hint of color, anything that would remind her that the world was something more than the monochrome nightmare she found herself in.

She spotted one or two fir trees, but even their greenery was muted and dull. It was like everything had a veil across it, a gray shroud that stripped the surroundings of life.

Siobhan shivered and huddled deeper into the cloak. "Are you sure this is a good idea? The weather doesn't seem favorable."

"The weather's never stopped Euan and his people having a celebration. Anyway, it can't be canceled. It's a tradition. They do it every year at this time."

Siobhan didn't respond.

"Trust me," said Conal, somehow sensing her unease. "I'll watch over you."

And she did trust him. She just didn't know why.

Time wore on. The deeper they rode into the woods, the more the winter-naked trees, the sycamores and the oaks, the birches and the junipers, all of them took on an aspect Siobhan had never seen before. The branches became more craggy, like the spindly limbs of some fantastical creature from a child's fairy tale. The trunks soared up into the air, some of them twisting all the way around as if the trees were trying to uproot themselves.

The forest started to oppress Siobhan, weighing down on her as if there were something heavy in the air. And try as she might, Siobhan could find no sign of a path. Conal guided Keir with light flicks of the reins, moving him between trees, around half-frozen rivers and fallen logs in a seemingly random fashion. Finally, Siobhan couldn't contain her curiosity any longer.

"How do you know where you're going?" she asked.

"Hmm? Oh, it's this." He lifted something from around his neck and held it over his shoulder for Siobhan to see. It was a round disk made from polished wood. Strange runes had been carved into it. They glowed a very faint orange. "Euan gave one to me and one to my father. It shows the path to where they live."

Siobhan looked to the ground, wondering if she had missed something. "What path? There's nothing here."

He grinned at her. "You'd see it if you were wearing this."

At one point, as they headed through a particularly thick clump of oak trees with branches intertwined into one vast canopy, Siobhan heard the fluttering of wings. She turned in the saddle to look, but all she caught was a faint flicker of movement out of the corner of her eye.

"Ignore them," said Conal. "It's just the brownies. They play a game to see who can hide from you the longest."

The deeper into the forest they went, the thicker and older the trees became. Siobhan felt like she was riding back through the years to a time when nature ruled over everything. She'd never seen trees as big as the ones they passed.

It was then that Siobhan realized they really were now following a rough track through the trees, Conal's horse plodding sedately along with its breath clouding the cold air before them.

They followed the track until it came to an abrupt stop up against a solid wall of trees. Siobhan frowned and looked around. The trees formed a barrier to either side as well. There was nowhere to go.

"Are we lost?"

"Just wait."

Siobhan heard a low creaking sound, and the trees in front of them shivered as if in a breeze. Then, with the scrape and groan of tortured wood, the trees pulled aside to form a dark opening before them. As she watched in amazement, the trees immediately behind this opening also moved aside, then the next row, and the next, until a tunnel formed that extended far back into the darkness. Siobhan glanced at Conal. He smiled reassuringly.

"It's all right. It's how we get into their village."

He tapped his heels lightly against Keir's flanks and clicked his tongue. The horse walked forward, heading into the tunnel without the slightest trace of fear.

Darkness surrounded them, but Siobhan could see a circle of gray light up ahead. The circle grew larger as they approached, sounds of life filtering back to them from somewhere beyond the opening.

Then they emerged from the tunnel, and Conal pulled Keir to a stop in the glade they now found themselves in. Siobhan looked around and felt a rush of fear unlike anything she had ever felt before.

The Fey walked everywhere. As at the river earlier that day, she saw their glamours first. Almost all of them wore a disguise of a humanlike being—just different enough to tell they were Fey, but not so different that the real humans would fear them. The only creatures who didn't wear glamours were those who looked otherwise harmless, strange creatures that flew through the air or slunk along the ground, creatures she had no names for. Here a caterpillar-like animal with the face of a crow, there a tiny sprite with leathery bat wings three times the size of her body.

"Just relax," said Conal. "No one will hurt you here."

He held out his arm for support so Siobhan could slide off the horse's back. She stood on stiff legs and stared around in fear. It took all of Siobhan's strength not to cower away from them whenever they drew close. But she held on to her sanity, remembering the slap Ilona had given her before they'd all set out on this journey. She raised her hand to her cheek, touching the spot where the hand had connected. She had to keep a hold of herself. She had a duty to find the stone.

At least her Second Sight was staying in check. It was fighting her. She could feel it trying to break free, to burst over her mind with all the violence of an earthquake, but somehow, if she concentrated, she was able to keep it trapped.

She wouldn't be able to do it forever. Already it was a strain on her mind—she could feel a headache developing that she knew would soon be debilitating. But for the meantime, at least, the Sight was under control.

She just hoped she would be able to control it long enough to get through the hours ahead.

The clearing they had entered was small. At the center stood two upright stones with a lintel laid across the top—all that remained of a moss-covered stone circle that now littered the ground, overgrown with grass and weeds. Strange trees overlooked the glade. Here a thorn tree with bright purple flowers blooming on its branches, so incongruous after riding through the dark forest. On the opposite side of the clearing was a low bush with some kind of bloodred fruit growing from its branches.

Siobhan looked around and wondered where the Fey actually lived. This was supposed to be their village, but Siobhan could see no sign of any dwellings. Maybe they lived beyond the clearing?

But then she saw one of the Fey approach the upright stones and gently lay a hand against one of them. A white light appeared inside the doorway, and the Fey stepped through and disappeared.

"It's magic," Conal said kindly. "It's how they get inside."

"Yes. Well, obviously," Siobhan said weakly.

"Conal!" someone shouted. "You made it."

Siobhan and Conal turned to see Euan striding toward them. Following close behind him were the other Fey Siobhan had seen accompanying him earlier that morning. They were all still wearing their glamours, and Siobhan wondered if Conal had ever seen their true forms. The disturbing Fey woman wasn't with them though, a fact Siobhan was very glad of.

As they approached, Siobhan noted that some of the other Fey walking about the glade gave Euan and his hangers-on a wide berth. She wondered about this, noting that those who avoided him seemed older than Euan. Their age wasn't revealed through wrinkles or anything like that, but more through their air of patience, of wisdom. It was hard to describe. Euan's movements were quick, abrupt. Like a fast-moving bird. The Fey who avoided Euan were more deliberate, more thoughtful. And Siobhan didn't feel the same fear she felt when looking upon the Fey Prince.

Euan stopped in front of Conal and gripped his arm in greeting. "You made it then."

"Of course. It's a special time."

Euan looked at Siobhan. "I see you brought your new pet."

"Leave her be, Euan. I'm taking her back to the manor with me."

Euan's eyebrows arched. "Feeling a bit frisky, are we?"

Conal opened his mouth to say something, but Euan turned abruptly and headed toward the standing stones. "Your people are already here," he called over his shoulder.

Euan touched the stone and stepped though it, vanishing instantly. His troupe followed him through. Then it was Conal and Siobhan's turn to stand before the stones.

"Where does it take us?" asked Siobhan nervously.

"Into the dwelling of the King and Queen."

Siobhan hesitated.

"Are you ready?" asked Conal.

Most definitely not, thought Siobhan. But she took a deep breath and nodded. "Ready."

"Good lass." He held out his hand. Siobhan gripped hold of it, and they stepped through the opening.

Siobhan felt nothing. There was no sense of movement, no sense of dislocation, nothing. One second she was outside, the next she was standing in an earthen tunnel. Torches lined the walls, held in place by brass sconces. Their flickering orange flames revealed smooth walls and a ceiling that was made from intertwined root tendrils.

The light also glinted on the carapaces of hundreds of black beetles scurrying between the roots, all of them heading down the passage toward a wide opening through which loud laughter and music could be heard.

Conal put a hand on her back and guided her gently forward. As they approached the doorway, the music grew louder, demanding more and more of Siobhan's attention. It was the most beautiful sound Siobhan had ever heard. It was a combination of flute and fiddle, the tune a restless, spritely song that drew you in and tried to get you to dance along. Siobhan became lost in the melody, seeing images in her head of a mischievous Fey creature that traipsed around the forest playing tricks on the unwary.

Something touched her arm. She started and turned to see Conal staring at her. She realized that she had stopped moving while listening to the song.

"Try not to get too lost in the music," he said. "It has a . . . distracting effect."

Siobhan shook her head, trying to shake the cobwebs from her head. She felt dazed, half-asleep. Conal was certainly right about the distracting effect.

The tunnel opened up into a huge room packed wall to wall with tables and chairs. Siobhan stopped in her tracks and stared around in awe. She never thought she'd ever witness something like this sight.

The chairs were filled with Fey and humans. They

laughed and joked with each other, sharing drinks and plates of food. At one end of the room, off to her left, was a raised dais. An elaborately carved table had been placed on this dais, facing into the room. Euan was already seated there, his feet up on the table. He saw Conal and raised his wooden goblet in greeting.

Conal nodded back and guided Siobhan through the room. As they moved through the crowds, Siobhan looked around at all the different people. She saw children, both Fey and human, running around and hiding beneath tables, just playing as if this were a normal playroom. Parents laughed and admonished them half-heartedly for their unruly behavior.

Siobhan smiled as a small boy ran into her legs and spun away into the arms of an older girl.

"What's going on?" she asked Conal, talking loudly to be heard over the din.

"It's a gathering," said Conal, smiling his greetings at those he passed. Some of them dipped their heads respectfully; others smiled and clapped him on the back. He was obviously well liked by the villagers.

"What kind of gathering?"

"Every few months the Fey are allowed to air their grievances before the King and Queen. We're invited to witness it so we don't think the Fey are trying to hide anything." He leaned close and whispered to her. "But it's really just an excuse to drink and eat."

He guided her to a table just below the dais. She sat down, while he looked around, obviously looking for something.

"I'll be right back. Just going to find some wine."

He disappeared before Siobhan could respond. She sank down in her chair and stared at the tabletop, suddenly very much aware that the Council's enemy, the Fey Prince himself, was only a few paces away.

As she stared at her hands clenched tightly together on the wood, she noticed for the first time that strange shadows were crawling all along the table. She looked up to the roof and saw that tiny glowing creatures lived inside the twining roots, casting distorted patterns of light and shadow on the polished wood.

Siobhan repressed a shudder of fear. Things were so different here. She wished Father Joe had warned her or at least told her what to expect. But things had moved so fast. She supposed all the girls were in the same situation. All he said was that they'd know what to do when the time came and that they were being sent into the Unhallowed Fey raths. Even on that point she wasn't sure he'd been entirely right.

Conal arrived back at the table just as the music stopped. He sank into a chair and turned with everyone else to stare expectantly at the dais. After a few moments portions of the wall separated and slid to either side. Two regal-looking Fey stepped through the opening, a man and a woman. The woman had her hand resting lightly atop the man's.

"That's the King and Queen," whispered Conal unnecessarily.

Siobhan studied them with interest. They were tall and graceful yet looked older than those around them.

Their hair appeared to be vines so thin, Siobhan could have easily mistaken it for normal hair. But she could see the difference in texture. It was heavier than normal, didn't move in the same fashion.

The royal couple wore white robes with bands of green encircling the sleeves and waists. But as they drew closer to their seats, Siobhan saw that they weren't just bands of color. They were actually live vines that had been intertwined with the fabric of the robes. The vines writhed gently, like a lazy cat enjoying the sun.

Siobhan turned her attention to their faces. The longer she was here, the more she was coming to realize there were two different types of Fey. The King and Queen fell under the category of what she would class as the friendlier Fey. They were nothing like Euan and his cronies. There was a patience in their features that the Fey Prince was completely without, and this patience humanized them, made them appear likeable. It flew in the face of everything she'd believed about the Fey, but she couldn't deny that she felt genuine goodness in these two regal beings. Siobhan suddenly realized that the King and Queen weren't wearing any glamour. What she saw was who they really were.

The royal couple sat down, and then others came through the opening after them. Next was a tall, distin-guished looking Fey with a golden sheen to his skin. Like the King and Queen, he appeared to be one of the elder Fey as opposed to Euan's younger friends. He approached the chair next to the King and sat down. Euan glared at him with dislike but the man simply ignored him.

"That's Elaphe, the royal advisor."

Siobhan drew in a sudden breath and looked sharply at Conal. "Elaphe?"

"Aye, that's right. Why?"

"Oh . . . no reason."

Siobhan waited for Conal to look away again, then she quickly turned her attention back to the golden-skinned Fey man. Elaphe. Could he be *the* Elaphe? The founder of the Council of Elaphe? The Council that Father Joe and everyone else was a member of as they tried to fight off the Unhallowed? But if that was true . . . Siobhan thought furiously, her mind racing with possibilities. If it was true, then it meant that Nephri's spell had sent her back in time. Elaphe had disappeared long ago.

Which would explain why Euan looked the way he did, why he looked so different from the Euan she had seen before. He looked so different because he *was* different. He hadn't become an Unhallowed Fey yet.

Siobhan tried to contain her excitement. What if she could find out what really happened here in the past? What if she could actually stop the Unhallowed from being born? Maybe that was why she had been sent here in the first place. Not to find the stone, but to stop the Unhallowed from coming into existence!

Siobhan looked up at the royal table. *I need to talk with Elaphe*, she thought firmly. If she told him why she was here, maybe he could help her. She was sure he would want to avoid the catastrophe that was to follow when the Unhallowed were born. If she was able to convince him that she spoke the truth, she wouldn't have to do this alone.

But there was no chance of approaching him now. As she watched him another figure entered through the door. All eyes turned to her as if drawn by an invisible force. It was the Fey woman Euan had been speaking with that morning in the forest. She paused, looked casually around, then walked slowly along the dais and sat next to him.

"That's Leanan. She's a priestess."

"Do the Fey believe in God?" asked Siobhan in surprise.

"No," said Conal evenly, and Siobhan could detect disapproval in his voice. "At least, not our God."

Now that everyone had arrived, the gathering got underway. Siobhan thought it would be a serious event, but it was more akin to a social gathering than anything formal. The disagreements brought before the King and Queen were not serious—two dryads arguing over the ownership of an ancient tree, a judgment over who was responsible for an accident while a troupe of Fey were out hunting one night—mostly small matters that Siobhan thought could have been sorted out without any outside help.

That was, until a group of four nervous-looking humans stood up. They moved around their table and stood before the dais. One of them took a step forward and looked up at the King, waiting.

"Speak, friend Mathew. What is your complaint?"

Siobhan saw the man glance sideways to where Euan was seated. The Prince had straightened in his chair so that all his attention was focused on the proceedings. He did not look happy.

"My lord," said the man, turning his attention back to the King. "Long have our people coexisted."

"This is so, Mathew."

"My lord, our closeness has been a boon for both our races. Trade, friendship, the exchange of culture—we have all profited from the relationship."

The Queen leaned forward. "What troubles you, Mathew?"

"Milady, it seems as if your rath . . ." Here he paused and glanced at the other men. He cleared his throat nervously. "It seems as though your rath has started to encroach into our lands."

Silence greeted this. Siobhan, watching the faces of all involved, saw Elaphe frown and look across to Euan and Leanan. The King himself looked troubled.

"I assure you, friend Mathew. This is not something we are aware of. Are you absolutely sure?"

"We are, my lord. Strange things are happening on the boundaries. My animals are going missing. I myself went to search for them and became lost in a forest I didnae recognize. I finally found my way out, but a whole day had passed when I thought I was gone only an hour." His eyes flicked across to Euan. The Queen caught the look and turned quickly to her son.

"Euan? Do you know anything of this man's complaint?"

Euan said nothing for a moment. He took a sip from his goblet and glanced to the table where another Fey sat, just below the dais. Siobhan didn't like the look of him one bit. He wore a glamour, but it failed to disguise his true character. His eyes were dark, his brow heavy. He stared at the Queen with a coldness that chilled Siobhan's heart.

Conal had also caught the exchange of looks. "That's Mordroch," he whispered. "Take my advice. Stay well away from him."

"Euan?" the Queen repeated.

"I know nothing."

"Are you sure?"

"I have answered your question, Mother. Would you have me answer it again?"

"*I* would," said the King.

Euan smiled. "Of course, Father. For you, I will repeat myself. I know nothing of this matter."

"Then who does?" demanded the King. "Who is breaking our treaties without our permission?"

Mordroch lazily raised a hand. "That would be me."

All eyes turned to Mordroch.

"Explain yourself," snapped the Queen.

"Explain myself? Perhaps it is you who should explain yourself."

The room stilled.

"What did you just say?" the King asked in a quiet voice.

"I think you heard me, my liege. I say it is my right to extend our lands. As it is *all* our right. What need have we for these . . . these *insects?* We could wipe them out in an instant."

The King did not take his eyes away from Mordroch. "My son, you would do well to control the behavior of your acquaintances. They begin to . . . displease me."

Euan did not look the least bit worried. "Mordroch speaks his mind, Father. I will not censor him. In fact, I think he speaks for a lot of your subjects."

The King finally broke eye contact with Mordroch, turning to Euan. "Is that so? And where do your loyalties fall in this matter?"

Euan shrugged. "Expansion is the way forward, Father. We need to extend our lands if our people are to flourish. I favor a more . . . politic approach than dear Mordroch here, but I do not condemn him for his eagerness. His interest is in our people. His heart is in the right place."

"His heart, if it even exists, is nowhere near the right place," snapped the Queen. "That is not how we do things, Euan. You know that."

Mordroch surged to his feet. "Then maybe it should be!"

"Sit down," said the King quietly.

"I will not—"

The King slammed his hand on the table. The crack echoed loudly through the room. "I said sit down!"

Mordroch hesitated, glancing across at Euan. Euan gave him a barely perceptible nod, and Mordroch dropped back into his seat. The King glared at him for a time, then the Queen rested a hand on his arm, and he forced himself to calm down.

Siobhan let her breath out in a rush. She hadn't even been aware she was holding it. She looked to Conal.

"These are your friends?"

Conal was frowning, concerned. "I've not heard

anything of this before. Mathew should have told my father. We could have talked to Euan privately." His gaze switched to Leanan. The Fey woman was whispering into Euan's ear. Euan laughed loudly and poured more wine into his goblet.

"It's her," Conal said, nodding at Leanan. "She whispers and plots and sets their minds onto paths best left alone." He glanced around at the worried faces of the humans. "I fear what she will set in motion if her influence grows."

So did Siobhan. Because she thought she had a very good idea of exactly what it was Leanan would set in motion.

Elaphe cleared his throat and stood up. Siobhan watched him carefully. She had been studying him surreptitiously since he had arrived at the table, trying to understand what set him apart from the others. She finally decided it was the feeling of calmness that surrounded him, an air of dignity far beyond the peacefulness that the other Fey seemed to possess, even the King and Queen.

He raised his hands in a placating gesture, stilling the room with his presence.

"Words have been spoken in the heat of temper," he said. His voice was deep and resonant. It put her in mind of summer days and sleepy afternoons, of cool streams and warm dusks. "Words I choose to believe were wrought out of misguided passion and nothing more." He turned, briefly, and looked upon Leanan, not Mordroch or Euan. The priestess looked away, frowning.

"So let us forget any unpleasantness. Know that we

will continue to live together as friends for a long time to come."

The King and Queen gravely nodded their agreement.

"And if proof was even needed as to the special relationship between our peoples, we have a special event to close off the afternoon and take us into the feasting of the night. Alfier?"

A Fey woman seated at Siobhan's table stood up. Her face was thin and long, pale as a cloud. She smiled and held her hand out to a young man seated next to her. He was not much older than Conal. He rose to his feet, and they both moved to stand before the dais. Elaphe sat down.

"Alfier," said the King. "You wish to ask something of us?"

The Fey woman bowed her head respectfully. "A boon, your majesties."

"Ask, dear Alfier," said the Queen.

"I would ask for your blessing on a life pledge between me and Thomas here." The man bowed his head so that he was looking at the floor. Siobhan thought he looked very nervous. Euan frowned and whispered something to Leanan. She nodded.

"A life pledge. And tell us, does young Thomas know what this entails?"

The man looked up. "I do, my lord."

"Tell us, then," said the Queen.

"To enter your rath and never leave. To stay here as long as I live and bind myself body and soul to Alfier."

41

"And you do this freely? Alfier has not bewitched you in any way?"

The man looked at the Fey woma,n and Siobhan could see the fierce love in his eyes. "Only by her beauty, my lord."

Alfier reached over and patted him on the arm. It was meant to be a gesture of affection, but to Siobhan it looked like someone petting a loyal dog.

"Then we give our permission. Thomas, welcome to our rath."

Everyone around the room stood up to applaud. Siobhan did so as well, but she couldn't help noting that the Fey applauded more loudly than the humans. And that the humans, despite Elaphe's words, cast nervous glances at Euan and his followers.

THREE

SIOBHAN SOON LOST TRACK OF TIME. AFTER THE KING AND Queen blessed Alfier and Thomas, the food and drink was brought in and laid out on the tables. The main feast was a huge stag the Fey Prince had taken from the forest that morning, and although everyone else seemed to enjoy it, Siobhan found herself not the least bit hungry.

Everything was so different here. There was so much information she needed to seek out if she wanted to accomplish anything. The humans and the Fey obviously lived together here, but it was plain to Siobhan that not everyone was happy with the way things were. As the night wore on, Siobhan could see the Fey were divided into two very distinct camps. The younger Fey all gathered around Euan and Leanan, while the Fey like Elaphe, those who were older in spirit, spent their time conversing with the King and Queen.

Siobhan was not an educated person, but having worked as a serving maid most of her life, she was very much aware of the low-key politics that went on wherever groups of people lived or gathered. There was a rift opening up inside the Fey, and Leanan and Euan were doing their best to widen it.

And Elaphe? What of him? He spent the night drifting between the tables, making conversation with everyone. He did not discriminate. Human and Fey, elder Fey and Euan's followers alike, he made sure he was not seen to be favoring any particular group. The more she watched him, the more she became convinced that he was the answer to her prayers.

As if sensing Siobhan's eyes on him, Elaphe looked up from his conversation with the King. She flushed and looked away, but the Fey stood up and approached their table.

"Conal," he said in greeting.

Conal stood up, and they gripped arms in greeting. "Elaphe. Good to see you again."

"And you." He shifted his gaze to Siobhan. "Who is your friend? I don't think we've met."

"No, you wouldn't have. I found her out in the forest this morning, miles from anywhere."

"Is that so? What were you doing there, child?"

Siobhan looked up into Elaphe's eyes. They were gentle but intense, dark pools of knowledge that demanded the truth. And she wanted to tell him the truth, all of it. But not here, not in front of everyone else. "My mistress," she said, her lips feeling awkward around the lie, "she left me there. Her husband was making eyes at me. She said it was my fault."

Elaphe stared hard at her. Siobhan got the impression he saw right through her lie. But he didn't say anything.

"I'm taking her to the manor house," said Conal.

"Yes," said Elaphe thoughtfully, staring at Siobhan. "Yes, I think that's a good idea." He looked at Siobhan again, and she couldn't escape the feeling that he was trying to read her mind, trying to dredge up her memories himself.

He shook his head slightly and turned to Conal. "If you are returning to the manor this night, you should be on your way. The snow is threatening, and I do not think it will hold off much longer."

"My thanks. My father will be wondering where I am."

Elaphe turned away, but not without one more lingering glance at Siobhan. She flushed and looked away, wondering what it was he was seeing. In doing so she happened to turn in the direction of Euan's table. Leanan was standing and staring at her. When she caught Siobhan's gaze, a slow smile spread across her pale face. Siobhan swallowed fearfully and turned away. She wanted to speak to Elaphe, but not with Leanan around. She would have to put it off until another time.

"Come," said Conal. "We'd best be off if we want to beat the snow."

An hour or so later, they were riding through the forests again. The moon was hidden behind thick, pregnant clouds, forcing Conal to take the path slowly. The night was cold and sharp. Siobhan's hands and nose were freezing cold, but she didn't mind all that much. It was fresh air. Normal air. She hadn't really noticed it till the end, but the fairy rath had been stifling. When

Conal had slipped off to say good-bye, Siobhan had felt the whole weight of the earth pushing down on top of her.

"What do you know of Elaphe?" she asked now that she could breathe. "He seems different from the others."

Conal laughed. "Aye, he is that. He's a fine man, but a bit . . . mysterious. I think he likes people to think he's some form of wise man."

"And is he?"

Conal was silent for a while. Then he chuckled. "Probably so."

It took them another few hours to get back to the village. By the time they arrived, Siobhan's teeth were chattering, and she could barely keep her whole body from shivering. Conal guided the horse down the sides of the vale and along the main street. Nobody was out in this weather. They drew level with a small inn, where warm light spilled out of a single, murky window. Siobhan peered inside as they passed and saw a group of people gathered around a huge fire in a stone fireplace against the far wall.

They passed the village square and turned onto a smaller road that led up the hill on which the manor house stood. Here, at least, there were signs of life. They passed through the thick wooden gate and into a huge courtyard. The horse's hooves clopped noisily on the cobbles as Conal guided the creature over to a long, low structure built against the wall. Piles of hay were tied up beneath the overhang, protecting it from the weather. They dismounted, and an old man came out of the small hut at the far end of the stables. He approached the two of them and touched his forelock.

"Evenin', young Conal."

"Evening, Jack. Warm him up, will you? He's had a busy day."

"Aye, sir," said Jack, taking hold of the reins and casting a sidelong glance at Siobhan as he did so. Siobhan wondered what everyone would think of her sudden presence. She wasn't even sure why Conal had brought her here. What did he expect her to do?

"Come," said Conal. "Let's find a fire and track down Brianna."

Conal led the way to the huge door that fronted the manor house. The door was constructed from a dark, grainy wood and was so big, Siobhan wondered how on earth Conal was going to open it. But then Conal pushed, and a smaller door opened up inside the larger one. He led the way inside and closed the door behind them.

Siobhan looked around. They were in a small room with rushes strewn across the floor. Thick jackets and cloaks hung on the wall, some of them leather, others made from thick wool. Opposite them was another door. Conal pushed it open, and Siobhan followed him into a huge hall.

The first thing that drew Siobhan's attention was the massive fire pit in the center of the room. Flames crawled lazily over the remains of that night's fire, casting a deep, penetrating warmth throughout the room. Siobhan sighed as she felt the chill thaw from her nose and cheeks. Finally, something to chase the cold away.

A large, U-shaped table ran around the fire, but it was empty at this late hour. The furs of animals had been piled up against the wall, ready to use when the cold got too much. Against the wall to her left was a small table on which three gold plates and some silver goblets were displayed.

"Come on," said Conal. "Brianna should still be up."

He led the way to a door opening into a corridor that stretched to the back of the building. Siobhan reluctantly followed, loathe to leave the heat and warmth behind. But she needn't have worried. Conal reached the end of the corridor, passing numerous closed doors along the way, and entered into the kitchens. Even from where she trailed behind him, Siobhan could feel the heat emanating from the room. She quickened her pace and stepped into surroundings so familiar to her, it was almost as if she were back home.

It was a large room dominated by a pitted and stained table that took pride of place in the center of the flagstone floor. From past experience, Siobhan knew that this table was the focal point of the lives of the servants. Here they gathered to eat, to gossip, to prepare food. Here they laughed and cried, told stories and listened to news brought from the outside world by stray travelers.

Against one wall was a huge, low stone oven with a fire-blackened door pushed tight against the flames. She could see red light flickering around the door where it didn't quite fit into the gap. Next to it was a large fireplace, the hearth swept clean, with several cooking implements dangling over an empty cook pot. A spit sat above that, a bit dusty as if it hadn't seen use in a while.

It was a comfortable room, and Siobhan felt instantly at ease.

That was, until the biggest woman Siobhan had ever seen entered through the back door, swearing and cursing at the cold. She was dusting ash off her hands as if she was the one who had just cleaned out the fireplace.

The woman froze when she saw Conal, her face flushing with embarrassment. "Sorry, your lordship. Didn't know you were there."

"It's fine, Brianna."

Brianna closed the door and hurried across to the oven, yanking the wooden door open and holding her hands so close to the coals, Siobhan was worried she would burn them. "Going to be a cold season. Not even winter, and we've already had the snow."

Conal smiled and shook his head. Brianna caught the gesture from the corner of her eye.

"Mark my words, Conal. It's a dark wind blowing."

Conal raised his hands in surrender. "I'm not arguing with you, Brianna. Have you found anyone to replace Maeve yet?"

Brianna glanced sharply at Siobhan, guessing Conal's intent. "Not yet. Have you heard? The stupid girl's only gone and got herself pregnant."

Conal smiled. "Isn't that what people do when they marry? Start a family?"

"Aye, well." Brianna sniffed. "Never liked the man, that's all. Something funny about him."

"There's nothing wrong with him. You're only saying that because she's moved away. Now, are you still needing that help?"

"Aye, well, our Niamh can't carry on doing the load of two." Brianna looked Siobhan up and down. "You're not meaning this one, are you? She looks as if a strong wind could blow her over."

"Believe me," said Conal wryly, "she's stronger than she looks."

"If you say so," said Brianna doubtfully. She turned her attention to Siobhan. "You. Girl. What's your name?"

"Siobhan."

Brianna's eyebrows rose in surprise. "Are you from over the water?"

Siobhan nodded, and it was as if this revelation had a magical effect on Brianna. Her demeanor changed instantly, going from slightly haughty mistress of the kitchen to amiable mother hen. She slammed the oven door back in its notch and bustled over. "Come on, then. Let's see if we can find some soup to warm you up." She pulled out a chair and pushed Siobhan into place.

"I'll leave you to it, then?" Conal asked. Siobhan thought she detected a note of amusement in his tone.

Brianna barely spared him a second glance. "Aye, you get off to bed now, young Conal. And don't sleep in. It's a sight hard to keep Eomen away from your food when you're late."

"I won't. Sleep well, Siobhan."

And with that, he was gone. Brianna scurried about the kitchen. She opened a smaller door underneath the oven where food could be kept warm and pulled out a covered iron pot. She poured Siobhan a large bowl of soup and slid it over. Siobhan stared at it doubtfully, unsure what it was they ate here. But it didn't look very different from what she was used to. She could see carrots, potatoes, some turnips.

"What are you waiting for? Get started."

Seeing as no spoons were on offer, Siobhan lifted the bowl and drank the soup. It tasted amazing, and as soon as the liquid slid down her throat and into her grateful stomach, she realized how hungry she was. She had picked at some food in the rath, but it hadn't filled her.

She finished the soup and laid the bowl down, sighing at the warmth spreading throughout her body. She yawned, feeling exhaustion coming to claim her. She had been on the move since dawn. So much had happened—so much she had to think about.

Brianna took the bowl away. Siobhan hoped she was going to refill it. She laid her head on her arms as she waited. A few seconds later, she was fast asleep.

~ Four ~

Siobhan was running desperately in a forest of pure black—no grass, no green, just the frantic inevitability of something grasping at her heels. She couldn't see her pursuer, but she knew it was there, and she could gain no ground on it. Every step she took raised a puff of ash from the blackened trees that spiraled up into the beams of weak winter sunlight.

With panicky gasps, she glanced at the possible paths she could take, but all directions looked the same. She had no idea where she was. Why was she running? Who was she running from? It didn't matter. Whoever—or whatever—it was, if it caught her, she was dead.

A loud crack echoed through the still forest—someone stepping on a fallen tree branch. And that branch was too close.

Siobhan ran again. She had been running her whole life, too scared to stand up for herself, too scared to draw attention to herself. Too scared to do the right thing. Her mother had always said, "Know your place, Siobhan. Don't speak out of turn."

Running. Always running.

She dared a glance over her shoulder. Puffs of ash settled slowly around her footprints. Nothing but black forest, swirling ash.

But there, in the distance, she caught a glimpse of something darting between the empty husks that had once been trees.

Siobhan sobbed and ran faster, but no matter how fast she ran, the creature following her always gained ground. There was no way she could escape.

But she ran anyway, and she could hear its breath as it gained ground. Loud, rasping, breathing onto her neck. Siobhan cried out in fear. She could smell the creature, its rank breath, filled with the stench of decaying meat. Coldness emanated from it, a coldness that spread across her back and her shoulders the closer it got.

The trees started to thin. Siobhan prayed that maybe salvation was ahead. Maybe the creature couldn't leave the forest. If she could only get out, get away from this deadness, maybe she could escape.

From somewhere inside herself, Siobhan found an extra burst of energy. She ran faster, faster than she had ever run in her life. She saw the end of the trees up ahead, a line of black, beyond which she could see the clear blue of the sky.

The line grew closer. She could feel her legs turning cold, her back seizing up with the chill. Just a little farther. Nearly there. Her knees ached. The cold reached inside, burrowing deep into her being and slowly draining her life away.

Close. The trees were so close. She could feel herself slowing down, feel the cold reaching up to her heart. She wasn't going to make it. The tree trunks were not more than twenty paces away. But the cold was spreading.

Keep running, she screamed silently at herself. You're nearly there.

She felt something on her shoulder, a blade of ice that shot down through her arm and made it fall useless by her side.

She screamed, furious that she was so close but no matter what she did, she would still be caught.

The trees drew closer . . .

A hand clasped over the back of her neck.

But then she jerked forward, and she was through the trees and onto a small sward of brittle grass.

She stumbled to a stop, staring ahead in disbelief. No. It wasn't fair. Not after everything she had been through.

The sward of grass swept ten paces away and ended at the edge of a cliff. She staggered forward. The drop descended to sharp rocks and crags. There was nowhere to go.

She began to shiver uncontrollably as the ice coursed through her veins.

"Siobhan," whispered a voice, and the voice was the very heart of ice, the cold that lies buried underground for thousands of years. It was the voice of ancient death, and it knew her name.

"Siobhan . . ."

" . . . Siobhan."

Siobhan's eyes snapped open, her breath freezing in her throat. She wanted to cry out, but her voice wouldn't come.

She waited, terrified, expecting at any minute to feel the icy hand close around her neck once again.

"Siobhan?"

A face appeared above her. She flinched, but it was only the face of a girl, maybe a year or so younger than she was. Siobhan blinked, then looked around in confusion. She was lying in a large bed. The rough straw of the mattress poked her in the back through her clothing.

"Are . . . are you all right? You were crying out."

Siobhan let her breath out in a rush of relief. It was only a dream. None of it had been real.

She fixed her attention on the girl hovering by her bed. She had brown hair, tied back at the nape of her neck. Her face was pale, her eyes large and blue. Siobhan sat up, fighting off a wave of dizziness.

"Yes. Sorry. I'm fine. It was . . . it was just a dream."

But even as she uttered those words, she wondered if that was true. Everything had seemed so real. The smells, the cold, the creature chasing her. What if it was a true dream? A Seeing?

She shuddered at the thought, the shudder changing to a shiver as she looked around the room. It was a small chamber with four roughly made beds. Weak gray light filtered in through a single window high in the wall. Judging by the light, it must be close to dawn.

What had happened? The last thing she remembered, she was waiting for a second bowl of soup. Then . . . nothing.

"Me ma brought you here," said the girl, as if reading her thoughts. "You must have been tired."

"Oh. You must be . . ."

"Niamh. Hello." The girl smiled nervously. Siobhan smiled back, trying to put her at her ease.

"I was coming to wake you anyway. Ma said you've to get up and help in the kitchen." Niamh looked suddenly concerned. "You can work, can't you? In the kitchen?"

"Oh, yes. It's what I'm good at."

Siobhan swung her feet around and onto the floor. She let out a squeal as her feet touched the freezing flagstones. She looked around for her shoes, finding them at the bottom of the bed. As she stood up, shivering in the cold, Niamh held out an old shawl for her. She accepted it gratefully and wrapped it around her shoulders.

"You won't need it once we start working, but the mornings are fair cold."

"What are we doing?"

"Making the laird's breakfast. We'd better hurry. He doesn't like being kept waiting."

Niamh led the way out of the room and out into the grounds of the manor house. The sleeping quarters were at the back of the enclosure, as were most of the other buildings, so as they walked toward the kitchen, Siobhan was able to get a good look at the surroundings. She could just see the stables from where she was. Jack, the old stableman from the previous night, sat on a small stool, sipping from a steaming mug. He watched the two girls without much interest. Off to the left were three other low buildings, roofed with thick straw.

"What are they?" she asked Niamh.

Niamh pointed. "The granary, the animal house, and the distillery."

All around them, the folk of the manor house were rising for the day ahead. Siobhan saw other servants already dressed and going about their chores. They cast sideways glances at Siobhan, probably wondering where she had appeared from.

The girls walked past a flock of chickens that clucked and flapped out of their way. A fenced-off enclosure held four huge pigs that snuffled and snorted through the hard mud.

Niamh led Siobhan up the steps and into the kitchen.

Brianna was already busy before the ovens. As soon as Niamh and Siobhan entered, she straightened up and wiped her greasy hands on her apron.

"Right. You two break your fast—your porridge and bread is in the warmer—then we need to get busy. There's a dinner tonight to welcome the new priest, and young Conal tells me that he's invited the Prince and his people. That means you two have to round up all the iron and take it down to the chapel. You'd better check all the wooden knives Conal made as well. Make sure their edges are sharp." She glared at them. "Well? What are you waiting for? Move it."

Niamh jumped to obey, and Siobhan quickly followed her example.

When it was ready, they carried the breakfast of porridge and kippers to the main hall where Conal and his father were waiting. Conal's father—his name was Guthrie, Niamh whispered—was a huge bear of a man, with long hair that fell to either side of his face and a bushy beard that grew to his chest. Siobhan looked to Conal. He glanced her way and smiled, but he seemed distracted. Or maybe just tired. They had done a lot of riding yesterday.

After breakfast Siobhan and Niamh went through the Great Hall and set about removing everything that was made from iron. That included goblets, decorations on the walls, everything.

"What's the point of this?" asked Siobhan.

Niamh stopped her work and looked at Siobhan skeptically. "You really not from around here?"

Siobhan shook her head.

"Oh. It's the Fey, you see. They don't like iron. My da says it burns them something bad. So whenever they come here, we have to hide it away. Most of the village is already without iron, just in case they come to visit. My da says a priest hid it all in the chapel years and years ago."

Siobhan used the opportunity to find out something more about where she was. "These Fey, they trade with the village?"

Niamh nodded, putting a plate into a sack.

"And there's no . . . problems?"

Niamh frowned. "What kind of problems?"

"Well . . ." She searched for an example. "The Prince, for example. Everyone likes him?"

"I wouldn't say *likes*. Well, Conal does, I suppose. But he hasn't done anything bad, if that's what you mean."

"And the Fey all live together?"

"Out in their rath, aye."

"They don't fight or anything?"

"Why would they fight?"

Siobhan pursed her lips thoughtfully. "No reason," she said.

They moved around the hall, packing away everything that could possibly hurt the Fey. Siobhan's thoughts raced as they did so. So the Fey weren't fighting amongst themselves yet. She wished she had paid more attention to Father Joe. Had he told them how the Unhallowed came into being? As far as she could recall, he'd just said something vague about the Prince and his followers being unsatisfied and breaking away from the others. Obviously, none of that had happened yet. Although from what she saw at the rath, the time when things would come to a boil couldn't be too far off.

Siobhan had no doubt anymore. Corrine and Mara's spell really had sent her back to a different time. But why? She was supposed to go where the rathstone was. Wasn't that the plan? That they would all travel to wherever the stones were hidden? So why was she here?

But then a thought occurred to her. What if this was the last time she could get hold of the rathstone? What if something was to happen to it soon, and it would disappeared? Then the spell would have had to send her back far enough that she still had a chance to retrieve it.

"Niamh," she said thoughtfully. "Do you know what year it is?"

Niamh stopped what she was doing and looked at her, puzzled. "Why would I need to know that?"

Siobhan shrugged. "Just wondering."

"I think I heard Conal mention it once. 1260? 1270? Not sure of the exact date."

So, she was right. She'd gone back through the centuries. The Unhallowed hadn't even been born yet. What if she could prevent it? What if she could stop whatever it was that had led to the Fey becoming Unhallowed? All those deaths—at Falston, at Sir James Campbell's estate. None of that would happen then, surely? Was it possible? Could she actually change history? Could she stop the Unhallowed from being born?

She wasn't sure, but she could certainly try.

But she would need allies. She needed to speak to

Elaphe as soon as possible, to tell him everything she knew. She was sure he would help.

"Are you sick?" Niamh's concern for Siobhan's health did not slow her work.

Siobhan snapped out of her reverie. "What? No. No, I'm fine." She took a corner of the sack. It was heavy now, laden with all the metal they could find. "Tell me, do the Fey come here often?"

"Not really," said Niamh. "Only for special occasions. Our new priest arrived yesterday, you see."

"Oh." Siobhan thought about this. "Why is the arrival of a new priest a special occasion?"

Niamh looked at her is as if she were mad. "We haven't had a priest in the village since Father Mathew disappeared."

"What happened to him?"

"No one knows. He just vanished."

Siobhan thought for a moment. "Does this new priest know about . . . you know . . . *them?*"

Niamh shrugged. "That's no business of mine. Or yours, for that matter."

Siobhan met Niamh's father after lunch. He was sitting on the stone steps, sharpening an axe, when she dragged a sack of washing out through the kitchen door. He was tall and thin, but his body looked hard as iron, his wiry muscles standing out against his skin. At first Siobhan wasn't sure who he was. Then he turned and looked at her, and she saw the resemblance to Niamh straight away.

He stopped running the whetstone over the blade and laid the axe to the side. "You'd be the new lass?"

Siobhan nodded.

"You're working here, then?"

"It seems so. For a time, at least."

"You're well spoken."

Siobhan flushed. "Sorry."

"What are you apologizing for? I wasn't telling you off."

"Oh. Sorry. I mean . . . sorry," she finished lamely.

Niamh's father just snorted with amusement. "The name's Eomen."

"Siobhan."

"Pleased to meet you, Siobhan. Now stop apologizing for breathing, and get on with that washing. But first grab a cloak from the room. The wind gets fair cold at the loch."

"Oh. Thank you." She hesitated. "Where . . . ?"

"There's a chest at the bottom of the beds. You should find an old one there."

Siobhan nodded and hurried across the yard, red with embarrassment. She ducked into the room where she woke up that morning and rummaged around in the lone chest until she found a woolen cloak, which she threw around her shoulders. It smelled musty, as if it hadn't been used in some time.

Niamh met her at the gates to the manor house. She was pushing an old wooden cart filled with sacks similar to Siobhan's. Siobhan hefted hers onto the top of the pile.

Niamh and Siobhan each took an arm of the cart and pushed it down the dirt road into the village. Actually, this wasn't exactly true. They both kept a firm hold of each handle and tried to keep the cart from pulling them off their feet as it trundled steadily down the hill.

They pushed the cart onto a smaller path that veered off to the left and led down to the edge of the loch. It was too awkward for them to push the cart over the pebbles and stones that marked the water's edge, so they had to drag each sack to the water one at a time.

Niamh smiled at Siobhan as she upended the first sack. "You looked tired," she said. "Rest up. I'll do the first lot."

"Thanks," said Siobhan gratefully. Niamh was right. She was exhausted. It had been work nonstop since she got up that morning. She should be used to it. After all, it wasn't much different from what her life used to be, serving the girls and faculty, first at Falston and then at Fearnan and in London. But the strain of keeping herself from running away screaming every time she thought about what she had to do was probably adding to her tiredness.

Siobhan sat down on a moss-covered boulder and stretched her knotted back. The afternoon sun shone brightly on the gray waters of Loch Tay, sparkling and flashing as the small waves rolled in and lapped against the pebble-covered shore. She turned her attention to the crannogs that Conal had pointed out yesterday. They sat in the water like an archipelago. There were still signs of the walls that had supported the huts and shelters. On the biggest of the islands, the one closest to land, the roof on the giant building was still intact, albeit covered in moss and lichen.

"Have the crannogs been used lately?" she asked.

Niamh squinted over the waters. "Not in my lifetime. I think they were used a while back when there was a bit of trouble with the English."

Siobhan nodded then went back to staring across the waters. Clouds drifted over, casting the occasional pall across the sun, the afternoon one minute dull and gray, then brightening again with rich sunlight.

She found her thoughts drifting inexorably to the rathstone. Even though she had decided to try and stop the Unhallowed being created, she realized she still had to find the stone in case her attempts failed. Then at least she could go back to the original plan. But where would it be hidden? Maybe she should be systematic. Just check every house she came across.

No, that was stupid.

And then she realized how truly stupid she really was. If the Fey weren't the Unhallowed yet, surely the rathstone would still be in the hands of the King and Queen. If they needed to use the stone to open Hallowmere, then they wouldn't let it out of their sight, would they? It would be a treasure, locked up and guarded in their rath below ground.

A wave of despair washed over Siobhan. She'd been there. She had already been in the rath. She could have snuck off and searched for it. It would have been dangerous, but the Fey had been distracted.

She'd already had her best chance at locating the stone, and she'd missed it.

~ Five ~

BRIANNA STOOD WITH HER HANDS ON HER HIPS AND studied Siobhan with a critical eye. "Too skinny by half. But I think it will do."

Siobhan looked down at the clothes she now wore. They had belonged to Niamh's sister when she worked at the manor house. Brianna had insisted Siobhan try them on, "seeing as the Gentry and the new priest are coming, and we can't have you looking like a plucked chicken ready to cook."

Siobhan wasn't exactly sure what that meant, but one of the first things she had learned was that there was no arguing with the woman. Besides, she'd noticed that her servant's garb from 1867 did make her stand out a bit.

Siobhan looked down at the clothes. The chemise and bodice laced up in the front and the back, and had the not-entirely-unpleasant effect of making her . . . attributes rather larger than they normally were. And beneath the long part of the bodice, which flared down past her waist to what Siobhan could only describe as a split skirt, Siobhan was wearing an *additional* underskirt. It made her feel like she had forgotten to take her nightdress off before dressing.

One of the things Siobhan found puzzling was the lack of pockets sewn into the dress. Here, what they called a pocket was simply a leather pouch attached to her belt. What was so complicated about sewing a piece of material onto their clothes? And no one used buttons, either. Everything was held together with laces. It was all so unwieldy.

Brianna pulled the chemise higher up on Siobhan's shoulder. "Are you ready?"

Siobhan nodded.

"You've served before, aye?"

"Yes, Brianna."

"Good. Now you listen to me, and listen good. Those Fey have a fair strange sense of humor, so ignore them if they say anything odd. You're there to serve, not talk." She glanced outside at the dark evening. A fierce wind had sprung up and was howling around the buildings. It was going to be a cold night. "The priest will be here soon. You'd better get on through."

Siobhan paused reluctantly, looking at the boar meat sizzling away on the spit in the huge fireplace. The smell of fresh bread wafted from the oven. Niamh had swept the coals out while they were still hot so that Brianna could use the heat radiating from the stones for her baking. Siobhan had been hoping for a taste of something before she had to serve.

Brianna caught the direction of her gaze. "Don't worry. I'll save some for you and Niamh. Now off you go."

Siobhan left the kitchen and walked down the hallway toward the Great Hall. She took a deep breath, mentally preparing herself for the night ahead. She planned on learning as much as possible about the Fey and their relationship with the humans. She knew she wouldn't be able to ask anything outright, so it meant she had to keep her eyes and ears open.

The large fire in the center of the hall was already roaring away. Flames and smoke soared up to the slanted hole in the roof, disappearing into the night. The damp wood spat and hissed. Sparks darted through the air as resin bubbled and cooked.

As Siobhan entered she could just see Conal's father on the other side of the flames. He was standing by the door, speaking to someone. Siobhan couldn't see who because the flames flickered in front of her vision, but it was probably the new priest just arriving. She moved around the table, wondering where Niamh was. Was she supposed to offer the men drinks? What did they even drink here anyway? Maybe she should go back and ask Brianna.

But then she caught her first glimpse of the priest, and all thoughts vanished in an instant. She stopped in her tracks, her eyes widening in shock.

"Father Joe!" she exclaimed.

Her first feeling was one of joy. He had come back for her. He had come back to take over the search for the rathstone, and she wouldn't have to worry about it any-more. The relief she felt was a painful rush that surged through her body. She almost wept with joy.

But then he looked over at her as she called his name, and she noticed things that didn't quite tie in with her assumption. It was Father Joe, yes, but he looked younger. And he was quite a bit thinner than the man she knew. His hair was longer as well.

She walked slowly forward. There was no recognition in his eyes—eyes, she noticed, that looked so much younger and more carefree than the haunted eyes of the man she knew.

"My name is Father Josephus, child. Do I know you?"

Yes! she wanted to cry. *Of course you do.* But this wasn't the man she knew. Well, it was, but a younger version of himself, one so far untainted by the battle against the Unhallowed.

But for that to be true, Father Joe had to be over five hundred years old.

Siobhan's brief flare of hope died, fading to ashes like a morning fire. "No," she said. "Forgive me. I was mistaken."

Father Joe nodded and turned away. He handed over a small cask to Conal's father, who looked pleased with the gift. Then he saw Siobhan just standing there staring at them.

"What are you staring at, girl? Here, pour some of this."

He held out the cask, and Siobhan hurried forward to take it from him. It may have been small, but it was still heavy. She staggered beneath its weight, just managing to hold onto it. She glanced out the corner of her eye at

Father Joe, but the man wasn't even looking at her.

"Come, Father Josephus," said Guthrie. "Sit with me, and we'll toast to your new placing."

Father Josephus smiled as he followed Conal's father to the head of the table. Siobhan took the cask and placed it on a table against the wall.

She stared at the small barrel for a while, wondering how she was supposed to open it. Then Niamh appeared by her side. "I'll do it. You get the goblets." She nodded to another table against the far wall where the goblets, wooden plates, and knives were stacked.

Siobhan hurried over and returned with two of the drinking vessels. Niamh already had the cask open. Siobhan poured the wine into the goblets and took them over to the two men. As she approached she could hear Father Joe talking.

"To be honest with you, Guthrie, I've heard disturbing things since my arrival."

"Disturbing? How so?"

"I've heard that you and your villagers . . . that you freely associate with *un-Christian* elements."

Guthrie barked out a loud laugh. "Is that so? Well, Father, if that's the case, then we've been associating with 'un-Christian elements,' as you put it, for generations now, with not even a failed crop to show for our blasphemy."

Father Josephus frowned. "Such flippancy is unwarranted. If you have truck with demons and monsters, then it is my duty as your priest to save your souls."

Siobhan placed the two goblets on the table. She

could sense the sudden tension erupting between the two men.

"Believe me, Father, our souls do not need saving. If you're looking for a crusade, I suggest you go join your brothers in Jerusalem. You'll find no sympathy for your cause here."

"It is not sympathy I am looking for. You seem to forget that you are lord of this manor only at the forbearance of the church. It is we who rule in the name of God. *We* who decide who is in need of saving."

They stared at each other for a long moment. Then Guthrie shrugged. "You can judge for yourself, Father. The . . . demons that you talk of will be here shortly to meet you."

Father Josephus narrowed his eyes. "They are coming here?"

"Of course. A new village priest is a momentous event. They wish to meet you. Did you think it would just be the two of us?"

"And your son."

"Conal, aye, he'll be here soon enough."

Father Josephus shook his head. "Your attitude is worrysome, Guthrie. I don't think you understand the peril you are facing."

"I understand well enough.. As I said, we've lived side by side with the Fey for generations. We trade, we marry, we feast. All is good. But surely you lot over at St. Fillan's know of such things? You are not so far away as to be untouched by the Fey and their kin."

Siobhan was watching Father Joe carefully, so she was

able to see the look that flashed across his face. Was it guilt? Or fear? Perhaps both.

He took a hasty gulp of wine to cover his discomfort. "We know of them. But Iamblicus, my superior, does not encourage intermingling."

Niamh tapped Siobhan on the back. She turned quickly, realizing she was just standing there watching Guthrie and Father Josephus.

Niamh looked at her curiously. "Are you all right? You look pale."

Siobhan rubbed her face. "I'm fine. Sorry. Just got a bit distracted."

Niamh nodded doubtfully. "Ma wants help with the meat. You'd better go. I think I hear the others in the front yard."

Siobhan nodded and hurried back to the kitchen. She helped Brianna turn the boar, which wasn't as easy as she thought it would be. They had to grip both ends of the spit with pieces of thick leather to prevent burns. Then they heaved the boar over so that it cooked evenly—it had to weigh as much as a pony. Once they had finished, Siobhan returned to the main hall, wiping the sweat from her brow. This was going to be a long night.

She had no idea how right she was. Euan and Leanan had arrived with the group of Fey that never seemed to leave his side. Siobhan was grateful her Sight was staying under control. She didn't think she'd be able to serve drink to the wolfman and the headless monster, who sat at the table trading insults and jests with each other.

Conal was also there, sitting at the head of the table next to his father and sipping wine from a goblet.

And Elaphe was there as well, attending in the stead of the King and Queen. Siobhan felt a rush of happiness when she saw him enter the Great Hall. Euan and his followers stopped talking when they saw him, but he ignored the sudden silence and politely greeted his hosts. Siobhan forced herself not to smile. Maybe tonight would be the night she would get to speak to him.

But it wasn't to be during the first half of the evening. Siobhan and Niamh were kept busy pouring out wine and filling up tankards of ale. Siobhan was shocked at how much the Fey drank. And they didn't even seem drunk!

As the time wore on, Siobhan found her eyes drawn more and more to Father Joe. Leanan had taken the seat next to him, and he looked trapped, like he wanted nothing more than to get up and run away. She was unused to seeing him like this. She was accustomed to a decisive and forceful leader, a man of the cloth in charge of the battle against the Unhallowed. To see him like this—young and seemingly afraid—it was a strange feeling for her. She actually found herself pitying him.

It was not a feeling she liked. Father Joe was a strong man. He did not deserve pity. He deserved respect.

During a lull in the conversation, when Leanan had vacated her seat to speak to the Fey Prince, Siobhan took the jug of wine over to Father Joe and tried to smile reassuringly. He held out his goblet with trembling hands and tried to return the smile, but it wouldn't come.

"Don't worry," she said softly. "This might sound

strange, but in time, you won't fear them anymore. You will lead the fight against them."

She wasn't sure why she said it. Just that she felt the need to reassure him.

He looked at her, puzzled. He opened his mouth to say something, probably to ask her what on earth she was talking about, but before he could say anything she quickly turned away.

And froze. Leanan and Prince Euan stood not three paces away, staring directly at her. Siobhan hadn't even heard them approach. Leanan's eyes glittered with malice, Euan's with something else. She couldn't quite place the look. Anger? Hunger? Fear?

Had they heard what she had said? She quickly turned away and sought out Conal, needing the feeling of protection he had given her the previous day. He smiled at her as she refilled his goblet, and she breathed slightly easier.

Dinner was served; wine and ale flowed freely. Euan's followers kept to themselves, not speaking to anyone else at the tables. Euan and Conal spent the night laughing and joking, each one trying to beat the other with the most outrageous hunting story. Siobhan watched them, wondering how Conal could be his friend. Euan was a monster, responsible for the deaths of people she knew, people she cared about.

Except, he wasn't, was he? At least, not yet. So what was it that turned him into that monster? What pushed him down that path, pushed him so hard he could not return?

As if in answer to her question, her eyes were drawn to Leanan. She was deep in conversation with Father Joe, and as Siobhan watched and listened to them she couldn't help feeling that they were somehow familiar with each other. Their glances and arguments were not those of newly met strangers.

"So your God made everything, did He?" asked Leanan in an amused tone.

"Everything."

"And yet you call us godless monsters."

"I called you no such thing."

"You are thinking it, though," she taunted.

Father Joe narrowed his eyes at her. He was probably wondering if the Fey could read minds.

"So how can we be creatures made by God and yet still be godless monsters?"

"Because you turn away from His glory. He created you, but He also gave everyone free will. You choose your own destiny."

Leanan smiled with amusement. "Ah, but if He gave everyone free will, then He cannot condemn us for using that free will. By not using it, surely we are spurning our God-given rights?"

Father Josephus frowned. "That's not what I meant."

"What did you mean, then? That's the problem with you Christians. You're always contradicting yourselves." Leanan abruptly leaned forward, so that she was very close to Father Josephus. "You are a good-looking man."

Father Josephus blinked. "Excuse me?"

Leanan tilted her head to the side, studying him. "You would sire good-looking children."

"I am married to the church."

"Strange," said Leanan thoughtfully. "I feel I've heard that somewhere before. And as I recall it didn't make a bit of difference."

Father Josephus flushed and looked away.

"And that's another thing," said Leanan. "Why would a church forbid its priests to marry and procreate? Surely it is the will of your god to bring more worshipers into the world? I know it's the will of my goddess."

She paused when she saw the look of distaste that showed plainly on the priest's features.

"What? You do not like to hear of other gods?"

"There are no other gods."

"Oh there are, Father. There are. She is called the Morrigan. We worship her through war and death and blood on the battlefield. She——"

"Leanan," snapped Euan. "Enough."

Leanan smiled. She reached out and gently stroked Father Josephus's hand. "I am only toying with you, priest. Mind me not."

Before Siobhan went to help Niamh with another cask of ale, she noticed that Father Josephus hadn't moved his hand away from Leanan's touch.

Siobhan yawned and rested her head on the kitchen table. How much longer could they go on? She had been running errands and pouring wine for hours and was exhausted. Yet the gathering in the Great Hall did not seem any closer to winding down.

Siobhan was disappointed with what she had learned this night. Even though she had hovered as close to the table as she could, she had overheard nothing of interest. Most of the talk was about the Harvest Festival that was coming up, a yearly fair where the local clans met up to trade goods and celebrate the end of the season.

Siobhan closed her eyes. Just a quick nap, she told herself. No one would notice. Just five minutes, then she'd head back into the hall. Surely they could get their own drinks for a little while?

No. Siobhan forced her eyes open and sat up. She couldn't sleep now. Not while Niamh was still working. It wouldn't be fair. And besides, she didn't want to disappoint Conal. He had showed faith in her by getting her a place at the manor house. She didn't want to let him down. She needed to wake herself up a bit.

She stood up and opened the back door, stepping out into the cold night. The wind buffeted her slight frame, slipping inside her clothes and chilling her skin. She shivered and turned into the wind, letting it chase the cobwebs from her mind. Five minutes of this and she would be wide awake again.

A noise from around the other side of the house caught her attention. It sounded like the front door closing. She felt a momentary pang of hope. Had everyone decided to retire for the night?

A moment later she saw Euan and Leanan walk through the courtyard. Siobhan watched them, not moving. Their faces were turned away from her as they walked toward the small chapel. They stopped and stared up at it. Leanan said something, but Siobhan couldn't hear. Euan responded, frowning.

Maybe this was her chance. If they thought themselves alone, maybe they would say something that could help her. She just had to get close enough to hear.

Siobhan descended the steps, but hesitated when she stepped away from the shelter of the house. She felt suddenly exposed, bereft of any protection. She swallowed fearfully. Could she do this? She wasn't a hero. She wasn't like Miss Brown and Father Joe. She wasn't even like Corrine and the others. They all seemed so brave. They all knew what they were doing. But Siobhan never wanted to be a part of this. She was just a serving girl, caught up in things she didn't understand—and that only because her family had its own difficulties. By rights she shouldn't even be here.

But I am here, she told herself. *And there's nothing I can do about that now. So I may as well do everything I can to figure out how to get the stone, otherwise I'll be stuck here forever.*

Siobhan shivered again, but this time it wasn't from the cold.

There was a large oak tree about twenty paces from the chapel. If she could get behind the tree, she should be able to hear what they were talking about.

Siobhan took a deep breath and hurried across the packed earth, making sure she didn't kick any stones or scuff her feet. She arrived behind the tree and laid her hands hard against the bark, sighing with relief.

She could hear Euan talking.

". . . not much to look at, is it?"

"It's pathetic," snapped Leanan. "They say they worship this god of theirs, yet this is the best they can do? It's a hut. Nothing more. At least the Morrigan demands respect. She would take my life if I tried to raise something like this in her name."

"They think differently—"

"Exactly! This is what I've been telling you."

Siobhan peered around the tree. Leanan turned away from the chapel and looked up at Euan. He was a head taller than she.

"Have you thought any more of what we talked about?"

"I have not, no."

"But don't you see? It is our best option. A way to avoid the death that Hallowmere brings. The King and Queen, they're old, Euan. We need a new ruler. One who will stay with us forever, not just for the next few years. One who can plan the future of the Fey in the long term."

Euan said nothing.

"Your parents have failed us. They are happy to allow their people to fade away to nothingness. Happy to allow these . . . these humans, these *insects* to take our lands, to breed like rabbits. We are better than these people, Euan. Why should they have free rein over this country, this world? Why not us?" Leanan paused. "You know they are going ahead with it? They plan to open Hallowmere for the renewal."

"We always knew they would."

"Yes, but not now! It is not needed."

"They think traditionally. Once a certain number of years has passed, they think it time. Affairs in the outside world do not affect this decision. They never have."

"Exactly my point! Now is the time to make your move."

"I am in talks with Guthrie—"

"Away with you," said Leanan contemptuously. "You heard him tonight. Every time you broached the matter of ceding some of his land, Campbell changed the subject. Mordroch has the right of it." Leanan paused, then said in a mocking tone of voice, "Perhaps he should be Prince. At least he has the best interests of the Fey at heart."

"You go too far, Leanan."

"No! I do not go far enough! You know I speak the truth. Campbell will not give you any land. And his sons are just the same. *Think*, Euan. If you say yes, we can map our future in the longest of terms. Our plans do not have to be acted upon in a year or ten years, or even a hundred! My lord, it is your duty to ensure the survival of your people. If you do not make plans for this, you have failed them, failed yourself. It is not a matter of choice. It is a matter of survival."

Euan turned back to Leanan, his movement bringing his gaze swinging past the tree. Siobhan ducked back into cover, holding her breath.

Leanan continued, her voice low and seductive. "Why must you descend into this . . . this pool and come out as different beings?"

"It is the price of immortality," said Euan doubtfully.

"That is not immortality. That is self-delusion. No matter how much you try and tell yourself you are being reborn, it is not *you* that comes out of the pool. You have no memories of your loves, your hates. No memories at all."

"Some would call that a boon."

"Not I. And not you either."

There was a moment's silence.

"You ask a lot of me, Leanan."

"I ask only what I know you can give. What you are strong enough to give. Leaders must make sacrifices for their people, Euan. That is what your parents, what all those *elders*, as they call themselves, do not understand. The world is a different place now. You know that."

"Perhaps . . ."

"Do you not want to live forever, Euan?"

"I do. But the price . . ."

"The price is worth the prize. My Prince, the Morrigan has talked to me. I have followed her orders to prepare for the coming war. All we need to start our war is the rathstone. We already have a small arm—"

Siobhan peered around the tree once again. But as she did so the kitchen door behind her opened, casting light out into the darkness. Leanan and Euan both turned to look, and Siobhan jerked her head back. She looked toward the door, but it was only Brianna throwing some old water out onto the earth. She shook the bucket out, then stepped back inside, closing the door behind her.

Siobhan breathed a sigh of relief. She had been lucky so far, but she shouldn't push that luck. She knew she had overheard something important, something she would need to think on, but if she stayed here much longer, they might sense her. She looked back to the kitchen. Should she try to sneak back, hoping the tree would mask her departure? Or maybe she should simply wait for Euan and Leanan to return to the Great Hall.

"And what do we have here?"

A hand grabbed hold of Siobhan's arm, yanking her out from behind the tree. Siobhan opened her mouth to scream, but Euan clamped his hand tight across her face.

"Little girls shouldn't be nosing around places where they're not wanted." He looked at Leanan. "How much do you think she heard?"

"What does it matter? Enough to be a danger."

"So what do we do with her?"

Leanan looked at Siobhan like an owl would look at a mouse. "Kill her. She is nothing to us."

Siobhan struggled in Euan's grasp, but the Prince was too strong. He pulled out a knife from his belt. It was wooden, but the edge looked as sharp as any metal blade she had seen.

"Don't struggle," said Euan. "It will just make it worse." He raised the blade.

"What's going on over there?" called a voice.

Siobhan's terrified eyes sought out the owner of the voice. A tall figure stood by the front doors of the manor house, peering over at them. Euan quickly put the knife away.

"Breathe a word of any of this, and I'll come

back and kill everyone in this house," he whispered. "Understand?"

Siobhan quickly nodded, and Euan removed his hand. Siobhan sank down against the tree as he and Leanan walked back to the hall.

"Nothing," she heard him say. "Just admiring the chapel. It's very . . . quaint."

The doors slammed and silence returned. Only then did Siobhan let the tears come. And once they started, she couldn't stop them. Everything that had happened, all the fear she felt, all the terror, the uncertainty, it all came out, released like water through a dam. She had been right. She wasn't meant for this. She couldn't do it.

"Here now."

This time Siobhan did scream. Her head jerked up, and she saw Elaphe standing before her. He quickly raised his hands in the air.

"I mean you no harm. I heard you crying, that is all. Are you well?" He shook his head in irritation at his own question. *"Are you well?* Will you listen to me? Of course you're not." He lowered his hands. "You're not hurt, are you?"

Siobhan stopped moving. She sniffed and wiped the tears away.

"Are you . . . hurt?"

Siobhan shook her head.

"No. I'm not hurt."

Elaphe looked over his shoulder to where Leanan and Euan had disappeared. "You must stay away from them, I think. They do not seem to like you." He turned back to Siobhan. "What is the reason for that? Have you done something to offend them?"

Siobhan swallowed nervously, trying to gather her thoughts. Now was her chance. "I think I have."

"Oh?"

Siobhan opened her mouth. But still she hesitated. So much depended on all this. If she trusted the wrong person, it could lead to the ruin of everything they had worked for.

But maybe there was a way to make sure.

She stared up at Elaphe and let her gaze unfocus. She searched for and found the deep, dark pit inside her mind, the hole where she had buried her talent.

Siobhan paused, but only briefly. She opened up the hole.

The Sight burst up out of the hole like a wild animal, furious at its captivity. Her vision swam and blurred. She saw Elaphe, as he stood before her. But she also saw him in the form of a golden snake. The two images bled into each other, his face flickering between reptilian and human.

That wasn't what she wanted to see. She wanted to see if Elaphe was trustworthy enough to speak to. She tried to focus her mind, tried to force it to do what she wanted it to. But as always, it felt like her mind simply snapped under the pressure. That it broke into a million tiny pieces and started to speed away from her grasp. And the farther it went, the less chance there was that she could pull it back.

She needed this to work. This one time, she needed

the Sight to work for her instead of against her. She tried again, tried to keep a grip on the sensation of Seeing, but the fragments slipped through her fingers. It was like trying to hold onto fine sand. She couldn't do it. She—

—she was aware of Elaphe standing close to her, his cool hand resting on her forehead.

"Gather it back," he said gently. "Pull it all back in. Remember your name. Repeat it. Who are you?"

"I . . . I . . ."

"You know who you are. Your name is Siobhan. Remember?"

"Siobhan . . ."

"That's right. Use your name. It is who you are. Repeat it. Use it to gather your mind back."

And she did. Somehow she managed to pull it all back under her control. Once she did that, she felt Elaphe helping her. He forced the Sight back into the pit and closed it up. She was glad he did so. She knew she wouldn't have been able to do it by herself.

She blinked and looked around. Mere moments must have passed, but it felt like hours. She was so exhausted, she could barely sit up. Elaphe stared at her with concern.

"Now," he said firmly. "Why don't you tell me your story. All of it. Including your little attempt to read me just now."

And so Siobhan did. She wasn't sure if trying to use the Sight had simply worn her down or if she was just afraid of doing this alone. Whatever the reason, she told him everything—starting with the fact that she had been sent back in time by a spell and then moving back to the day Corrine first arrived at Falston. She told of the fire, then the boat trip to Scotland. Her possession by ghosts. She told him about the Prince and his search for the stones, and how he wanted to gain control of Hallowmere and rule over the mortal lands as well as the Fey raths. She even told him about before Falston, bits and pieces of her childhood that no one in the Council but Miss Brown knew, about her mother's dementia, about all the secrets she told no one and rarely thought of herself.

As she spoke, Elaphe said nothing, his head bowed to the ground as he listened.

The story came full circle, back to the spell cast by Corrine and Mara at St. Fillan's well and her waking up in the forest. She then told him what she had overheard Leanan and Euan talking about only moments before and finished with what they had said about wanting the rathstone.

Elaphe stood in silence. Siobhan had to look away from his gaze. She feared if she stared too long at the pain and hurt in his eyes, she would burst into tears and not be able to stop.

"So the day has finally come," he said.

"You believe me?"

"Of course I do. I can tell when someone speaks untruths."

"What are you going to do?" she asked.

Elaphe looked surprised. "What am *I* going to do? 'What are *we* going to do?' is what I think you mean."

He gazed thoughtfully up at the sky. "I'll have to speak to some others. We will need allies."

"Who?"

"Well, Father Josephus, obviously. Although I think you should be careful what you tell him. No man should know his own future before it happens."

"I don't know anything to tell," said Siobhan. "I've only become involved in the Council recently. There wasn't time to tell me everything. And they keep their secrets well."

"I suppose that is good. Although a bit more information would have been helpful. Your very being here may change history for all we know. But no matter. First things first. I must safeguard the rathstone from Euan and his followers, then gather the others. And you, my girl. You need to learn to control that gift of yours. I'm surprised it hasn't driven you mad by now."

"Sometimes I think it has."

"Why didn't Father Josephus help you? If, as you say, he is aware of the magic of the Fey, it would not be difficult for him."

Siobhan flushed. She was glad it was dark so Elaphe couldn't see. "I . . . I wouldn't let him. My power . . . it is the work of the devil. But so are the means he wanted to use to teach me. I will have nothing to do with Fey magic."

"Siobhan," said Elaphe gently. "Another way to look at it is that God gave you this gift because He saw your life as a whole. He saw that your destiny was to help rid the world of the evil of the Unhallowed. God wouldn't send His soldiers into battle without weapons, would He?"

"I . . . I don't know," said Siobhan doubtfully. Then she shook her head firmly. "But it is a taint. I feel it every time it overwhelms me. It wants to take control, to devour me."

"Anything you let take control of your life is a taint, Siobhan. The way we stop it being so is to take charge and claim it as our own. If you allow me to teach you methods to take command of this gift—and believe me, it is a gift—then you shall be one of God's warriors. It will no longer be a taint, but a boon."

Siobhan said nothing.

"Think on it," he said. "I would like you to come to the church in the village tomorrow evening. Those whom I trust enough to tell will be there, but I think they should hear this story from your mouth as well. Will you come?"

Siobhan nodded. "Of course."

Elaphe smiled. "Good." He held his hand up, palm facing out. Siobhan hesitated, then did the same. Elaphe pressed them together. His skin was cool to the touch, and she thought she could feel scales brushing against her skin.

"We are bonded, Siobhan. I do not know where this journey will take us, but I will do my best to protect you on the path ahead."

"And I you," said Siobhan. She didn't know why she said it. It just seemed right. But the words seemed to satisfy Elaphe. He nodded brusquely.

"Till tomorrow." Then he turned and walked back to the Great Hall.

~ Six ~

THE NEXT DAY PASSED IN A BLUR OF NERVOUSNESS AND anticipation. Siobhan did her chores, making only a few mistakes due to her distracted thoughts. But the night before had been a late one, and Brianna just thought she was tired.

The day finally ended, and Siobhan managed to slip away and make her way down the hill into the village. The main street cut a swathe right through the houses, carrying on out through the low wall and into the forest beyond. She walked along the deserted stretch, listening to the sounds of life spilling out of the small huts and buildings, noting the torch- and firelight that flickered between ill-fitting stones and doors.

The church stood almost exactly in the center of the village. Unlike the other buildings, the church didn't sit right next to the road. The village green took that honor, with the church itself built on the other side of the large sward, up against a hill that marked the village's eastern boundary. Siobhan walked across the grass and stopped before the iron gate that led into the churchyard. It was a long, low building made from large gray stones. Thick, well-crafted double doors made from heavy oak stood open to the early evening. Warm light spilled onto the path.

Siobhan pushed open the gate and walked up the path. She hesitated briefly at the door, then steeled herself and walked inside.

She was immediately surrounded by an air of quiet calm and serenity. Siobhan paused involuntarily and closed her eyes. She took a deep breath, inhaling the atmosphere of tranquility and letting it wash over her like a soothing balm.

She stood like this for some time before opening her eyes again and looking around. Directly opposite her, high up on the wall, was a small, stained glass window depicting the Virgin Mary. This surprised Siobhan, as the elaborate window was the only one like it in the whole village—not even the manor house had something like this, which seemed to be an expensive piece. But maybe Conal's father had donated the money.

No one was around. Siobhan walked down the aisle and sat on a stair near the front of the church. She stared at the altar, watching the lowering sun stream through the colored glass and scatter puddles of red, blue, and yellow across the stone floor. Dust motes danced in the light. She watched them drifting back and forth, mesmerized by their slow movement.

There was a soft click off to her right, and Elaphe stepped through a door that had previously been hidden by shadows.

"Hello, Siobhan," he said. "I'm glad you decided to come."

Siobhan stood up. "I didn't have much choice."

"There is always a choice." He stepped to the side and gestured to the door. "Shall we?"

Siobhan nodded, and Elaphe opened the door for her. She stepped into a room lit by a large fire. Chairs had been set in a circle before the hearth. Father Josephus sat in one of the chairs. So did another stern-looking priest. In the chair next to him—Siobhan blinked in surprise— was Jack, the smith from the laird's house. He nodded briefly at her.

Elaphe touched her back and guided her to an empty chair, then took the one next to her.

Siobhan looked around at the faces, all of them staring at her. She tried to look confident and grown up, but she knew she probably looked exactly how she felt—like a frightened girl.

The stern-looking priest spoke first. "So, child," he said, his voice clipped and abrupt. "Elaphe here tells us a rather fantastical story."

"Very fantastical," muttered Father Josephus.

Siobhan turned her attention to Father Josephus, wondering at the tone of his voice. He seemed . . . angry. Siobhan looked closer at him, sensing something—and then it was gone again.

"That's enough, Josephus," said the priest.

Father Josephus opened his mouth to say something else, but Elaphe spoke first.

"Perhaps we should deal with the introductions first. Siobhan, Father Josephus you already know. Jack is the blacksmith for the village."

Jack looked up and briefly held Siobhan's gaze. He nodded almost imperceptibly.

"And this is Father Iamblicus. He is the priest for several nearby villages and comes to visit us from time to time, though he is based at St. Fillan's Kirk. Before Father Josephus was appointed to us here, he studied under Iamblicus."

"Pleased to meet—"

"What proof do we have she speaks the truth?" asked Father Josephus, cutting her off.

Elaphe and Iamblicus frowned at this show of bad manners.

"I mean"—he turned to Elaphe—"you yourself didn't even know about this."

"Because they knew how I would react if they had approached me."

Father Josephus frowned angrily and leaned back in his chair. "Well, I don't believe it."

Siobhan could hardly believe what she was hearing. The one person she thought would be on her side from the beginning was turning out to be the one person most strongly against her. "You've certainly changed your tune from last night," she said, struggling to keep her voice from showing her anger.

"I beg your pardon?"

"What was all that about Guthrie having dealings with demons and exposing his soul to danger?"

"That was a private conversation."

"So? You still said it. I heard you."

"I'm not denying I said it. Sometimes you have to . . .

overemphasize the dangers to the simple folk. Just to make them think about what they are doing, you understand. I feel that this village is intermingling too freely with the Fey." He paused and looked apologetically at Elaphe. "So I present a worst-case scenario in the hopes that people will take at least a part of my warning to heart."

"That is not how we teach the faith," said Iamblicus disapprovingly.

Father Josephus turned to Iamblicus. "This isn't about teaching the faith. This is about protecting the flock."

Siobhan noticed that Elaphe was staring at Father Josephus rather intently, like he was trying to see something beyond the priest's words. He frowned and opened his mouth to say something, but Iamblicus spoke first.

"This isn't the time for such a discussion." He turned his attention back to Siobhan. "And I say again, your story is rather fantastical."

"Even so, it is the truth."

Iamblicus raised his eyebrows. "I think we will be the judges of that."

"I have already judged," said Elaphe. "She speaks the truth."

"And because you say so, we are all simply to believe?" asked Father Josephus.

"No," replied Elaphe. "With your permission—with all of your permission," he said, looking at Siobhan as he said this last bit. "I would like to show you Siobhan's thoughts. I want us all to see what she knows."

Silence greeted his words. Siobhan stared hard at Elaphe. He hadn't said anything about this.

"I will link our minds with Siobhan's while she tells the story. That way we can experience the events first-hand." He turned to Siobhan. "With your permission, of course."

Siobhan swallowed nervously. She wasn't sure she liked the idea of these men seeing her thoughts, but if it would get them to believe her any quicker, then maybe it was worth it. She nodded once. "It's fine."

"Friends?"

"Eh . . . this won't work both ways, will it? You won't be able to see into my mind?" This was Father Josephus, and Siobhan thought he looked rather nervous.

Jack cleared his throat. He hadn't spoken once since she had arrived. Siobhan had almost forgotten he was there. "Scared we'll see your guilty secrets, Faither?" He spoke with the thick, almost unintelligible accent of the local villagers, even thicker than Conal's. "Father" came out as "Fay-thir." Siobhan was just glad Niamh and her family were Irish. Their accent was much softer on the ears.

Father Josephus flushed red. "No," he said defensively. "I just wondered how it worked."

"If the girl is brave enough to put up with us in her head, then I think we cannae complain ourselves."

"N-no. Of course not. Well said, Jack."

Jack merely grinned and stared at Father Josephus until the priest looked away.

"This won't be anything dramatic. I will link our minds and ask Siobhan to recite her story. That is all. You will simply see more in your heads, probably a lot you do not understand. Are you ready, Siobhan?"

Siobhan nodded.

"Then we will begin."

Elaphe closed his eyes and mumbled something under his breath. After about half a minute, he opened his eyes and nodded at her. "Go ahead."

So Siobhan told her story for the second time in the space of twenty-four hours. She left out the most personal information she'd shared with Elaphe, speaking only to her broad mission as set forth by the Council. As she talked she heard gasps and curses from the men around her, particularly when she told of the attack on Falston itself.

When she finished she trailed away into silence and looked at those surrounding her. Their faces had changed drastically from what she had seen before. Now they were pale, unsure. Father Josephus looked like he was about to be sick.

"Can I take it that we all believe her?" asked Elaphe quietly.

There were mumblings of "aye" all round.

"Then I propose we officially form ourselves into a group dedicated to fighting the plans of the Unhallowed." He turned to Siobhan. "Does this group have a name in your time?"

"It does. It is called the Council of Elaphe."

Jack chuckled to himself.

"Well," said Elaphe awkwardly. "If that is what it is called. My friends? Any objections?"

Iamblicus shook his head. "None here."

"Father Josephus?"

"What? No. Fine. I have to go." With these words Father Josephus lurched to his feet and took his leave. Iamblicus watched him go with concern plain on his face.

"Excuse me," he said. "I must attend Josephus."

Elaphe nodded, and Iamblicus left the room. Jack stood up and stretched. He nodded at Siobhan and Elaphe, then left without another word.

"Well," said Elaphe wryly. "Not exactly an auspicious start for a society dedicated to wiping out the evil of the Unhallowed."

"At least it's a start," said Siobhan quietly.

"Yes. That is true. And you," he asked, turning to face Siobhan, "are you ready to make a start?"

"To what?"

"To controlling your gift."

"I . . . I'm not sure."

"Come now, Siobhan. Forgive me for speaking so plainly, but in the light of what you have shown us, it is irresponsible of you to pretend you can hide away from your powers. What will you do if you realize you could have saved someone's life, if only you had learned how to harness your gift? Would you be able to live with that kind of guilt?"

Siobhan said nothing.

"It will not be difficult, child. Just a matter of learning certain techniques. Learning and mastering them. I can teach you the first right here. It will not take long."

Siobhan stared at Elaphe, thinking how nice it would

be not to be bothered by the Second Sight. "How will you teach me to control it?"

"There are many ways, cants and charms that can be uttered to dull the effect. Or to switch it off altogether, if you so wish. Although that only works for a short time. The Sight is a tool, Siobhan. Nothing more."

"All my life," she whispered. "All my life it has controlled me."

"I will teach you," said Elaphe gently. "I will teach you to control it. It is not hard."

In a way, that made it worse. All her life she'd been cursed with the visions. And to be told it was easy to control . . . She shook her head dumbly. What kind of person would she be if she had been able to do just that—control the visions? What kind of a person would she have grown into if she hadn't had to live in fear her whole life, constantly thinking she was going insane?

She sighed, giving in. "Fine."

"Good lass. Now, sit down."

Siobhan sat on the chair close to the fire.

"Now, the Sight, when you first feel it stirring, is a feeling of your mind opening up, like you are *feeling* your surroundings instead of seeing them, yes?"

Siobhan nodded.

"Your mind branches out. It feels like you are reaching for things, but with your mind instead of your hands. Is that accurate?

"It is," said Siobhan.

"Then that is the first lesson I will teach you, and it is probably the most important thing you must remember:

Do not focus on the tendrils if you do not wish to use the Sight. The more you focus on them, the stronger they get, the more they will fragment your mind. If you want to switch the Sight off, simply close your eyes and gather them in, like you are . . . like you are coiling rope. Keep them close to your mind."

Siobhan swallowed. His description was much like what she'd done in the forest the other day, though she hadn't known what she was doing and probably did it wrong. That must be why the Sight had always had so much control over her. Always, when she had sensed her mind branching out, she had helplessly followed each and every tendril, searching frantically for some kind of answer at the end. Her mind would fragment until she could no longer think, would no longer even know who she was anymore.

Yet still she would pursue each strand. Some false instinct would keep her seeking until her mind could no longer take it, and she would fall unconscious. That or descend into a fit.

And all the time she was doing this, she was actually strengthening the Sight, increasing its hold over her mind. Such a simple fact, one that would have helped her fight the madness. And she'd had no one to tell her.

Elaphe laid one hand over Siobhan's eyes and the other over her chest. He spoke a chant beneath his breath. Siobhan tried to hear, but she couldn't grasp the words. They slithered through her hearing like an eel in the water slipping through her hands.

She felt a sudden bloom of pain in her head. The

hole that she had pushed everything into opened up, the Sight pouring out in a torrent. She cried out, raising a hand to her temples. Immediately, she felt her mind fragment, like the shattering of glass, each tiny piece spiraling in a different direction. Her mind's eye flicked back and forth, fixing on each and every one as she reached out beyond herself, touching everything and understanding nothing. Her mind tried to follow the strands, like she had always done. It was habit, instinct.

Then Elaphe was standing before her. He had her face in his hands, and he was staring straight into her eyes.

"Siobhan. Do not follow them. They are not you. They are simply pieces of the Sight. Do you understand? It is not your mind that is fragmenting. It is not you. You do not need to control it. You cannot control it. That way lies madness. Just let it go. Just release it."

Siobhan blinked, pulling her mind back from the brink of wherever it had been heading. Part of her watched as the tendrils probed outward, invisible streamers that walked over Elaphe's face, over the walls of the room, over the closed door, and out into the church beyond. But she pulled back from them, letting them venture out on their own, without feeling the need to follow them. She focused on Elaphe's eyes.

"That is better. Just let them be. You will always know they are there, but they will not bother you unless you focus on them. That is an exercise you must practice, Siobhan. Without letting the Sight overwhelm you, try to follow one strand at a time, only for as long as you are comfortable. If you feel your thoughts slipping away, pull back. If you do this, you will soon be able to control your visions. You will soon see only what you want to see."

Siobhan nodded, unsure but hoping she was putting her trust in the right person.

Elaphe stood up. "It is a wonderful gift, Siobhan. You can even use it to find objects you have lost. Use it wisely, and it will probably save your life any number of times."

~ Seven ~

THE NEXT FEW DAYS WERE TAKEN UP WITH PREPARATIONS for the Harvest Festival that Niamh had previously mentioned. Siobhan hadn't been sure if she would be going, but it turned out that nearly everyone attended. It was a yearly tradition everyone took very seriously.

Her waking hours were filled with lifting, washing, carrying, and cooking, and she was so exhausted by the time night fell that it was all she could do to crawl into her bed. She tried to practice the exercises Elaphe had given her, but she usually ended up falling asleep.

But today she had some time to herself. The chests were packed, the horses readied, the food and drink prepared and loaded. They were leaving the next day for Killin, a village at the other end of the loch. Apparently it wasn't too far. A couple of hours on horseback, a couple of hours extra if they were walking.

Brianna had told Siobhan and Niamh to go and have some free time before the busy days ahead. Niamh had gone for a nap, saying she never got to sleep during the day.

Siobhan decided to go down to the loch and practice

her exercises. It was the only place she knew of where she would be left alone.

The loch was choppy today, the iron-gray waters ruffled by the cold wind, small jagged peaks rising and falling. Siobhan walked across the pebbled beach, thinking about the million-and-one things she should be doing.

She felt like she was failing, that events were passing her by. She thought it was the correct decision to postpone her attempt to retrieve the stone and instead concentrate on stopping the Fey from becoming Unhallowed. But what if she couldn't do that? What if she failed, even with the help of the newly formed Council? Should she not have a backup plan? Maybe she should start thinking of a way to get the stone back. She may not need to use it, but if she did . . .

Well, if she did, then at least she would be prepared.

Siobhan looked up from her reveries and found herself at the bridge that led to the first of the crannogs. She rested her foot on the wood, testing its strength. It creaked but held. She pushed down harder and waited, but the only sound she heard was the water lapping gently against the supports. She thought it would hold her weight.

Siobhan walked across the bridge, avoiding any of the boards that looked like they had rotted from exposure. Up ahead, the bridge led directly into the round building with the peaked roof. The building itself was raised high above the island on stilts. Siobhan walked through the empty doorway and found herself in a large common room. Daylight filtered in through small gaps in the roof covering. Her footfalls raised clouds of dust that caught the light and hazed the air. She tried to imagine the villagers from years before sheltering here from attackers. It didn't seem very comfortable. But then, if you're fighting for your life, what did comfort truly mean?

On the opposite side of the room was a second doorway leading outside. She exited the hut and found herself on a walkway that circled around the building. The walkway led to a short flight of stairs, which took her down to the surface of the island. The island was covered with rocks and boulders and looked to be about a hundred paces across. Thick wedges of yellow grass had managed to find root here and there, but that was the only sign of vegetation she could see.

She walked to the water's edge and picked up a small stone, throwing it across the water. It skipped three times before sinking beneath the surface.

"Not bad," said a voice behind her.

Siobhan whirled around in alarm. She was shocked to see Conal sitting on a rock a few paces away.

He smiled at her. "Sorry. Didnae mean to frighten you."

"You didn't," said Siobhan defensively.

"That's all right, then."

"Did you follow me here?" asked Siobhan suspiciously.

"Me?" Conal's eyebrows raised in surprise. "I was about to ask you the same thing. I've been here since the noon bell rang."

"Oh. Of course." Siobhan felt foolish. Of course he was already here. What possible reason would there be for Conal to follow her?

He got up and joined her by the shoreline, stopping to pick up a handful of the smooth stones. He threw one across the water. It skipped five times before disappearing.

"Beats yours, I think."

He handed her a stone. She threw it, but it sank again after three jumps. She stared at the expanding ripples in disappointment. "Let's call it a draw," she finally said.

Conal laughed. "Fine." He dropped the pebbles into the water, then sat down by the shore. Siobhan hesitated, then did the same, squinting out over the water.

"How are you settling in?" asked Conal.

"Fine."

"I've been meaning to come and see you, but I always seem to get sidetracked."

Siobhan said nothing. Why would he want to come see her?

"Getting on with everyone?"

"Mostly."

Conal laughed again. "You don't say much, do you?"

Siobhan flushed and looked away. He had a nice laugh, did Conal. It was carefree, unashamed. She could never laugh like that. She'd be too worried about people looking at her.

They were silent for a while, staring out across the waters. A family of geese drifted past. They watched them disappear around the island.

"What made you come here?" asked Conal.

"Peace and quiet," said Siobhan. "Brianna gave us some time off before the festival, and I wanted some privacy."

"Oh," Conal said. Siobhan sensed his hesitation. "Do you . . . want me to go?"

"What?" She looked at him in surprise. "Oh, no, I didn't mean it that way," she explained hastily. "Just that I wanted away from the house for a while."

"Ah. I feel the same way, actually. Quite often, as it goes."

They were silent again. Then Conal cleared his throat. "You're quite an enigma, you know."

Siobhan looked at Conal in surprise. "Me?"

"Oh yes. Quite a few people are talking about you."

Siobhan thought about this for a while. Finally she asked, "Why?"

This time it was Conal's turn to show surprise. "You mean you don't know?"

Siobhan shook her head. Conal looked thoughtful for a moment before continuing. "You're very . . . mysterious. Very secretive."

Siobhan smiled. "Not mysterious at all, I'm afraid."

"And secretive? What about that?"

"Maybe a bit secretive. I'll give you that one."

They locked eyes for a second, and Siobhan quickly looked away. An awkward silence descended.

"Can we talk about something else?" asked Siobhan finally.

"Aye, of course. Whatever you want."

Siobhan was silent for a moment as she thought. "How long have you been friends with Prince Euan?"

"Years. I've known him most of my life." He smiled. "Actually, I think I used to irritate him."

"Why?"

"When I was a child, I used to follow him and his friends around. I thought they were magical knights or something." The smile faded. "It nearly got me killed."

"Why? Did he threaten you?"

Conal looked at her in surprise. "No, nothing like that. In fact, he saved my life."

Siobhan tried to imagine the Euan she knew saving someone's life. Her imagination failed.

"I followed him into the forest one time. A pack of wolves caught my scent. They must have thought me easy prey. Euan heard my cries and came for me. He saved my life."

"He saved your life?"

"Aye, he did."

"Euan? Euan saved your life."

"Aye, Euan," said Conal, starting to sound annoyed. "Why are you finding this so hard to believe?"

Siobhan hesitated, staring into Conal's eyes. How easy it would be to tell him. To tell him everything. They could do with someone like him in the Council. Elaphe wouldn't mind, surely?

She opened her mouth, then snapped it shut again. How could she expect him to believe her? He and Euan were friends.

"Siobhan?"

"It's . . . nothing. I don't trust him, that's all."

"Why? Because of his jests? You shouldn't mind that. He doesn't mean anything."

Siobhan sighed. No. He wouldn't believe her. He would have to figure it out for himself.

"Tell me about this festival," she said, trying to change the subject.

Conal frowned at her suspiciously, then he shrugged and turned back to look out over the loch. "We have it every year at the tail end of harvest. All the local villages gather. We trade, we drink, we feast."

"And the Fey also attend?"

"Oh, aye. They wouldn't miss it for the world. They like a good party, do the Fey. Even the King and Queen, actually. Just one big party."

Conal picked up another handful of stones. As he did so his hand brushed Siobhan's fingers.

"Sorry—"

Siobhan quickly snatched her hand away and stood up. "I've . . . ah . . . got to go."

"Siobhan, don't be silly. I didn't mean—"

"What? No. It's not . . . It's Brianna. She'll want me to help. To get ready for tomorrow. That's all."

"Siobhan—"

But Siobhan was already hurrying away, unable to look him in the eyes.

~ Eight ~

THE NEXT DAY DAWNED COLD AND WINDY, THE SKY A SOLID slate of gray that hung low against the horizon. Siobhan and Niamh helped Eomen load the cart with the items that had been left to the last minute. Siobhan saw that this meant mostly barrels of ale and casks of wine. Eomen told her they hadn't loaded them earlier for fear of them being stolen. There was also a huge, folded square of canvas that was laid out on the base of the cart. Niamh said it was the tent that Conal and his father would be staying in for the three days of the festival.

"If we're lucky, we'll get to sleep in it as well," she said.

Siobhan eyed the dirty-looking canvas dubiously. "What do you mean, 'if we're lucky'?"

Niamh looked at her as though she were insane. "They'll have a fire going inside. Would you rather sleep outside? In this weather?"

Siobhan looked up just as a handful of brown leaves blew past her face. She smiled at Niamh. "Fair point."

"We'll be off soon," said Eomen, making sure everything was tied down tightly in the cart. "Niamh, go see if your mother needs me to take anything else."

Niamh hurried into the kitchen. Eomen glanced at Siobhan. "You got all your things?"

Siobhan held up a small bundle that held all her worldly possessions—the dress and the hair combs she'd been wearing when she woke up in the forest that day. She was wearing the dress Brianna had given her. "Not exactly a lot to carry," she said.

"Aye, well. There's folk with less than that, lass." Eomen looked over her shoulder and straightened up. Siobhan turned to see Elaphe approaching through the gate.

"Elaphe," said Eomen respectfully.

"Goodman Eomen. Can I have a moment of Siobhan's time?"

"Siobhan?" Eomen looked at her, puzzled. "Aye, of course. Siobhan?"

Siobhan hurried over to Elaphe, trying to ignore Eomen's curious looks in their direction.

"Siobhan," said Elaphe. "How are you?"

"Fine."

"Have you been doing the exercises I gave you?"

"When I can. I've been busy preparing—"

"Siobhan, forgive me, but it's very important that you persevere with them. You *must* learn to control your talent. It may save your life."

Siobhan looked at the ground, shamed by Elaphe's disappointment. "I will, Elaphe. I promise."

"I am sorry, child. I didn't come here to chastise you."

"Why did you come? Eomen will be wondering . . ."

"I know. But I needed to see you before you left. You must do something for me—for the Council."

Siobhan straightened her back. "Anything."

Elaphe smiled. "I need you to keep a watch over Euan and his followers at the festival."

"Why? Won't you be there?"

"No," said Elaphe, his voice troubled. "Iamblicus and I are greatly troubled by the reports of missing villagers. We didn't think of it much before now—we thought it was wolves or simple unpreparedness—but after what you have told us . . . Well, we fear the worst, especially with what we know from Mathew's report at the last gathering. We are hoping to track them while Euan and Leanan are otherwise engaged."

"You want me to keep an eye on them? On my own?"

"Not on your own. Father Josephus will be there. As will Jack. We don't want you to do anything. But as a servant you can get closest to them without being noticed. Just see if they say anything of use. That is all. Can we count on you?"

"Of course. I'll do my best."

Elaphe smiled. "That's all we can ask." He looked up. "I think it is time for you to depart now. We will speak soon." He raised a hand in farewell to Eomen, then turned and walked back through the gate.

Siobhan rejoined the others. Eomen was busy checking that the horses were firmly attached to the cart. He threw a sideways look at Siobhan but didn't say anything. Instead he pulled himself up onto the front board of the cart. A moment later Niamh reappeared carrying a huge pot filled with raw potatoes and onions. Siobhan hurried forward to help her, and they both manhandled it into the cart. Then they climbed up after it.

"Ma said she'll see you tonight and that you're not to drink too much when you get there," said Niamh to her father.

Eomen smiled and flicked the reins. The horses gave a snort, then set off through the yard. They passed Jack as he prepared the other horses for Conal and his father. He nodded as they passed. Siobhan hadn't had a chance to speak to him since the Council meeting, but he seemed content to carry on as before. Eomen lifted his hand in farewell, and then they were out through the gate and trundling down into the village.

Siobhan looked about as they passed the small houses and shops. The village was a hive of bustling activity. Siobhan could sense the excitement in the air. Even the elderly were getting ready to travel.

"Does everyone attend the festival?"

"Of course," said Niamh. "It's the highlight of the year. The crops are harvested; the cold hasn't hit with full force yet. It's the one chance everyone gets to relax and enjoy themselves."

Siobhan watched as a brother and sister chased each other around the street. Their mother watched them from inside the doorway of a small hut, an amused smile on her lips. The children were thin, and the mother looked tired and worn. But they looked happy. Siobhan supposed that Niamh was right. People needed something to look forward to, even if it was just one simple feast every year.

Eomen followed the road out of the village, then turned onto a track that led up the hill through the trees and out of the shallow, protective valley. The blue and pink heather covering the green landscape seemed brighter this morning, their colors contrasting with the dark gray of the sky.

"Here," said Niamh, rummaging through a bag and pulling out an old, woven blanket. "Might as well get used to it. It'll be keeping us warm through the nights."

Siobhan snuggled under the blanket, trying to ignore the smell of must and animals. It kept them warm. That was all she needed.

The road circled around the village and then followed the edge of the loch as it headed west. Siobhan spent her time staring across the water, watching the high hills on the opposite shore slowly pass them by. Behind the hills was a line of mountains, the jagged, snow-covered peaks hazed by distance. Siobhan snuggled even deeper into the blanket, wondering how cold it must be so high up.

As the morning progressed they came across other travelers making their way to Killin. Some of them waved as the cart trundled past, and Eomen nodded his greetings back at those he knew.

They arrived at the huge field outside Killin later that afternoon. People were already milling about, setting up tents and wooden stalls, shouting greetings to friends, laughing over a shared drink. Children ran across the wide open space, screaming and laughing, covered in dirt and mud from their romping. The smoke from numerous fires drifted up into the sky, mingling invisibly with the gray clouds. Eomen guided the horses through the narrow thoroughfares around the outside of the camp, calling greetings to old friends and warnings to those who got in the way. The cart rumbled jerkily across the uneven ground, jarring Siobhan. She clenched her jaw tight and looked over the side to see what was causing the discomfort. The ground was covered in pieces of broken bark—probably to keep the track from becoming a huge mud puddle in the event of rain.

Eomen worked his way closer to the center of the field, where a huge open space was kept clear of tents and stalls. A massive, unlit fire had been built in the center, logs the same size as Siobhan pushed up on their ends and piled against each other. Inside this structure was a man-shaped figure wearing a wooden mask.

"What's that?" she asked.

"He's the Winter Spirit," said Niamh. "He's burned every year to make sure the winter will end and spring will come."

"Oh." Siobhan stared at the figure half-glimpsed among the wood. It was dressed in a black robe, and the mask was carved to resemble some kind of demon. She shivered, trying to shake the feeling that the cloth and wooden figure was looking at her.

Finally, the cart shuddered to a stop. Eomen jumped off and stretched. "Right. You two. We'd better get the tent up before Guthrie arrives. We'll want the fire going as well. I'll find someone to help with the ropes. Before we get started, you can go buy some firewood." He tossed Niamh a small purse. "And no spending it on anything else. I know how much is in there."

He turned and walked off. Niamh turned to Siobhan with a grin.

"Let's go. I've been dying for some stew all day."

"But your father said . . ."

Niamh waved Siobhan's protest aside. "He didn't mean it. Anyway, a bowl of stew isn't going to use up all the coin."

After a few minutes of searching, they found a stall run by an old woman with no teeth, and Niamh bought two bowls of stew. They stood by the woman's fire, sipping the hot, watery liquid and watching the chaos flowing around them. Siobhan tried to take everything in, but it was impossible. So much was going on, it would take a full day to inspect every stand and all its wares. She contented herself by watching a skinny man juggling five balls through the air. He was rather good, until a small child darted forward and stamped on his toes. He cried out in surprise, dropping the balls. The child stuck his tongue out and ran, disappearing into the crowd amidst much laughter. The man glared at them, then picked up the balls and stalked away through the cramped aisles, pushing aside anyone who wouldn't get out of his way fast enough.

They handed the bowls back to the old woman when they had finished. "Now," said Niamh. "Let's get some firewood."

They found a seller on the outskirts of the market. The boy, who was about Siobhan's age, had piles of wood, and as Niamh stood talking to him, a younger boy arrived with another bundle tied to his back. He dropped it to the ground and turned wearily, heading back into the forest. Siobhan listened carefully and could hear the sharp sounds drifting toward her through the cold air of axes cutting wood. Niamh finished talking and returned to Siobhan. "Let's go," she said.

"What about the wood?"

"He's going to bring it to the tent. Unless you want to carry it, that is?"

Siobhan grinned. "No thanks."

By the time they returned to the campsite, Eomen and four other men had pulled the massive tent upright. The three men were holding the long ropes taut while Eomen hurried around the perimeter, hammering long wooden pegs into the ground to secure them. Once he had finished he thanked the men and told them to come back later for a mug of ale.

"Wood's coming, Da," said Niamh.

"Good lass. Put up the dividers, will you?"

Siobhan and Niamh entered the dim tent where there were two extra pieces of canvas lying on the ground. Niamh took the end of one, indicating for Siobhan to take the other. They opened these out and attached them to eyelets in the tent walls, creating two smaller partitions along one side of the tent.

"That's their rooms sorted out. Now it's just the fire, and we're done."

The wood arrived soon after, and they set about building the fire in the center of the tent, directly beneath the small hole that would allow the smoke to escape. Niamh disappeared outside and reappeared a minute later with a burning brand from someone else's fire. She thrust it into the wood, and they both watched as the logs smoked, then caught alight. A few minutes later Niamh and Siobhan were warming their hands near the flames.

"That's better," said Niamh, smiling.

The afternoon wore on, and the chill deepened. An hour or so before dusk, Conal and his father arrived on their horses, Jack following along behind them. They dismounted, and Jack took their reins, leading the horses behind the tent.

"The fire going, Eomen?" asked Guthrie, rubbing his hands together vigorously.

"Aye. And the wine is on the heat as well."

"Forget that. Break open the whiskey. That'll soon put fire in my bones."

"Right you are."

"I'll have the wine, Eomen," said Conal as he took his gloves off. "Come and have some yourself. You look like you're freezing."

As he passed them by, Conal glanced over at Siobhan. Their eyes locked for a second, and it looked like he was about to say something, but a shout went up from across the empty circle of ground in the center of the camp. She looked up, and beyond the unlit fire she could see a procession of horses approaching through the darkening afternoon.

The Fey had arrived.

~ NINE ~

SIOBHAN SAT ON A FALLEN TREE TRUNK AND WATCHED THE spirit of winter burn.

It was nighttime, and the festival was well under way. Drunken laughter could be heard from every nook and cranny. Bagpipe music shrilled and wailed, the tune horribly off-key. Siobhan had seen the man who was playing the pipes drinking five mugs of ale, one after the other. She was surprised he could even stand.

She looked beyond the fire to the Fey encampment across the field. They had raised their own tents and shelters, their extravagance humbling the simple pieces of cloth and sack the villagers used. The Fey tents looked as though they were made from silk, and yet the material barely shivered in the cold wind.

She could see the King and Queen. They sat on wooden thrones carved to resemble large trees. The backrests of the thrones were the branches and leaves, and they curved up and over to shelter the occupants from any rain. They sat just outside the largest of the tents, with a long line of local village leaders queuing up to say a few words.

She could see Euan as well. He and the four Fey who always followed him around sat almost directly opposite Siobhan, so she caught glimpses of him through the roaring fire. He was laughing and drinking, his eyes glittering with reflected flames.

Conal was there as well, seated on a low stool as he drank the ale his father had brought.

Siobhan had been trying to get close to Euan all evening, but she was hampered by the fact that it would look suspicious if she simply stood around and listened to him talk. But now, with Conal there, it gave her the perfect opportunity.

She collected a jug of ale and walked around the fire to where Conal was sitting. She offered the ale, and Conal held his cup out before looking up and realizing it was she. A flicker of surprise crossed his face, but Siobhan ignored it.

Euan laughed. "Already got her trained up, eh Conal?"

Siobhan ignored the jibe and moved back into the shadows. She hoped that if she just sat there, she might overhear something worthwhile.

But hope springs eternal, as the saying went. She waited for the next two hours, occasionally leaving the cover of the shadows to quietly fill Conal's cup. And in all that time, Euan didn't say anything of interest. He spent most of the night boasting of past hunts with his lackeys. Conal joined in the jokes, but steered clear of contributing to the cruder stories.

Siobhan thought she should just go to bed. There

wasn't much chance of Euan saying anything with Conal around anyway.

But then an opportunity presented itself. Conal's father had been drinking steadily all night, and he finally succumbed to the effects of the spirit. He passed out and fell off his chair, landing face-first in a puddle of spilled whiskey, amidst much laughter from those around him. Conal got up, and he and Eomen carried him into their tent so he could sleep it off.

Siobhan stayed where she was, frozen in the shadows. And her patience was finally rewarded when Euan leaned close to Mordroch and whispered the words: "We take the stone tonight. Pass the word."

Siobhan felt a thrill of fear soar through her body. Tonight! She had no idea their plans were so far advanced. No one did. Certainly, Elaphe would not have disappeared if he had known.

What should she do? He had to be warned.

Father Josephus. Elaphe had said to tell him if anything happened.

Siobhan slowly stood up, careful not to make the slightest sound. Then she slipped around the back of the crowds and went in search of the priest.

She eventually found him, but he was of no help to her at all. He was passed out on an old blanket, his arms curled around a skin of wine. Three empty skins were strewn about his body, and no matter how much she shook him, he wouldn't wake up.

That left only Jack, but she couldn't find him either. Siobhan stood outside the tent, shivering with the cold and with frustration. Where was everyone? Didn't they realize how important this was?

She knew she wasn't being fair. No one had thought anything would happen so soon after Siobhan told them the story. Siobhan got the impression that Elaphe was thinking in terms of weeks and months. Years even, if they were lucky.

But no. It all started tonight. And if Euan got hold of the rathstone, he would be one step closer to controlling Hallowmere.

Their fight would end before it had even begun.

She had to do something. The realization hit her like a blow to the stomach. She sagged down onto a fallen tree trunk. She tried to think a way around the fact, but she could see no other option. Elaphe and Iamblicus were gone. Father Josephus was passed out, and Jack had vanished.

She was the only member of the Council of Elaphe who could stop Euan from stealing the stone. Even then she tried to come up with reasons why she couldn't do it, avoiding the fact that it was fear, plain and simple, that was talking. She couldn't get into the rath. The path was hidden.

The answer presented itself almost immediately. Get hold of Conal's talisman. The one he used when he took her to the rath. That would gain her entry.

How was she supposed to find the stone?

Elaphe had said it was underground, deep beneath where they'd had the feast. Find some stairs and keep going.

The stone was protected.

Here she paused. Elaphe had said he was going to set wards around the stone to protect it against Euan and his cronies. How would she break them?

Siobhan thought about it, then decided it didn't really matter. She had to try, no matter how scared she was. If she didn't, she would never forgive herself.

And the night was growing old. So she had better get a move on.

Siobhan had thought that with the decision made, she could simply spring into action and be on her way, but in reality that meant she had to wait for Conal to retire for the night, sneak into the tent, and steal the talisman from around his neck.

But Conal wasn't cooperating. He was drinking slowly, laughing and joking with his friends, and Siobhan realized with a rising sense of despair that he wasn't going to get drunk enough for her to carry out her plan.

She shivered as she wondered what to do. The night was growing colder, and all the positions around the fire were taken up. Siobhan turned and headed into the warm tent. Conal had said they could all sleep around the fire, seeing as the night was so cold. She could at least keep warm as she pondered her next move.

Eomen was off somewhere drinking with his friends, but Niamh had already turned in for the night. Siobhan could see her bundled beneath the old blanket, as close to the fire as she could get. A grunt and snort from the back of the tent told her that Guthrie was still passed out.

She stopped suddenly, her breath catching in her

throat. Something Conal had said the first day she was here came back to her. Hadn't he said that he *and* his father had a talisman? That the Fey had presented each of them with means of gaining entry to the rath?

She glanced behind her to make sure the tent flap was pulled down, then watched Niamh for a few seconds to make sure she was still asleep.

Her heart thudding painfully in her chest, the blood pumping in her throat, she carefully made her way around the sacks of food and casks of drink, careful not to knock anything over.

She arrived at the partition dividing Conal's and his father's rooms from the rest of the tent and laid a trembling hand on the material.

A burst of laughter came from outside as a drunken group stumbled past the tent. Siobhan froze, her breath catching in her throat. Niamh muttered something. Siobhan looked over her shoulder, but she was only rolling over in her sleep.

Siobhan waited while the revelers disappeared. Her hands were sweating despite the cold. She was sure that Guthrie must be able to hear her heartbeat. It was thudding so loudly in her own ears, she thought it impossible no one else could hear it.

She waited like this for a few minutes, making sure Niamh and Guthrie were still in a deep sleep. She nervously pulled the material aside and peered into the small room. A shuttered lamp cast a dim orange glow over the small area. Guthrie lay sprawled on a blanket, his mouth hanging wide open.

Siobhan steeled herself, then stepped inside. She slowly approached the sleeping form, freezing every time he twitched or groaned or thirstily smacked his lips. She kneeled next to him, wrinkling her nose at the smell of sweat and drink.

Now what? There was no easy way to do this—the talisman wasn't sitting out where she could just grab it. She just had to hope the alcohol kept him asleep.

She gingerly opened the cloak that Conal had wrapped around him. Then she gently pushed aside the shirt beneath, revealing a chest full of thick hair. There it was, attached to a leather thong and tied around his neck— the same kind of charm Conal had used to gain access to the rath.

Siobhan breathed a sigh of relief, a smile coming to her face. Finally. Something was going right. She reached forward—

And stopped, the smile fading. How was she supposed to get it from around his neck? She couldn't untie the thong. That would take too long. And besides, he'd probably feel it. She looked around the small room for something to cut the leather, panic threatening to overwhelm her. She didn't have time for this. Why was nothing ever easy?

Then she heard a voice outside the tent. It was Conal. He was calling good night to someone.

Siobhan groaned inwardly. Why hadn't she just waited outside, like she had originally intended? She felt around the floor, searching frantically for something, anything, that she could use to cut the cord.

She didn't even have a knife of her own . . .

A knife. She pulled Guthrie's cloak aside and found what she was looking for. A small dirk tied to his belt. She tried to untie the dirk with fingers that felt huge and clumsy.

Come on! Come on! she cried silently, fumbling with the knot. She grunted in triumph when it finally parted, grabbing hold of the small knife. She paused and listened. Conal was laughing, telling someone that tomorrow was the real party; tonight was the warm-up. Siobhan leaned forward and slit through the leather thong. She pulled on it, but it wouldn't budge. She pulled harder. Guthrie groaned and rolled toward Siobhan. She froze, then in one swift movement, she yanked the charm away from Guthrie's neck.

His eyes fluttered open.

Siobhan didn't move. Her breath caught in her throat as she stared down at the bleary-eyed man. He tried to focus on her, found that he couldn't, then simply closed his eyes again and drifted off.

Siobhan sighed with relief and quickly replaced the dirk and left the small room. She had only moved two steps when Conal stepped inside the tent and saw her.

He stopped. Siobhan quickly tucked the talisman into her dress and tried to smile.

"What are you doing?" asked Conal.

"Oh . . . just . . . looking for another blanket. Not for me. For Niamh. I saw she was shivering."

Conal glanced across at the sleeping form of Niamh. She wasn't shivering. In fact, she looked quite warm.

"Anyway, I'll just get to bed," she said quickly. "Have to get up early tomorrow to organize breakfast."

Conal watched her as she lay down next to Niamh and pulled the threadbare blanket over her. She rolled over and turned her back to him.

Even so, she could feel his eyes on her back for some time before he carried on through to his own bed.

~ Ten ~

SIOBHAN WAITED A FULL HOUR BEFORE MOVING. SHE WANTED to be absolutely sure everyone in the tent was asleep before she set out. If worse came to worst, and someone did wake up, she would simply say she was going to use the longdrop. No one would ask her any more questions after that, she was sure.

She carefully pushed the blanket back and sat up. The fire was still burning strongly, and by its light she could see Niamh sleeping peacefully. Siobhan tiptoed around her and slipped out into the night.

The party was still going strong, though the crowds had thinned somewhat. The Fey had all disappeared, their tents dark and sealed tight against the cold night air. Siobhan felt a rush of urgency and hurried around the tent to where Jack had tied the horses. He still wasn't back yet. She wondered if she should be worried about him, but she shook off the thought quickly. He was a grown man. He'd probably just passed out drunk like Father Josephus.

Siobhan decided to take Jack's horse. She felt too guilty taking Conal's or his father's. Besides they were too big for her, and the horses that pulled the cart didn't have any saddles. Jack's did, however rudimentary it was—nothing like the saddles she was used to from 1867. Siobhan pulled it out of his small tent and dragged it over to the mare. She nickered softly when Siobhan approached.

"Easy girl," Siobhan whispered. "Easy now."

The horse chuffed her breath into the air and tossed her head. Siobhan waited a moment for the mare to settle, then heaved the saddle onto her back and secured the straps. She threw the reins over the horse's neck and pulled herself up.

Siobhan leaned forward and patted the mare's neck. "Are you ready?"

Siobhan pulled the reins to the side and guided the horse quietly through the narrow thoroughfares of the camp. It took a while, but once she was free of the field, she guided the horse onto the road they had arrived by and increased the mare's speed to a steady canter.

The way Siobhan saw it, it took them about four hours in the cart to get to Killin from Ballach. So it shouldn't take her more than an hour on horseback to get back from the rath, which was a little over halfway back to Ballach, if she traveled at a reasonably fast pace.

The moon was full, the clouds dispersed by an afternoon wind, so the road was lit as clearly as she could possibly wish it to be.

The only problem was the cold. She held her shawl around her shoulders and hunched forward so she could keep a grip on the reins, but in ten minutes she was shivering just as much as if she were lying naked in the snow. There was nothing she could do about it though. Nothing but push on and hope it would all be worth it.

Time stretched on and on, so much so that Siobhan eventually had to pause to make sure she hadn't taken a wrong turn somewhere. She hadn't. The cold just made the journey seem longer.

She eventually led the mare over a rise and spotted the road Conal had taken her down that first day, the road that led to the fairy rath. She pulled the horse to a stop. The forest sprawled out below her, the treetops lit white by the moon. Everything was silent—the night, the forest. Even her own heart had stopped beating so hard.

This was it. Once she ventured down that road, there was no turning back. She shook her head and smiled wryly. There had never really been an option. She may have told herself that she could hide, but the responsibility would always have found her. She had to do this. That was all there was to it.

Siobhan dug her heels in, and the horse leaped forward into a gallop. The mare whinnied her pleasure, happy to finally be allowed her head. She stretched out and thudded down the incline, steadily gaining speed. The wind whipped through Siobhan's hair, stinging her cheeks with the cold and bringing tears streaming from her eyes. She felt exhilarated, alive—as if nothing could stop her.

The mare's hooves threw up clumps of dirt as they

galloped along the road. In what seemed like no time at all, they arrived at the bottom of the hill. Siobhan pulled on the reins, slowing the mare to a walk. The horse tossed her head, breath chuffing into the cold air as Siobhan guided her toward the line of trees. As before, there were no paths she could see.

Now she would see if the amulet worked the same for her as it did for Conal. She reached into her pocket and withdrew the talisman.

As soon as she did so, she heard the rustle of branches in front of her. She looked up and saw that an opening had formed in the trees, a dark tunnel that extended away into the darkness. Siobhan smiled and tied the talisman around her neck. Then she dug her heels in, and the mare leaped forward into the tunnel.

Siobhan didn't pause until they got to the next wall of trees. Like Conal before, she didn't have to do anything to gain entry. She simply waited a few moments, then the trees groaned as if in pain and pulled aside, forming another passageway.

Siobhan took a deep breath. "This is it, girl," she said, patting the horse on the neck and urging her into the tunnel. The mare went willingly, and it was Siobhan who constantly checked over her shoulder to make sure nothing was about to jump out at them.

Nothing did, and it wasn't long before she saw a difference in the darkness up ahead. It was less solid, more like natural night than the unnatural shadows that surrounded her. As she drew closer she could see the stars in the night sky, and after a few more minutes, she emerged into the Fey village.

She stopped the horse and looked around. The clearing was the same as before, the only difference being that it was now deserted. She hoped Conal was right about *all* the Fey attending the festival. Her plan hinged on the fact that the rath was deserted.

Siobhan dismounted and tied the reins loosely around a low branch. Moonlight spilled down, casting a soft glow over the standing stones as she approached them. The moss and lichen that covered the pitted surfaces looked black in the cold, ivory light.

Siobhan glanced around once, just to make sure no one was watching her. Then she gripped the talisman, clenched her eyes closed, and stepped between the two stones.

~ Eleven ~

SIOBHAN OPENED HER EYES AGAIN AND FOUND HERSELF surrounded by hundreds of faceless creatures, all of them turning in her direction.

She screamed, then quickly clamped her hand over her mouth as her eyes darted frantically around the tunnel. The creatures clung to the earthen walls and hung from the roots in the ceiling. They covered the floor like a moving carpet.

At first glance they looked like monkeys. Except that their heads were those of old men, wrinkled and covered in liver spots. Some of them even had a few stray wisps of gray hair. But the only features on each miniature head were two wide gashes where the nose should be. Nothing else. No eyes, no mouth, no ears. Just a blank, egg-shaped head with two dark slits in the center. The creatures tilted their heads like birds, the gashes opening and closing, opening and closing, as if they were trying to catch an elusive scent.

And that's exactly what they're doing, Siobhan realized. All the creatures in the tunnel, every single one of them, had turned blindly in her direction. She could actually hear the intake of air as they sniffed.

Siobhan backed up, intending to leave as quickly as she could. Her heel slid up against something, and she felt a sharp pain in her calf. She turned and saw she had bumped up against one of the creatures. The sharp pain had been it, swiping at her leg with tiny claws.

The creatures were blocking off the exit. Siobhan turned in a slow circle, realizing with a sinking sensation that she was totally surrounded.

As one, the creatures moved slowly forward, swinging along the roots or leaping along the walls, coming closer to Siobhan.

And all the time she could hear the constant snuffling as they tested the air.

There was nowhere for her to go. But she was damned if she would simply stand there and let them get her. Siobhan took a careful step forward. The creatures froze in place, then they started to sway up and down in obvious agitation. Siobhan stopped moving, and immediately they stopped as well. One of the creatures at her feet leaned in and sniffed her foot. Its tiny damp hands gripped her leg as it walked around her, sniffing as it went. Another one, right by Siobhan's shoulder, leaned in and sniffed her face. She could hear the snuffling loud in her ear, could smell the faint stench of decay from the creature's body.

It lifted her hair, inhaling deeply.

And sneezed.

At least, Siobhan thought it sneezed. It leaned away from her, then jerked suddenly forward, an exhalation of air and something wet striking Siobhan on the cheek. She winced and used her sleeve to wipe it away.

She didn't know what the creatures were doing. Were they some kind of guardians? Something the Fey leave behind to watch over their rath? Then why weren't they attacking her?

Then she realized, and she felt a fool for not thinking of it sooner.

The talisman. She was protected while she wore it around her neck.

She reached up with trembling fingers and pulled it out from beneath her dress. She held it away from her chest, allowing the closest creature to lean in and smell it. It did so immediately, grabbing the disk with tiny fingers and bringing it close to its nose. It snuffled and sniffed for what seemed like an age, but then, apparently satisfied, it released the talisman and turned away from Siobhan. So did the others, all of them retaking their positions along the tunnel, no longer the slightest bit interested in her.

Siobhan took a shaky breath, then walked slowly forward, careful not to step on any of the guardians. She had to move slowly, because now that they had accepted her, they ignored her entirely, which meant they didn't even bother to move out of her way.

She made it to the banquet hall. All the tables had been removed, the space now feeling huge and empty. She looked around, but she didn't think the stone would be anywhere in here. What had Elaphe said? Somewhere underground.

She turned her attention to the doors through which the King and Queen had entered on the night of the feast. They were as good a place as any to start searching.

The doors led into a small room where another three doors opened off from the room, one per wall. She sighed, looking between them. One was as good as the other, she supposed, picking the one directly ahead. It led into a brightly lit corridor, although Siobhan couldn't see the source of the lights. Doors opened off either side of the passageway. She pushed the first one open and found a small, sparsely furnished bedroom. For some reason this struck her as odd. She had never thought of the Fey as needing sleep or rest. To do so would make them seem, too . . . human.

Or perhaps they simply used the rooms as places to be alone? Maybe even the Fey needed private time.

She walked farther down the passage, but it was all the same. Large and small rooms. Some with musical instruments, some without. A few had strange games laid out on ornately carved tabletops. Siobhan studied them, but the patterned inlays hurt her eyes. The tiles were formed into deep pools of color and shapes that tried to draw her deeper and deeper, until she staggered and almost fell over.

She blinked and looked away. She had a feeling she was wasting her time in this corridor.

She retraced her steps and took the door to the right. This one led into a short passage, then to a flight of stairs that led downward. That felt more like it. Siobhan followed the stairs down.

And down. And down. They seemed to go on for-ever, so that her calves soon ached, and she wondered if the stairs actually led anywhere. What if it was some kind of Fey joke? What if she ended up walking and walking forever?

She shook her head against such a fancy. But she did pause, wondering if she should go back and try the other door. She eventually decided against it. She had come this far. She might as well keep going and see where the stairs led.

She set off again. The lower she went, the colder it became. Her breath clouded the air before her. She wrapped her arms around herself, shivering in the frigid air.

After a while she noticed that the walls had started to recede, the stairs themselves growing wider and wider, until all she could see to either side was darkness. Siobhan's feet echoed as she walked, and she could sense a growing space all around her. The darkness started to deepen as well. Whatever light had lit her way thus far had faded to a twilight resonance. Everything was shaded in hues of gray.

She finally reached the bottom. There was no warning. One second she was walking down the stairs, the next her knees were jarring from the sudden flat ground.

She stumbled forward a few paces. She caught herself before she fell to her knees, coming to a standstill. At the same time a soft white light blossomed from somewhere, growing in strength until she was soon able to see her surroundings.

She was in a vast, cavernlike chamber. She knew that

from the echo brought on by her slightest movement. She still couldn't see the walls, though. The white glow only lit a circle up to twenty paces around her.

In the center of this circle, no more than a few arms' lengths in front of her, was a polished wooden statue, carved into the shape of a small boy.

He was holding an ordinary stone in his outstretched hand—a pebble, really, or so it seemed. The rathstone.

Siobhan almost sobbed with relief. The white light shone down on the statue like the glow from heaven itself. It struck highlights from the deep brown wood, accentuating features so detailed that it seemed as if the boy were actually alive.

She walked slowly forward. The boy was shorter than she, his hair long and flowing down his naked back. Siobhan hesitantly reached forward, her free hand gripping the talisman around her neck. She touched the rathstone.

The boy's hand closed around her own.

Siobhan cried out in shock and tried to pull free, but her hand was stuck fast. She looked up.

The boy's eyes were open. He was looking at her.

"Who are you?" asked the boy.

Siobhan stared in astonishment. Again, she tried to pull her hand free.

"Let me go."

"Who are you?" repeated the statue.

"My name is Siobhan," she said. She could feel her bones grinding together in her wrist. She winced in pain.

"You are not Prince Euan."

"What?" Siobhan blinked in confusion. "Of course I'm not."

"Prince Euan is not allowed here."

"But I'm not Prince Euan."

The statue cocked its head to the side, studying her.

"What do you want?"

Siobhan hesitated. "The stone. Elaphe . . . Elaphe sent me to get it."

"No person may touch the rathstone. It is forbidden."

Siobhan's heart sank. She hadn't thought of this. She had assumed she would simply be able to walk in and pick up the stone from its resting place. She hadn't thought about a guardian.

"Please let me go."

The statue said nothing.

"What are your instructions?" asked Siobhan desperately.

"My instructions are to keep the rathstone from the Prince and his followers."

"But I am not one of his followers. I am here on Elaphe's request."

"Then what is the password?"

"The password?" Siobhan's thoughts raced. What password would Elaphe set? It had to be something Euan wouldn't guess, no matter how much he tried. Eventually, Siobhan allowed a small smile to form on her lips.

"The Council of Elaphe," she said.

There was a long moment of pause. Then the statue

released her hand. Siobhan stumbled back, still staring at the wooden boy.

Then she looked down. There, resting in her palm, was the rathstone.

She couldn't believe it. She had done it. She had achieved what Father Joe originally sent her here to do. She had actually managed to get the rathstone. And without any kind of help. She felt a wave of pride. Who would have thought? Who would have thought that a simple washing girl from Ireland would be able to accomplish something of such importance?

Her face broke into a giddy grin, but the grin soon faded. Things had changed now. She was no longer here just to get the stone. People were relying on her to help them. She couldn't just desert them—couldn't desert Elaphe or any of the good people she could now call friend. And she wasn't sure how she was supposed to get back anyway.

No. What she needed to do now was to get the stone as far away from here as possible, as far away from Euan as possible.

Siobhan hid the stone in her pocket and retraced her steps back up the staircase. It was a lot harder going up than down. She was soon breathing heavily, her brow prickling with sweat. But she eventually reached the top of the stairs and hurried through the small antechamber into the banqueting room beyond. She hesitated at the door that led out into the tunnel. Those creatures would still be there. Would they simply let her walk through their midst holding the rathstone?

Only one way to find out. She lifted the talisman over her neck and held it out in front of her, then she pulled open the door.

The faceless creatures immediately turned in her direction. She held the talisman out to the one closest to her. Like before, it gripped the edges of the charm with soft, padded fingers and brought the disk close to its face. It sniffed and sniffed, turning the talisman around and around. Then it released its grip and moved away.

Siobhan walked slowly forward, trying to make sure she didn't stand on any of the creatures. The exit to the rath was just ahead of her.

Then one of guardians snaked between her ankles like a cat rubbing against its master. Siobhan stumbled, throwing her hands out to steady herself against the wall. The talisman flew from her fingers. She steadied herself, watching in horror as the disk spun through the air. It landed on the ground a few paces away from the exit.

As one, the guardians all turned their blank faces to Siobhan.

She straightened up, swallowing nervously. The creatures followed her every move. She took a slow step forward. A rustle of agitation spread through the creatures. Siobhan froze. But surely she was already accepted? They had let her in. *They must remember.*

Mustn't they?

The door was three paces away. She glanced nervously to her left. One of the creatures was no more than a hand's breadth away. She could feel the breath exhaling from its nostrils. Was it her imagination, or was its breathing getting faster? Another was reaching out a tentative hand for her pocket—the pocket where the rathstone was hidden.

She hesitated, then decided she couldn't put it off forever and leaped forward.

The creatures all jerked upright. Wings that before had lain invisibly along their backs flared out behind them. Siobhan felt tiny fingers grasping at her clothing, her legs. The guardians dropped from the ceiling. One landed on her back. She screamed and reached around to jerk it away.

She bent down and swept up the talisman into her hands, and then she was diving through the dark opening and out of the rath.

~ Twelve ~

Siobhan rolled on the ground and scrabbled quickly to her feet. She hurried backward, staring at the opening between the standing stones. The grass was visible on the other side. No sign of the rath she had just escaped from.

More importantly, no sign of the guardians. Maybe because she had picked up the talisman again, they had decided to leave her alone. Siobhan exhaled with relief, then quickly felt in her pocket for the rathstone. It was still there.

She looked around the glade. It was still night, although the chill was deepening. Dew dappled the ground. Morning wasn't far off.

The mare stood where Siobhan had left her, happily cropping the grass. Siobhan had never been so happy to see a horse before. She ran across the clearing and hugged her around the neck.

"You waited for me," she said softly. The horse nickered. "Thank you," said Siobhan. "Thank you so much."

She found a stump to stand on and hauled herself into the saddle. Now she had to give the rathstone to

Elaphe. Hopefully, he would know what had to be done to keep it safe.

The mare's ears suddenly flattened against her head. She backed up, spooked by something. Siobhan fought with the reins, trying to keep her pointed in the right direction. But the mare had other ideas. She turned around until she was facing back into the glade. She neighed nervously.

Siobhan glanced around the clearing. Nothing. She looked to the horse, trying to see what had spooked her.

The mare was looking directly at the entrance to the King and Queen's rath. A second later there was a flutter of darkness, and the air was filled with a swarm of the enraged guardians.

Siobhan screamed and yanked the horse around, jabbing her heels hard into the mare's ribs. She bolted forward, needing no further encouragement from Siobhan. They galloped back through the open tunnel, throwing up clumps of packed earth as they went. Siobhan threw a quick glance over her shoulder and saw the guardians flying after them, their wings flapping hard as they picked up speed.

Sobbing and whipping at the reins, Siobhan tried to urge more speed from the mare.

The road flew by beneath them, and they somehow managed to stay just ahead of their pursuers. They exited the long tunnel of trees and entered the forest.

As they rounded a sharp, U-shaped bend, she looked to her right and saw the guardians cut straight through the trees. Despair washed over Siobhan. There was no way she could keep this speed up. The road wound around the twisted landscape here. Siobhan was forced to slow down or risk the horse stumbling over a root and breaking her leg. The guardians would have her in no time.

As the road straightened again, Siobhan tried to coax another burst of speed from the mare, but the animal was already giving everything she could. The guardians were no more than a few paces away from her, reaching out with their tiny, clawed fingers. Siobhan leaned forward, trying to make herself as small a target as possible. Something grabbed her shawl, and she let go of the reins with one hand to swing her arm behind her. It connected with one of the creatures just as the mare leaped over a fallen log, almost dislodging Siobhan from the saddle. She quickly grabbed the reins with both hands again, pushing in hard with her thigh muscles to keep her seat.

She chanced another look over her shoulder. They were no more than a hand's breadth away. They drew closer, stretching out with their claws, fumbling at her dress. The rathstone! She slapped her hand over her pocket, pushing the tiny hand away. But others were there to take its place. One of them landed on the saddle behind her. It scrabbled on her back, trying to reach around for the stone. Then another one sunk its tiny claws into her neck. She screamed—

And was answered by a loud shout from up ahead. Siobhan whipped around and saw Conal's horse leaping over a fallen tree trunk. Conal drew his sword while his horse was still in the air, the iron glinting darkly in the moonlight. The horse thudded to a landing, and Conal swung the sword, slicing into the creatures with each movement. Siobhan moved away from the fight, watching with wide eyes as the guardians tried to get to Conal's head, swiping at his eyes with their tiny claws. But Conal didn't let them get close enough. The sword blade whirled around him, both a shield and a weapon, letting nothing come within his guard.

Within moments a dozen of the creatures lay dying on the ground. The others reconsidered their attack and flew out of reach. Conal brandished his iron sword at them, shouting curses at the top of his voice. He urged his horse forward. The guardians flinched, then turned and fled.

Siobhan sobbed with relief. Then she took a long, shaky breath, watching as the dead guardians underfoot melted into black, oily pools. Conal looked around to make sure no more of them were about, then guided his horse over to Siobhan.

"Are you all right?"

Siobhan nodded, not sure if she would be able to talk.

"Siobhan, what are you doing here? What were those beasts?"

Tell him the truth. The words echoed in her head. *Just tell him the truth. It would be so easy.* She hesitated, then decided against it. He wouldn't believe her. She knew that. The whole story sounded insane, a stupid fancy thought up by a writer those penny dreadful novels that Ilona had been so fond of buying back in London.

No. She couldn't tell him. Not yet.

"How did you know I was here?" she asked, hoping to distract him.

He scowled at her, aware that she had avoided his question. "Earlier tonight, I entered the tent and saw no one around. Then someone called me outside. When I came back in, there you were, next to my father's room. I wondered what you were up to. It kept me awake, so I got up to ask you, but you'd already gone. So was Jack's horse—he's going to kill you if he finds out, by the way."

Siobhan flushed and looked at the ground.

Conal carried on. "I went into my father's room to see if I could discover what you were up to. That's when I saw his talisman was missing."

Conal urged his horse closer and took hold of Siobhan's reins. "Siobhan, what are you doing here? You can tell me."

Siobhan looked into his eyes. She saw earnestness there, concern for her. She shook her head stubbornly. "I can't, Conal. I can't involve you. It's too dangerous."

Conal barked out a laugh. "Dangerous? Who's the one who just saved your life?"

"And I thank you for that," said Siobhan softly. "Truly I do. But this is . . . different. Important things are going on, Conal." She shook her head helplessly.

Conal stared at her a moment, then wheeled his horse around. "Come on."

"Where are we going?"

"Where do you think? Back to the camp. We have

to get the talisman back to my father before he wakes up."

They pushed the horses hard. As they drew close to the camp, Conal slowed down to a walk, allowing Keir to get his breath back. Steam rose from the horse's flanks into the early morning air.

Siobhan was grateful for the change of pace. The events of the night were catching up with her. She didn't think she had ever felt as tired as she did now, and her legs trembled from the unaccustomed horse riding.

As they made their way through the forest, the sky lightened to a dull gray. Morning mist twined between the boles of the trees. It reminded Siobhan of the morning she had arrived here, when she had first met Conal.

She glanced over at him. He was slightly ahead of her and off to one side, so all she could see was his profile. He was frowning, still irritated that she wouldn't take him into her trust. Siobhan sighed. Maybe she should. After all, what did she have to lose? She already had the stone. At least if she told him everything now, he might understand her actions. Maybe he wouldn't judge her so harshly.

"Conal, I need to tell you—"

He turned in his saddle to look at her, but before he could say anything, a voice slid out of the trees.

"Isn't it a bit early to be out riding?"

Conal and Siobhan both stopped their horses. Siobhan looked around, but could see no one. Conal laid his hand on his sword hilt as he searched the mist-shrouded forest for the source of the voice.

"No need for that, old friend," said the voice.

A moment later, Euan emerged from the mist, flanked by Leanan on one side and Mordroch on the other. The three nameless Fey who always accompanied him hovered in the background. Conal chuckled with relief and slid off his saddle.

"Euan. You shouldn't creep up on people like that."

"Really? I sometimes find it better to stay in the shadows. You discover more about people that way."

"Some would say simply talking to them was an easier option."

"Alas, no. People have a habit of . . . lying, of deceiving. It is human nature."

Conal frowned. "Human nature? What about Fey nature?"

Euan didn't answer but simply stared at Conal in a calculating manner. Leanan put a hand on Euan's arm and whispered into his ear. He shook his head sharply. She said something else, and he hesitated, then turned back to face Conal.

"Conal, we are friends, yes?"

"Of course we are. Euan, what is all this?"

"I've known you a long time. You wouldn't lie to me, would you?"

"No. You know I wouldn't."

"Then where have you been?"

Conal hesitated. It was for the briefest fraction of a second and under different circumstances might easily have been mistaken as something completely innocent. But to Siobhan the pause screamed their guilt just the same as if they had admitted the truth.

"Siobhan and I were out for an early morning ride. That is all."

"I see. Off for a bit of rough-and-tumble?"

"Don't speak like that, Euan. I've warned you before."

"Oh have you? You've warned me, have you?" he paused and looked down at the ground, shaking his head. He smiled wryly, but then the smile vanished, replaced instantly with a snarl of anger. "Nobody warns me, Conal! Do you understand? Nobody!"

Conal stepped quickly forward, moving between Siobhan and the Fey. "What's wrong, Euan? Why are you speaking like this?"

"Why am I speaking like this?" Euan shook his head wearily. Siobhan was watching Euan's face, so she caught the look that flashed across his features. It was a look of pain, of sadness. A look of hurt and betrayal. He stared at Conal for some time, deep in thought. Then he turned to Leanan.

"Are you sure? Maybe you made a mistake."

"I do not make mistakes. I sensed its release, Euan."

Euan turned back to Conal. He shook his head sadly. "What have you done, my old friend?"

"Damn you, Euan! I haven't done anything!"

"I wish I could believe that. Really I do." He stood thoughtful for a moment, then looked at his followers. "Take them."

147

Mordroch grinned and led the others forward. Conal pulled his sword from the scabbard.

"Conal," said Euan. "Don't. Otherwise I might hand your young friend over to Mordroch. He likes them fresh."

Conal looked over his shoulder at Siobhan.

"Just throw it down," repeated Euan.

Conal bared his teeth and turned back, throwing the sword onto the grass. Mordroch and one of the Fey grabbed hold of his arms. The other two pulled Siobhan from the horse and dragged her to stand next to Conal.

Leanan then walked slowly forward. She stopped before Conal, reached up and stroked his face. Conal jerked his face away, but Leanan grabbed his chin and stared deep into his eyes.

"Euan is mine," she said softly. Then she leaned forward to whisper into his ear. "And we will destroy you all." Her tongue snaked out and licked his neck. She breathed in deeply, then let go of his chin and turned to Siobhan.

"And what have you been up to, my pretty?"

She reached out and felt around Siobhan's dress. Siobhan tried to pull away, but the two Fey holding her tightened their grip on her arms.

"Leave me alone!" cried Siobhan.

Leanan ignored her and reached inside Siobhan's belt pouch. Siobhan struggled, but there was nothing she could do. She watched, sick to the stomach, as Leanan withdrew the rathstone.

Leanan stared at it in awe. Then she turned to Euan,

raising the stone high in the air. Euan's eyes widened. He strode forward and grabbed it from her, a look of such triumph on his face that Siobhan suddenly realized she had cursed them all.

"Finally," whispered Euan. He looked up at Leanan, his face alight. "After all these years."

Mordroch peered at the stone. "Is it real?"

"It's real," said Leanan. "The King and Queen will regret the way they have treated us, my Prince. Our revenge will be sweet."

Euan said nothing, just stared at the stone nestled in his hand. "Such a small thing," he whispered.

Leanan leaned close to him. Siobhan could see the raw hunger in her face, the naked need to see her will done.

"It is as I have always said, my lord. The humans cannot be trusted. Surely you can see that now. They never intended to share their lands. It was always a ruse—a ruse so that this . . . this *girl* could sneak in—"

"No," said Conal. "That . . . that was me. I did it. I took the stone."

"NO!" shouted Siobhan.

"Siobhan!" snapped Conal. He turned to look at her, his face full of command. "Be silent." He faced Euan again. "I took it."

Leanan was delighted. "Do you see, my Prince? Their true colors come forth. They have wanted this all along. It has always been their plan—to steal the stone and use it to force us to their bidding. Even one you thought your friend. One you treated as a brother. See how they betray us?"

"Why, Conal?" asked Euan. "Leanan always warned me, but I refused to believe. All those times we talked about our peoples' futures. Was it all lies?"

Conal said nothing.

Euan's face twisted with bitterness. "So be it." He turned to Leanan. "They have saved us the effort of taking the stone ourselves. We move our plans forward. Spread the word."

Leanan bowed. "At once, my *King*."

~ THIRTEEN ~

THE COLD SUN FILTERED THROUGH THE SMOKE OF THE campfires, dancing across the clearing in ever-shifting pillars of hazy light. Siobhan watched them move, trying to ignore the activity in the camp around her. She couldn't, though.

Leanan had led them here after a forced march that Siobhan thought took about two hours. When they arrived in the clearing, Euan had lit the first fire, then tied Siobhan and Conal to a tree.

Then it was simply a matter of waiting while the Fey arrived. They did so in groups of three and four, nodding respectfully to Leanan and bowing down before Euan.

"They have been planning this for a long time," whispered Conal from the opposite side of the tree.

Siobhan still hadn't said anything about the rath-stone to Conal. And he hadn't asked. "Why do you say that?"

"Look at these Fey. They're not asking questions. They knew exactly where to come. They've set up this meeting place before now."

"What are they going to do?"

"I'm not sure. But it won't be good."

And he was right. Sometime later, the first humans arrived, tied up and linked together by lengths of rope. They were pulled into the camp, confused and afraid, and were made to sit in neat rows on the grass.

"What's going on? Why are they bringing humans?"

"I'm not sure." He peered hard at the dirty, bedraggled faces before him. "These are the villagers who have gone missing over the past months," he whispered, surprised.

When there were over a hundred Fey gathered around the various campfires, and an equal number of humans, Leanan walked to the center of the glade. The conversation stopped. All eyes turned toward her.

"Long have I waited for this day," she proclaimed proudly. "A day when a new generation of Fey take what is rightfully theirs. A day when we cast off the shackles of Hallowmere and say no, we will not fade away. We will not age quietly like timid mice, forced to renew ourselves when our bodies grow old and tired. For it is not renewal. Make no mistake about that. We are expected to submit to the pool and come out bereft of our memories, bereft of who we were before. 'Born fresh,' they call it. I say it is dying by another name.

"I have told you all of another way, another way to live forever, a way for an immortal life, one where we will not fade away, but continue strong, knowing and remembering who we are. Remembering all our years of knowledge. All our experiences, our loves, our losses. We will remember them all and be stronger Fey because of it."

She looked contemptuously at the rapt audience.

"Let the elders descend into Hallowmere. Let the King and Queen dip their withered bodies in the pool and come out . . . come out a lowly spriggan. Or a selkie. With no memories of the power they once held. Well, not for us!"

She paced around the fire. "You are all here because you believe in what the Morrigan revealed to me. You are all here because you are visionaries. You are all here because you feel the need to save our race. You *know*. You know that if something is not done, the humans will take all that is ours."

She looked around once more. Her amber eyes shone with fervor. It reminded Siobhan of the time a traveling priest had come to her village when she was a small girl. He had stood all day in exactly the same spot, delivering fire-and-brimstone sermons about the evil of all mankind.

Euan had been standing by while Leanan delivered her speech. When she finished he walked forward and surveyed the assembly.

"Siobhan," whispered Conal.

"What?"

"I've been cutting at your rope with a piece of slate. I think it's almost parted. Now listen to me. It's very important that you listen to me. All right?"

Siobhan said nothing.

"If you get the chance, you must flee. As soon as some kind of distraction presents itself."

"I'll not leave you behind."

"Don't be stupid! This is more important than me. Can't you see that? They're planning on building an army. They're going to attack our people, probably the elder Fey as well. That's what this is all about. Someone has to warn them."

"You should do it, not me. I'm no good at this kind of thing." She had proved that by getting herself in this situation in the first place. She wished she could have found Elaphe and gotten him to take care of this. Where was he?

"Quiet! This isn't a game, Siobhan. I don't know your part in this, but I do know you're involved somehow. You have to get back and tell everyone what's going on. Tell my father to gather the villagers. We need to stop the Fey now, before it's too late."

Siobhan said nothing.

"Siobhan?"

"I understand," she whispered.

"Good lass. You have to be strong, Siobhan. I know you don't have much faith in yourself, but it's time to grow up and take a stand."

Conal said no more, so Siobhan turned her attention back to the Fey. Euan was talking now.

"I understand that more than a few of you are worried about the rite," he said. "That is understandable. I am worried about the rite, even though it has been explained to me over and over during the past weeks." Here he stopped and smiled at his people. "But I trust Leanan. I trust the Morrigan. And to prove that trust, I will be the first." He turned and pointed to Conal. "You all know

Conal. You all know of our . . . our friendship over the years." The other Fey nodded. "Then watch, and you will see how serious I am about our future."

He nodded at two of the Fey. They marched over to Conal and untied him from the tree. They then dragged him through the clearing and brought him before Euan.

"Kneel before your king," said Leanan.

"He's no king of mine," snarled Conal, not once breaking eye contact with the Fey Prince.

Leanan nodded at one of the Fey, and he pulled out a bronze sword. Siobhan's heart stopped, thinking they were about to run him through, but the Fey shifted his grip on the weapon and hit the flat of the blade against the back of Conal's legs. He fell to his knees.

"That is better," said Leanan. She walked slowly around Conal, tracing her finger across his face. "You all know this man," she called. "To show Prince Euan's commitment to our cause, he has chosen a friend to be the first sacrifice. Call it . . . a gesture of intent."

Leanan came to stand before Conal again. "You have a choice," she said. "Either you submit to Euan's power willingly, or you die."

"I'll not bow to him."

Euan stepped forward. "I think you will." He leaned over and whispered something in Conal's ear. Conal half-turned to look at Siobhan. His face was torn with anger and frustration.

"Fine!" he said, turning back to Euan. "You will have me willingly. Are you satisfied?"

"Oh, it's not as easy as that, I'm afraid," said Leanan. "There is a . . . rite that must be undertaken."

She pulled a knife from her belt. "Are you still willing?"

Conal hesitated, then nodded. "Aye," he said heavily. "Do what you will."

Leanan grabbed his arm and sliced a deep cut down his forearm. Blood welled to the surface. Siobhan saw the hunger in Leanan's eyes as she saw it. The Fey witch leaned forward and inhaled, her tongue flicking out like a snake to taste it. She shuddered with pleasure, then stood aside.

"My King, he is yours."

Euan stepped forward, hesitantly, it seemed to Siobhan. He gripped Conal's arm. They locked eyes for a moment—two friends, now enemies—then he lowered his mouth to Conal's arm and drank his blood.

Siobhan gasped, watching in horror as Euan gradually transformed before her very eyes. When she had first seen him in the forest, he was filled with raw power, almost crackling with energy. She remembered thinking it was as if all of nature were condensed into one body. The energy of spring, the power of summer, the coldness of winter, and the willfulness of autumn. The vitality of nature had burst through him, blazing through eyes that knew all her secrets. And it wasn't just him. The same power had shone through all the Fey she had met. It was as if nature was given form by these creatures, that the natural world experienced life through them.

As she watched, this all faded.

It was akin to experiencing a warm, sunny day, and then a bank of dark clouds comes suddenly from nowhere to cover the sun. Everything about Euan simply dulled. He was diminishing before her eyes as he became Unhallowed.

Siobhan knew she should feel anger. She knew she should feel hatred. But at that moment, the only emotion running through her body was one of pity. She'd seen where this path led him and all of the people involved, human and Fey. She wouldn't wish that on anyone.

Siobhan looked at the other Fey, thinking that surely if they saw what the rite had done to Euan, they wouldn't want to participate. But all she saw in their faces was raw hunger, a desire for power, for immortality.

Euan finished up with Conal. He dropped him to the ground like a discarded piece of food. Siobhan saw that Conal was still breathing. *At least that's something,* she thought with relief.

But then his head flopped to the side, and she saw his face, pale and drained of blood. His eyes were dark orbs of pain, and they looked at Siobhan without the slightest hint of recognition. Euan had done something to him, something more than just drained him of blood. She was sure of that.

But then he reached out a hand across the grass. She looked back to his eyes, and something of who he was came back into focus. He stared at her, mouthed a single word.

Flee.

It was at this moment that Siobhan realized

everything depended on her. It was as Conal had said. There was no one left who could warn the others. If she didn't escape now, Conal's sacrifice would be for nothing. The Unhallowed would rise up and attack everyone they saw as a threat.

Now Siobhan felt the anger. Before she'd come here, she had always thought she was removed from what was happening back at Falston. She'd felt that she was dragged into events simply because she could see through Fey glamours or because Father Joe needed another body to make up the numbers.

And that may have been true. But it was different now. Now it was full circle. What started as something personal, a family tragedy she fled from because she didn't have the power to change it, Euan had made again personal by attacking Conal, someone she had come to think of as a friend. Siobhan had always known the stakes involved, but seeing Conal lying on the grass clarified everything in her mind. She could no longer hide behind the excuse that she was just a serving girl, that she wasn't meant for any of this. No one was. That was the point. You fought because you had to. You found your own reasons for doing what you had to do, and then you made sure you did it.

She had found her reason.

She pulled her wrists apart. The ropes strained, then gave way. The main rope had already been untied when they took Conal to Euan. She was free.

Siobhan looked about to make sure no one had seen her. Leanan was standing before the captive humans.

"As you can see, Conal is still alive. You can either submit like he did or die. The choice is yours."

Siobhan got to her feet and darted into the undergrowth, running faster than she had ever run in her life.

~ Fourteen ~

Siobhan's chest was burning from the exertion of running. There hadn't been any signs of pursuit yet, but that didn't mean they weren't coming. She needed to get back to the festival as soon as possible. She needed to tell Father Josephus. They needed to find Elaphe.

And then they had to tell the King and Queen.

She tried to run for as long as she could, but after an hour she had slowed to a walk. Her legs were weak with the strain. How far away was she? Nothing looked familiar. The trees were sparse here, and she couldn't remember it looking like this when Leanan and Euan led them away from the camp.

Siobhan stopped and dropped into the grass. She may as well admit it to herself: She was lost.

She covered her face with her hands and tried to control her breathing. How could she let herself get lost now? She had to warn the others before it was too late.

What would Elaphe say?

Siobhan paused, dropping her hands into her lap.

Thinking of Elaphe had made her remember something he had said when he was teaching her how to control the Sight. What was it? That she could use it to find lost objects? Something like that. But was it possible somehow to use her Sight to find lost people? Could she use the Sight to guide her back to Niamh?

She had no choice but to try.

Siobhan closed her eyes and retreated inside her mind, concentrating hard on what she was about to do. She opened up the black hole, allowing her talent to escape into her mind. She had done this a few times since Elaphe had taught her how to control it, and every time she was finding it easier and easier to stop the Sight from over-whelming her.

She thought about Niamh, picturing her face, her hair, her smile. The way she kept pushing stray strands of hair from her eyes, the shy smile, the friendly laugh. She pictured her in as much detail as possible, then she sent that picture out into the tendrils of her mind, letting it drift of its own accord.

Almost straight away, she sensed one of the tendrils quicken, almost as if it were alive and its breathing grew faster. Siobhan figured out which tendril it was and followed it as it picked up speed, darting through the trees, dodging around boulders, and twining around branches. She tried to do as Elaphe had instructed her, gathering just the one thread to her as if she were coiling rope.

Siobhan scrambled to her feet and ran after it, hoping that she had gotten it right and that it wasn't leading her back to Conal and Euan.

It wasn't. After another half hour of running, she

stumbled through the trees and saw the first signs of life—two boys, playing with a stick in a large puddle by the side of the road. Siobhan paused, her breath rasping in her throat. There had been a few moments when she thought she heard the sounds of distant pursuit, but she had managed to avoid being seen by anyone. She had thought she wouldn't be able to keep up the pace, but her desperation had given her extra strength.

That and the need to avenge Conal.

She ran into the campgrounds and made her way to the tent. Her first instinct had been to seek out Niamh. She wasn't sure why. Maybe it was the need to share what had happened with someone who she knew would be sympathetic, someone who wouldn't judge her or tell her what to do. Besides that though, she had no idea where Father Josephus had pitched his tent, and she was hoping Niamh could help.

She found the girl carrying an armful of wood to the small campsite behind Conal's tent. Niamh dropped the wood next to the smoldering embers of last night's fire when she saw Siobhan.

"Siobhan! Where have you been? Da's furious! You can't just up and leave when you want to. You're a servant, you're not allowed."

"That doesn't matter now," replied Siobhan.

"Doesn't—of course it does. Look, we better come up with an excuse. We'll say you drank something last night. That you didn't know what it was . . ." She trailed off when she saw the expression on Siobhan's face. "What? What is it?"

So Siobhan told her. Everything. About what Euan and Leanan had done to Conal and what they would do to the other humans they had in their grasp. She told her what she had overheard, of Euan and Leanan wanting to rule over everything.

"You need to tell someone," Niamh whispered, once Siobhan had finished.

"So you believe me?" asked Siobhan in some surprise.

"Of course. Why wouldn't I?"

Siobhan struggled to find the words. "It just sounds so . . . outlandish. If I wasn't there I don't know if I would believe it."

Niamh shrugged. "They are the Old Ones. My Da has told me stories from the old country. The Fey are fickle, Siobhan. Always have been. I think you'll find that most here will believe you."

Siobhan felt relieved. "Do you know where Father Josephus is sleeping? We need to tell him what has happened."

Niamh nodded. "I saw him this morning already. Come on."

Niamh led Siobhan through the camp to Father Josephus's tent. It was a humble affair, nothing like the tent Conal and his father stayed in. Siobhan and Niamh hesitated, aware that there were voices coming from inside.

Siobhan felt a flutter of hope. Maybe Elaphe had returned already.

"Father Josephus?" called Siobhan hesitantly.

The voices stopped. A moment later the tent flap was

pulled aside, and Father Josephus appeared. Siobhan was surprised. The priest looked quite different from when she had last seen him. His face was thinner, and dark circles smudged the skin beneath his eyes.

"Siobhan. What can I do for you?"

"Something has happened, Father. The Fey . . . It has started."

Father Josephus stared at her for a moment, then he heaved a huge sigh and stepped aside. "You'd better come in."

Niamh and Siobhan stepped into the dim interior. A small fire burned in the center of the tent, the smoke drifting lazily up through the hole in the roof. Siobhan blinked, waiting for her eyes to adjust. It was only then that she saw Iamblicus standing on the other side of the fire.

"Iamblicus!" She looked around, wondering if perhaps she had missed Elaphe. Iamblicus saw her look and shook his head.

"Elaphe has not returned, child. He still searches for the missing villagers."

"There's no need anymore. I know where they are."

Iamblicus took a step forward. "What are you talking about? Explain!"

So she did. She told the two priests exactly what she had told Niamh. Their faces changed as they took in her words. They exchanged fearful looks as she told them of Euan's plans to take what the humans refused to give them freely. They paled as she described what Euan had done to Conal.

When she was finished, she trailed off into silence. Iamblicus was the first to speak.

"We must tell the King and Queen. Come, Siobhan. We cannot waste any more time."

Iamblicus led the way out of the tent and over to the area where the Fey had set up their shelters. The camp was waking up properly now, even those who had indulged in too much wine venturing from their beds.

The way into the King and Queen's tent was blocked by two Fey guards. Their bronze spears were crossed before the opening.

"Out of the way," snapped Iamblicus. "We need to see the King."

"The King is busy," said one of the guards.

"Then perhaps you would like to explain to your liege why you refused to admit those of us who have information on their only son's . . . what would you call it? Rebellion? Desertion? Betrayal, certainly."

The guards glanced at each another, then the one who had spoken to Iamblicus ducked inside. He returned a few moments later.

"You may enter."

Iamblicus impatiently swept past him, the others following behind. The entrance led into a narrow corridor made from walls of silk. The material gently undulated, like waves on a balmy summer's day.

The makeshift passage opened into a small waiting area complete with wooden chairs that were carved into the likenesses of mythical beasts. At least, Siobhan thought they were mythical. Who could tell these days?

"You girls wait here," ordered Iamblicus. "We will call you if you are needed."

Niamh and Siobhan sat down in the chairs while Father Josephus and Iamblicus disappeared into another section of the voluminous tent.

"What do you think will happen?" asked Niamh.

Siobhan said nothing. What could she say? That this was the beginning of a centuries-long fight that would see humankind used as pawns in a game of otherworldly power? She didn't think Niamh would be happy to hear that.

Time passed. Siobhan soon grew restless and paced back and forth in the small chamber, looking for something to distract her. But there was nothing of interest to be found except for the chairs.

She was just considering heading back outside for a breath of fresh air, when the Fey King walked in.

He crossed immediately to Siobhan. "Child. Is it true?"

Siobhan nodded.

"My girl, this is very important. You saw it? Everything? Euan taking this boy's blood?"

"I saw it."

A shadow descended over the King's face. He dropped heavily into one of the chairs. "I would never have thought . . ." He shook his head sadly. "So it has come to this. After all these years."

Siobhan and Niamh exchanged glances. The King glanced up and caught their look. He straightened and tried to smile, but it died on his lips.

"Still. You girls mustn't worry about things that don't concern you. I'm sure we'll sort it out."

"I think it concerns all of us, sir," said Siobhan softly.

The King fixed her with a shrewd stare. He nodded. "My apologies. Your age . . . I sometimes lose track of when your people mature. You are, of course, correct. There are dangerous times coming. But I'm sure we'll all pull together to overcome the difficulties that lie ahead."

Siobhan thought about her time, six hundred years in the future, where they were still fighting the Unhallowed. Something of her thoughts must have shown on her face.

"You do not agree?" asked the King quietly.

"I . . ." Siobhan didn't know what to say. "I think it will be a long fight," she finished.

The King was about to say something more to her, but Fathers Josephus and Iamblicus entered the room and distracted him.

"Come, girls," said Father Josephus. "In the light of recent events, the festival has been canceled. Word needs to get out to those families . . . affected by what has occurred."

He looked at Iamblicus. "It will be an unpleasant task."

"Ours is not to shy away from unpleasantness, Josephus. Ours is to help our flock when we are needed. Now is such a time."

Father Josephus bowed his head. Siobhan could see

his face flushing with chagrin. "Of course, Iamblicus. I didn't mean—"

Iamblicus cut him off. "No, no. My apologies, Josephus. All this . . . it has made me uneasy. Forgive me. We must do our best, that is all. We can do no more."

Father Josephus nodded. "Farewell."

Iamblicus nodded at the King, then left the tent. Father Josephus hesitated, then put his arms around the girls' shoulders.

"Come. You must pack up your belongings and return to the village."

"What will you do?" asked Siobhan.

Father Josephus sighed. "I must tell Conal's father what has occurred."

~ Fifteen ~

Conal's father took the news of what had happened to Conal hard. When they returned to the manor house, he closeted himself in his chambers and refused to come out, calling only for spirits and ale and leaving untouched the plates of food Brianna prepared for him.

"It's not healthy," she said to Eomen as she stood before the kitchen table, preparing ingredients for soup.

"He needs to grieve, Brianna. Think how you would feel if you lost Niamh."

Brianna's face darkened, and she turned her attention back to peeling the potatoes.

They had been back from the festival for two days now. The village was in a state of shock. On top of the villagers who had disappeared over the last few months, twenty people had vanished from the festival as well. No one in the village was left untouched. Even if no one from their immediate family was taken, then friends or neighbors had been. Questions were being asked, questions with no answers.

Why them? Why had they lost a child or a husband, while others had not? What had they done to deserve

169

such a fate? Why not the family across the street?

And to say it was random, that there was no cause or reason behind who was taken—why, that was worst of all. The villagers needed answers, and no one was there to give them.

Three times now since they had come back, Guthrie had ordered Siobhan to his room and demanded she go over every detail of what had happened. He would question a terrified Siobhan, scream and shout, demand to know how she had gotten free while his son had not. He would accuse her of being in league with the Fey, accuse her of killing Conal, and then a second later would shower her with sobbing apologies. Brianna had put a stop to it the last time, storming into the room and seizing Siobhan by her arm. She had raised a finger to Guthrie.

"Enough of this. You're terrifying the girl. You're not the only one who lost someone, Guthrie. The whole village mourns."

Then she yanked Siobhan out of the room. Guthrie hadn't called her back since.

There was a tentative knock at the kitchen door. Eomen opened it to reveal a young boy standing on the steps.

Brianna looked at him. "Well? What is it? Spit it out, boy."

"Father Josephus would like to see Siobhan. In the village."

Brianna and Eomen both turned to look at her. "You'd better go," said Eomen. "Not polite to keep the father waiting."

"But tell him not to keep you long. You've the washing up to do before it gets dark."

Siobhan nodded and slid off the chair. The boy had turned and run back toward the village as soon as he'd delivered his message. Siobhan followed at a slower pace, wondering what Father Josephus could want. Maybe they had come up with a plan?

The village was mostly deserted, those out in the cold, grieving silence doing so only because of errands that wouldn't wait. Siobhan shivered as she folded her shawl tightly about her shoulders and walked along the main village road. The church was just up ahead, a long building with thick, double doors barring the entrance.

A door slammed behind her.

"Wait!"

Siobhan turned and saw a pale-faced woman hurrying toward her. Siobhan paused, waiting for the woman to catch up.

She stopped in front of Siobhan, her breath coming in ragged, nervous gasps.

"Can I . . . can I help you?" asked Siobhan.

"You were there. They say you were there."

Siobhan didn't need to ask what the woman meant. She knew.

"Did you see my husband there? He's this tall—" She indicated with her hand. "He has no hair. Bald as the day he was born." The woman chuckled, but the sound turned into a sob. "I just need to know. Was he there?" The woman grabbed hold of Siobhan's arm. "Is he still alive?"

Siobhan tried to extricate her arm, but the woman's grip was tight with desperation.

"I . . . I don't know. I'm sorry."

"But you were there! You must have seen—"

"Here now," said a gentle voice. Siobhan looked up with relief and saw Father Josephus standing there. He took hold of the woman's hand and gently lifted her fingers from Siobhan's arm. "Let's just leave the girl be, shall we?"

"But she was there. She saw . . ." The woman broke down and started crying. Siobhan could hear the same words, repeated over and over through the tears. "She saw. She saw."

Father Josephus turned her around and led her back to her house. He looked over his shoulder at Siobhan. "Just go inside."

Siobhan nodded and hurried toward the church, afraid that someone else would stop her, demanding answers. She passed through the large doors and saw someone standing at the front of the church. The figure turned, revealing his face.

"Elaphe!" Siobhan ran forward and wrapped her arms around the surprised Fey. "Oh Elaphe, it's been terrible."

Elaphe hesitantly stroked her hair. "I know, child, I know. Father Josephus told me everything."

"They . . . they have the stone. I took it. I didn't know what to do."

"Don't worry. You did the right thing. They would have taken it regardless. This is my fault, not yours. I underestimated them. I thought their plans were years away from fruition."

"What are we going to do?"

"We must set up defenses around the village. I do not think Euan will be content with what he has done. He will want more sacrifices. More victims so he can turn his followers into Unhallowed. We must gather everyone together for a meeting—"

The door burst open behind them, and Father Josephus stumbled inside. "Elaphe!"

Elaphe turned in his seat. "What is it, Father Josephus?"

Father Josephus could barely contain his excitement. "It's Conal. He has returned. Hale and hearty, by all accounts."

Elaphe and Siobhan exchanged troubled looks.

"Where is he?" the Fey asked.

"Up at the manor house."

Elaphe stood and pulled his cloak tight about his body. He looked down at Siobhan. "Let us attend."

~ Sixteen ~

Elaphe led the way through the manor grounds and into the kitchen. Niamh was the only one there. She was busy stirring the soup Brianna had made earlier.

"Did you hear?" she asked excitedly when Siobhan hurried through the door. She stopped talking when Elaphe followed Siobhan, and she looked uncertainly at them both. "Siobhan? What's going on?"

Elaphe strode across the kitchen and opened the door, checking the hallway beyond. He turned back to the girls, his face troubled. "I don't like this," he said. "Something feels amiss." He locked eyes with Siobhan.

"You think it's the Unhallowed?"

"It may be. My people . . . well, you would know better than anyone, Siobhan. We have the ability to hide our true selves. It might be Conal. It might not be." He sighed and rubbed his forehead. He looked uncertain. "I'm afraid you're going to have to use your Sight, Siobhan."

Siobhan nervously bit her lip. "Can't you do it yourself?"

"I plan to. But think, Siobhan. If it is not Conal, then

I will need you to go into the village to use your Sight and see if there are other Unhallowed about, disguising themselves as humans."

"Do you think they are about to attack?"

"It is a very good possibility, don't you think? On the other hand, I could just be looking for demons in the smoke." He tried to smile at the girls, but it came out as more of a wince. "Can you blame me? After all that has occurred?"

He opened the door again. "Come. Let us seek out young Conal and hear how he managed to escape."

Yes, thought Siobhan, picturing Conal writhing across the ground in pain. *I'd like to know that as well.*

They walked through the manor house to the Great Hall. The table was bare—obviously no one had had time to prepare a feast for Conal's return. Siobhan was sure that his father would want to celebrate, though. Elaphe looked around.

"Not here." He frowned. "You girls just . . . I think you should wait here," he said thoughtfully.

"Where are you going?" asked Siobhan.

"To find Conal and Guthrie." He looked at the two of them. "I won't be long. Don't worry."

Elaphe hurried across the hall and out the front door. Siobhan and Niamh exchanged looks.

"Do you truly have the Second Sight?" Niamh asked, looking troubled.

"Yes. But I'm not sure how to properly control it. It sometimes . . . takes over. Overwhelms me. Honestly, I thought I might be going mad."

They heard the sounds of someone approaching along the corridor. A bellow of laughter burst into the hall. Siobhan would recognize that laughter anywhere: Conal's father, Guthrie.

Siobhan felt a rush of excitement. Was it true? Had Conal really escaped?

Maybe, but she had to be certain. Siobhan closed her eyes and opened the locked door to that part of her mind where she had been keeping her Second Sight. The Sight flooded out, but Siobhan took Elaphe's advice and pulled back, letting it wash over her whole being without trying to stop or control it. Immediately, the tendrils flung themselves outward, probing, searching, devouring other peoples' thoughts and feelings.

Niamh, wishing she had the Second Sight, thinking it would make her different from all the others, special. Guthrie, beyond the door, ecstatic that this son had returned and could now carry on the family name. Elaphe, off in the grounds somewhere, worried that this was the end of humankind.

All these sensations barreled through her head, but instead of shying away from them, retreating in fear and trying to close off her mind, she simply stood firm, letting them buffet over and around her. As they disappeared she focused on the tendrils while they flicked and prodded everything close by, like bolts of lightning arcing into the closest tree. They probed ever outward, searching, seeking.

Siobhan suddenly realized that no one could hide from her. She could read minds, judge motives, sense betrayals. If she studied her power, really studied it, she could be truly powerful. No one could stand against her.

Siobhan opened her eyes again, watching as the door opened. Guthrie walked in, looking over his shoulder at someone, still smiling at a shared joke. He crossed the threshold, and Conal walked in behind him.

Only . . . it wasn't Conal.

It was Euan.

"Ah, my son. You have no idea how glad I am to have you back," said Guthrie.

"I'm glad to be back, Father," said Euan.

"Siobhan?" whispered Niamh. "Is it . . . ? Is it himself?"

Euan looked up, and their eyes locked. There was a moment's hesitation before Euan realized she could see his true form. The smile dropped from his face.

"By the gods!" he snarled. "Why is it always you?"

"Conal?" asked Guthrie uncertainly.

"Shut up, you old fool." Without a moment's hesitation, Euan whipped out a bronze knife and stabbed it into Guthrie's throat. The huge man's eyes widened in shock. His hands flew up to the wound, trying to staunch the flow of blood. He fell to his knees, staring up at his killer, at the person he thought was his son. His eyes glazed over, and he fell forward.

"Animal!" Siobhan screamed. "Why did you kill him?"

"What?" Euan seemed puzzled, then he looked down at the body at his feet. He shrugged, then stepped over Guthrie and walked toward them. "Call it a whim. He irritated me. Always has done."

Siobhan and Niamh stumbled backward. "What have

you done with Conal?" asked Siobhan.

"Oh, he's around somewhere. In fact," Euan paused, putting on a look of mock thoughtfulness. "He's probably leading the attack on this village right at this very moment."

Then Siobhan heard it. The bells in the village church, tolling their mournful call into the early evening air.

Euan nodded in satisfaction. "Yes. That will be them now."

The door burst open, and Elaphe ran in. He froze when he saw Euan standing a few paces away from the girls. Euan gave him a mock salute.

"Elaphe. Say hello to my parents for me."

Then he turned and sprinted back the way he had come. Elaphe ran after him but returned a few moments later.

"He's gone. What did he say to you?"

"They're attacking the village! Elaphe, we have to do something!"

Elaphe hesitated. He looked momentarily lost, like he didn't know which course to take. Then he nodded firmly. "Yes. You are right. Do you have any iron around? Anything at all?"

Siobhan looked at Niamh. The girl looked on the verge of panic. "Niamh! Iron."

Niamh snapped out of it. "What?"

"Iron. Is there any iron here?"

"No. Conal thought it would seem impolite—" She paused.

"What?"

"Jack. He still uses iron to make horseshoes. Says nothing else will do."

Elaphe headed for the doors. "Let's go."

~ SEVENTEEN ~

*T*HEY FOUND PLENTY OF IRON IN THE SMITHY BEHIND the stables. The smithy was a separate structure, built up against the outer walls of the village so that the chances of a fire ignited by the fierce heat were lessened. Elaphe stood uncomfortably in the doorway while Niamh and Siobhan searched through the dim light for something to use as a weapon.

Siobhan found a heavy iron poker next to the cold hearth. It was covered in gray ash. Jack must have used it to stoke up the fire. Niamh found a half-made horseshoe, a piece of thick iron that had been curved slightly but then abandoned because of some defect the girls couldn't see.

They both turned to Elaphe. He eyed the iron nervously and kept a safe distance from the girls.

"What do we do?" she asked.

"We need to get everyone down to the loch. Niamh— you come with me. You'll have to help me spread the word. I'm not sure people will trust me under the circumstances."

"The loch?" asked Niamh. "But we'll be trapped against the water."

Elaphe shook his head. "We will use the crannogs. I'll prepare a spell over the water, something to protect the villagers once they cross." He turned to Siobhan. "Can you warn Father Josephus? He will still be in the church."

Siobhan nodded.

"Avoid any confrontations. Do you understand? The Unhallowed are stronger than you. Use the iron only as a last resort."

Siobhan and Niamh looked at each other, both suddenly aware that this might be the last time they saw each other alive. Siobhan grabbed Niamh in a fierce hug. "Take care, Niamh."

"And you."

They separated. Siobhan tried to smile bravely, but it felt false on her lips, like a lie to a priest. She reached out one last time and gripped Niamh's hand, then she turned and ran from the smithy before Niamh saw her tears.

Siobhan hurried through the gate, abandoning the relative safety of the manor house. She ran along the road until she came to the top of the hill that led down into the village, noting the lurid sunset that turned the distant clouds orange and red.

She hesitated. Sunset had already come and gone, hadn't it?

Siobhan breathed deep and crossed the last few paces to the top of the hill.

"Mother of God," she whispered, as she surveyed the horrific scene below her.

The village was ablaze. Houses burned in the early

evening air, the flames spreading across the damp thatch and sending thick, choking smoke roiling into the sky. Siobhan heard screams and shouting and the occasional clang of metal as someone tried to defend themselves. Dim figures could be seen running back and forth, but at this distance Siobhan couldn't tell if they were the Unhallowed or the villagers. The church bell was still ringing, the clanging peal echoing over the sounds of attack.

Siobhan felt the terror in the very pit of her soul. She watched as the flames leaped from one house to another, the lurid glow of fire brightening the scene of panic and slaughter below her. Bodies lay sprawled in the street, villagers cut down as they fled for their lives.

She watched a mother and child dart out from behind a small hut and run toward the church. But before they made it, a huge, spiderlike figure detached itself from the shadows and crawled after them. Siobhan's heart leaped into her throat. There was no way they would make it.

But just as the Unhallowed was drawing close, the church doors flew ope, and Father Josephus ran out brandishing some kind of long weapon he held with a cloth, as though it might burn him. Siobhan wasn't sure what it was. He sprinted to the woman and waved her and her child past, then stood firm in the road, blocking the path of her attacker. The monster slowed to a walk, then stopped. Father Josephus shouted defiantly, and the spider turned and scampered into the shadows. Father Josephus quickly retreated into the church.

Siobhan steeled herself, then hurried down the hill, sticking to the shadows of the trees along the road. As she descended into the village, Siobhan started to feel the fear building within her, rising higher and higher until it threatened to overwhelm her. It was as if standing on the hill overlooking the village put her at a distance from the attack. She could look at it once removed. But as she descended the hill, as the houses and walls started to first draw level with her eye line, then rise above her, she was drawn directly into the events. Her vision of what was going on was reduced to what she could see immediately around her. And at the moment that was an ivy-covered wall to her right, the road ahead that dipped over a rise a few paces away, and darkness to her left. She looked around in fear. The Unhallowed could be anywhere.

Siobhan staggered to a stop. She couldn't do this. She just couldn't. Panic welled up within her. She looked frantically for some way out, for somewhere to run, to hide, but there was nowhere to go. Screams sounded from all over the village. Weapons clashed together. She tried to cover her ears, but the sounds were in her head. There was no escaping them.

She turned and looked back up the hill, thinking maybe she could run back to safety, but she saw Niamh and Elaphe standing there. Niamh raised a hesitant hand in farewell. Siobhan sobbed, then returned the gesture.

She had to go on.

Siobhan followed the street into the outskirts of town. She slipped behind a line of small houses that were, so far, untouched by the fire, and she skirted the vegetable patches in the back gardens until she thought she was close to the village green. She slid along the side of the house, her hands running over the packed and hardened mud of which the wall was constructed.

As she approached the opening that would take her out to the village green, a high-pitched ululation froze her to the spot. Three Unhallowed ran past, so close Siobhan could have reached out and touched them. She heard another scream, this one human, and the Unhallowed started laughing as they gave chase.

Siobhan peered out from behind the house and saw the Unhallowed chasing a woman toward the church. To Siobhan's dismay she saw another group of Fey, these almost ten feet tall, thin and craggly and looking for all the world like dead trees, chasing a second family across the grass. The family and the woman made it to the church, banging frantically on the doors and screaming for sanctuary. Father Joe appeared and ushered them in, quickly slamming the doors shut again. The two groups of Fey joined up with each other, then retreated a small distance. They formed into a line and waited, staring directly at the church.

Siobhan cursed beneath her breath. She needed to tell Father Joe of Elaphe's instructions. How was she supposed to do that with a gang of Unhallowed guarding the entrance?

She searched the area around the church. The building itself backed up against a steep hill and fronted the sward that was the village square. Houses lined the square to either side, but one of the rows was engulfed with flame.

Luckily, there were gaps between the last houses on either side and the church grounds, so the fire couldn't leap across the space to the church itself. Lucky for the church and those inside. Not so lucky for Siobhan. The Fey would be able to see her while she ran to the church.

But there was nothing else for it. She'd already left Conal behind. There was no way she would do the same to the villagers.

She retraced her steps to the back gardens and worked her way around the outskirts of the village. It took her longer than expected because three of the houses were on fire, and she had to leave the gardens altogether as the heat was so intense. She prayed that whoever lived there had made it out in time.

She also had to stop moving every time she heard screams and shouts echoing nearby. She would wait for the sounds to move away before setting off again.

By the time she reached the last few houses, her heart was beating so fast she thought it would burst in her chest. The slightest sound made her jump, and she was terrified that at any moment she was going to be discovered.

She crept down the wall of the last house and peered around the side. There were more Fey standing before the church now. It looked like there were about twenty of them, limned by the orange glow of fires behind them. The shouting and screaming had all but fallen silent now. That made Siobhan feel slightly better. Either the Fey had done what they had come to do, or Elaphe and Niamh had gotten everyone to the loch. Siobhan hoped for the latter.

The grounds of the church were about fifteen paces away. A low fence surrounded a small graveyard, and beyond that was the side wall of the church. Her best bet would be to head around the back and look for a rear entrance, but to do that she still had to get over the fence without the Fey seeing her.

She peered around the corner again. They were still there, silent, unmoving. What were they waiting for?

And then she saw. A dark figure sauntered along the main road of the village. She couldn't see his features, but she would know that arrogant walk anywhere.

Prince Euan.

He left the road and walked toward his comrades. When they heard him coming they all turned to await his arrival. Siobhan realized that this was her best chance, to move while they were distracted. She sprinted out from behind the house, her breath coming in frightened gasps. She smacked into the fence, wincing at the creaking noise of the rickety wood. She threw her iron bar into the church grounds, then grabbed hold of the slats, trying to pull herself over. She was halfway up before the damp wood snapped beneath her hands, sending her sprawling headfirst onto an ancient grave.

A cry went up from the square. Siobhan froze, then peered around the stone grave marker. The Fey were looking toward the church, but not directly at her. They had obviously heard something but couldn't place the sound. The church was only a few paces away. Could she make it before the Fey caught her? What if there wasn't a back door? She would be trapped against the hill with nowhere to run.

She drew a shaky breath and picked up the iron bar. For a brief second she had the strange notion of what it would be like to tell a younger version of herself what she was doing. The person she was only a month or so ago would be absolutely terrified by these circumstances. She supposed that hadn't really changed. She was still terrified. But she did it anyway.

She scrambled to her feet and ran as fast as she could for the rear of the church. A shout went up behind her, but she refused to look back. Doing that would only panic her, and knowing her luck, she'd probably trip over her own feet.

She skidded around the corner and sobbed with relief when she saw the recessed doorway. She hurtled into it and banged on the wood, ignoring the sharp pain in her hands.

The wood was thick and weathered, and her banging barely made any kind of sound. She redoubled her efforts, then decided there was no need to keep quiet any longer, so she shouted at the top of her lungs and started using the iron bar on the door.

"Father Josephus! It's Siobhan. Let me in. Please!"

She carried on banging, but it was no good. Father Josephus obviously couldn't hear her. She leaned forward, her head resting on the rough wood. "Please open," she whispered, exhausted. "It's me. It's Siobhan."

She heard a noise behind her. She turned quickly, but there was nothing there.

Then she looked up.

The Unhallowed Fey looked down on her from the

top of the bank that the church was built against. Euan stood at the front. He crouched, his hands dangling between his legs.

"You are very troublesome," he called down to her.

Siobhan said nothing.

"May I ask why? It seems . . . personal."

"Personal?" shouted Siobhan, unable to keep her silence any longer. "Look what you did to Conal! Of *course* it's personal."

Euan flashed a wicked grin at her. "I had no idea you and Conal were such good friends." He straightened up. "Would you like to say hello?"

"What . . . ?"

Before she could say anything more, a shadow moved forward to stand beside Euan. Euan put his arm around the figure's shoulder. "Conal, say hello to Siobhan."

Conal said nothing. He just stared down at Siobhan, unblinking.

"Conal?"

Nothing.

"What's wrong with him?"

"Not a thing. He's very well. Aren't you Conal?"

Conal didn't move.

"Nod your head, Conal. There's a good boy."

Conal nodded once.

Tears ran down Siobhan's cheeks. What had Euan done to him?

"You *do* know I'm going to kill you?" said Euan. "Actually, no. Ignore that. I'm going to get Conal to kill you."

"Why don't you just do it then?" Siobhan screamed. "I'm sick of you! Ever since you got your claws into Corrine, we've all been living in fear of you. But not anymore! If you're such a dangerous person, come down here and do it! Kill me!"

Siobhan stopped screaming and glared up at him, her chest heaving. He frowned at her.

"Who is Corrine?"

Siobhan gulped down her anger. She had let her emotions get the better of her. She shouldn't have said any of that. But now she had piqued his curiosity. Had she just changed history? Or rather, had she started him on the path that would eventually lead to Corrine? She shuddered. *Don't think on it*, she told herself. *Just deal with him now.*

She heard a creaking behind her. She whirled around to find the door slightly ajar and an eye staring out at her. The eye turned to the top of the hill, where Euan and his people were waiting. A hand snaked through the gap, gripping an iron cross in a handkerchief.

"Hold this," said a voice, and Siobhan realized it was Father Josephus. She grabbed the cross and stared into his eye. She also held up the iron bar she was holding.

"Father Josephus," called a voice behind them.

Siobhan glanced over her shoulder and saw Leanan staring down at them, smiling.

"How are you, Father? Keeping well? We'll have to get together sometime soon. Have another little chat. Yes?"

The door in front of Siobhan opened wider.

"Come inside. Quickly."

Siobhan stepped into the church. The door slammed shut behind her. She looked around and saw a wide-eyed Father Josephus leaning against the wood.

Sanctuary. The Unhallowed couldn't cross over Hallowed ground. She was safe. For now.

And Siobhan started to cry. She didn't want to, but she couldn't help herself. Everything that had happened, all the events up to this moment, they all came crashing down on her in a wave of pain and fear. The tears came in great, heaving sobs that wouldn't stop no matter how hard she tried.

Father Josephus hesitantly took her into his arms. She cried into his shoulder, wondering if she was going to come through this alive.

~ Eighteen ~

"WE CAN'T JUST STAY HERE," SIOBHAN REPEATED, frustration ringing from her voice.

"Why not?" asked Father Josephus. "God will protect us."

Siobhan looked around the nave of the church. There looked to be about twenty or so villagers huddled together in fear. About half of them were children.

"Like he protected everyone else tonight?"

"That's different."

"It is not. Father, God protects those who protect themselves. We may be safe for the moment, but what's to stop the Fey throwing a torch through the window? We'll all burn alive."

Father Josephus paled. He swallowed nervously, looking at the many leaded glass windows that surrounded them.

Siobhan stepped closer to the priest and lowered her voice. "We have to get out of here. For the sake of these people. Euan will wait out there as long as the game amuses him, then he will finish it. I know what he is like."

Father Josephus sighed. "What do you suggest, then? I thought I was doing them right by bringing them here."

"You weren't to know." Siobhan looked around, wondering how she was going to get the villagers down to the loch. How would they avoid the Unhallowed?

Father Josephus saw the expression on her face. "We're trapped, aren't we? I've doomed us all."

Siobhan's eyes fell on a small door behind the transept. "Where does that lead?"

"The cellar. The previous priest kept wine and such down there. Supplies."

Siobhan pulled open the door and was greeted with pitch blackness. She took a torch from the wall and held it inside the opening. Stone stairs descended into the cellar. They were uneven, the path of years wearing a depression in each step.

"There's nothing down there, girl. Although, perhaps bringing up the casks of wine might not be a bad idea."

Siobhan ignored Father Josephus's attempt at a joke and headed down into the cellar. There were only ten or so steps, and they opened into a room the same size as the church above her head. The floor was paved with huge flagstones. Placed around three of the walls were trunks and wooden containers. Against the last wall were the casks of wine. Obviously the previous occupant liked his drink.

Or maybe he used them for communion, thought a more charitable part of her mind.

She heard the scuff of footsteps behind her, and the light in the cellar brightened as Father Josephus entered with his own torch.

"They grow restless."

"So do I."

Father Josephus sighed. "What are you expecting to find down here?"

"*Something* . . . anything. I'm not going to sit up there and simply wait for them to come for me."

"No. No, you are right." Father Josephus smiled at her. "You are a brave girl, Siobhan."

Siobhan snorted. "No I'm not. I'm terrified. There's just no other choice." And it was true. There was no one else to protect her. Siobhan almost wished Mara or Ilona were here. They were so much braver than she. They would know what to do.

"That *is* bravery, my girl. The realization that we must act despite our fear." He placed his torch in a wall sconce and clapped his hands. "Right. Let's get started, shall we?"

He moved to one side and lifted the lid of the first chest he came to. "Linen," he said in disgust, slamming the lid and moving on to the next. Siobhan followed his lead, turning to an ornate trunk and lifting the lid. She lowered the torch, seeing the glint of silverware and glass. Nothing of use to them.

She looked in each chest and box as she moved around the wall, but there was nothing they could use. If she was honest with herself, she hadn't really expected there to be. But she had to keep moving. She had to hope. Without that, she may as well just walk out of the church and hand herself over to Euan.

Father Josephus closed the last lid. "Come, Siobhan,"

he said gently. "We must think of something else."

Siobhan sighed and looked around the cellar one last time. Father Josephus moved to the stair and took his torch from the sconce. Siobhan started to follow him, then stopped suddenly. There was something . . . something Niamh had once said to her.

"What is it, Siobhan?"

Siobhan tried to think. *When was it?* Then she remembered. Back at the manor house. When she and Niamh were clearing out the iron in preparation for the feast. She had said something about there being no iron in the village, that the church held it all hidden away so it couldn't harm the Fey. What had she said? That a priest had buried it beneath the church.

She looked down at her feet. Could it be? "We need to find a flagstone we can pull up."

Father Josephus frowned. "Why?"

"Niamh told me that when the Fey and humans made contact, they had to get rid of all the iron as it was harmful to the Fey. She said the priest at the time refused to throw it away. He thought the Fey evil and suspected a trap."

"Wise man," said Father Josephus wryly.

"But Niamh said he buried the iron beneath the church. Don't you see? If it's here, we could use it against the Fey."

"It's probably nothing more than a legend, Siobhan."

Siobhan bristled. "Do you have a better idea?"

"Sadly, no."

They got down on their hands and knees and tried to

get their fingers into the grooves around the flagstones. Immediately, Siobhan could see it was an impossible task. The stones were too heavy. They would have to be levered up with something.

Father Josephus straightened up. "I'll be back in a moment," he said, then hurried up the stairs.

In his absence, Siobhan walked slowly around the cellar, trying to see if any of the flagstones looked different from the others. She was just about to pull the trunks away from the wall when Father Josephus returned with a long crosier. He jammed it into the gap between two flagstones, then smiled at Siobhan.

"I'm sure God will forgive me," he said, then pushed down on the metal rod.

Nothing. But at least they had something they could use. Father Josephus started at one end of the room and tried to lever up every flagstone. While he did this, Siobhan pulled the chests and containers away from the walls, onto the stones he had already tested.

Father Josephus was soon sweating profusely. "Are you sure of what Niamh said?" he panted, leaning on the crosier.

"Yes. Her da told her the priest buried it beneath the church."

"He didn't say buried it in the church grounds?"

Siobhan hesitated. Now that Father Josephus said it, she wasn't sure.

Her doubt must have shown on her face, because Father Josephus got to work again. "No matter. We will try what we can and deal with the unknown when we have to."

A few minutes later, they found it. Father Josephus had placed the rod between two flagstones up against the wall and heaved down on it. The flagstone flew up into the air, and Father Josephus, expecting a heavy resistance, stumbled and fell hard to his knees. The flagstone flipped and hit the ground, smashing into pieces. Siobhan hurried forward to inspect the shards. The stone had been cut a fraction of the thickness of the others, allowing it to be easily moved by anyone who knew its location. She turned to the hole to find Father Josephus seated at its edge, wincing and rubbing his bruised knees.

Siobhan joined him and leaned down, holding the torch out in front of her. The hiding place wasn't just a small opening. It was a space about half the size of the actual church. A small ladder had been cut into the stone wall.

Siobhan turned around and quickly clambered down. She had to duck to get into the hole, but what she saw made her heart sing with relief.

Iron. Everywhere she swung her torch, the flickering flame revealed dull gray swords, daggers, bowls, and horseshoes. Helms and shields were heaped in low piles, the shields wooden but inlaid with studs of iron and bound with metal bands to reinforce them. Everything they needed was right here.

"Siobhan?" called Father Josephus. "Have you found anything?"

Siobhan smiled. "Yes, Father. I think we have."

The villagers helped move everything up to the church. There were enough swords for the men to carry and even one or two for the women. The children were given the helms and as much iron as they could possibly hold. Some of them even carried candleholders and brandished them like weapons. *Which they are,* thought Siobhan. One touch of any of this and the Fey will run screaming. Siobhan herself had replaced her poker with a short sword and a small iron dagger.

Father Josephus stood before them all, leaning on his own sword, one he had picked especially—an iron blade with an ivory guard and leather grip. "We have to get to the loch," he said to the villagers. "Elaphe is guiding the others there, and we need to join them. If that means fighting, if that means dying, then so be it. But if we make it to the loch, Elaphe will help us repel these abominations."

"How will he do that?" asked one of the villagers, a thin, hatchet-faced man Siobhan thought was called Curin. "He is only one person."

"And how do we know he's not in league with them?" asked Lyra, one of the servants from the manor house.

"We have to trust that God sent him to help us," replied Father Josephus. He looked around at them all, meeting the eyes of the adults. "This will be hard," he said. "But it is something that must be done. The children are our priority. Our first goal is to make sure they get to the water. Once that is accomplished we can die knowing we did our duty."

He looked around at the frightened, resolute faces. Then he nodded once and walked to the doors. Siobhan went to his side and the others followed, forming a protective circle around the children.

"Are you ready?" the priest asked.

Everyone assented, faces grim. Father Josephus smiled, a flash of teeth that looked to Siobhan more like a hunter readying to stalk his prey than a man of the cloth. Then he pushed open the door and stepped outside.

It was like stepping out into one of her worst nightmares.

The Unhallowed formed a dark line before them. They were silhouetted against the rising flames behind them as more houses caught fire. The roar of the flames was loud in the night. Siobhan faltered, then felt Father Josephus grip her arm.

"Be strong, my girl."

Siobhan swallowed. It was like an image from hell itself. The Unhallowed simply stood, waiting for them to come. And it wasn't just the human-looking Fey. All manner of creatures stood before them. Hunchbacked monsters with yellow eyes, hags with tentacles writhing from their faces, stick-thin dogs with ribs bursting from emaciated skin. Every possible abomination stood before them, grunting and snarling, rasping their breath or cursing their names, eager and ready for them to leave the protection of the church.

And in the center was Euan, his face hidden in darkness.

As they left the church grounds and drew closer to the line, Siobhan saw doubt enter the ranks of the Fey. One or two of them stepped back, others glanced uneasily at Euan. The Fey Prince stood his ground, though Siobhan could see him trying to hide the pain he felt at the closeness of the iron. As they drew nearer, Siobhan saw the cold fury in his glittering eyes.

Father Josephus stopped five paces from them.

"You think you have won, priest?" asked Euan softly.

"No," replied Father Josephus, just as softly. "I think this war has only just begun."

They locked eyes for what seemed like an age, and then Father Joe moved forward again, the villagers following closely behind. The Fey parted way before them, like a tide of water pulling back from the shore. Once they passed the line, the Unhallowed closed ranks behind them once again.

Father Josephus increased their pace and took them along the road and past the burning houses. Siobhan heard some of the villagers cursing as they caught sight of their homes. Homes that were now gone forever.

This is the beginning, she thought. *All the centuries of pain and warfare to come. It all started here.*

They reached the path that took them down to the loch. As they approached the water, Siobhan saw many torches bobbing around on the crannog.

Elaphe was waiting for them at the edge of the bridge.

"Father Josephus," he said, "I am glad you made it. And Siobhan, well done."

Siobhan said nothing. She was looking out over the water, trying to count how many villagers had survived. It looked to be quite a few.

Elaphe followed the direction of her gaze. "I think forty or so are missing."

Siobhan did a quick calculation. "That's almost a fifth of the village!"

"I know."

"What did they want?" asked Father Josephus. "If their aim was to kill us all, why not simply lay siege to us? They would last longer than we would."

"They do not want to kill you. At least not yet. They want you alive so they can use you to turn their followers into the Unhallowed. Think. They must be getting new recruits all the time. They will need humans to keep up their stock of blood."

"What can we do?" whispered Father Josephus.

"You will have to rebuild all the crannogs. It is your best protection."

"Why?"

"I have made the spirits of the water aware of the situation. They will bar the Unhallowed from crossing without invitation. You will be safe. I advise you to get everyone together come first light and salvage as much wood as you can get your hands on. This first bridge is sound, but the others linking the crannogs together will need to be rebuilt. You will see the islands beneath the water where they used to stand."

"But . . . how long will we have to live on the water?"

Elaphe shook his head sadly. "I do not know. I'm sorry. It is the best I can do at the moment."

Father Josephus's face softened. "Do not apologize. You have done more than enough. If it wasn't for you . . ." Father Josephus shook his head. "Well, who knows how many would still be standing?"

"Do not lose hope. The King and Queen are not taking this lightly. In five days' time our brethren from all over the world will bring together their rathstones, and we will meet for our Gathering. Traditionally, it is a time of hope, but this time it will be a war council. We will formulate a plan to deal with Prince Euan and his traitorous friends."

Siobhan heard these words and felt sick to her stomach. All *was* lost. Elaphe was dissembling with Father Josephus. He knew the rathstone was gone. The Fey wouldn't be able to join together at this Gathering. Not now.

Elaphe looked down at her. "Siobhan," he said gently.

Siobhan looked into his eyes. They were sad, lined with worry and pain.

"What?" she asked, her heart sinking even further. "What is it?"

Elaphe took hold of Siobhan's hand and gripped it tightly. "It's Niamh, Siobhan. They took her."

~ Nineteen ~

As Father Josephus hurried his charges across the small bridge, Siobhan stood before Elaphe.

"Are you sure?" she asked him.

"I'm afraid so."

"You saw it? You saw them take her?"

"I did."

There was a wail from over on the crannog. Siobhan looked over the water to see Eomen hugging Brianna tight against his chest. She felt relieved that they had both survived, but now they had to face the fact that their youngest daughter had been taken.

"There is hope yet, Siobhan. She is not dead."

Siobhan turned back to Elaphe. "Why did you lie to Father Josephus about the rathstone? You know you do not have it. Euan does. You can't just tell them that and abandon them."

"I never planned on abandoning them."

"Then what are you going to do?"

"The same thing I have been trying to do, track Euan to his lair. Only now it is more urgent." He bent over so that he could look Siobhan in the eye. "We need to retrieve the stone. We need to get it back to the King and Queen so Hallowmere can open as planned."

Siobhan frowned. "You can't go on your own. Where's your army? Find out where he is and lead an attack. Take back the stone by force."

"Force is not always the answer," said Elaphe gently.

"But you can't do this on your own."

"I must. I will endanger no other."

"*I* will come. I can help rescue her. And the others."

"Child, listen to me. No matter how much you have been through, you cannot accompany me on this. It is too dangerous."

Elaphe straightened up. "The best thing you can do is help the villagers rebuild the crannogs. They will be safe on the water." He smiled at her. "You are a brave child, but this is not your fight."

Siobhan was close to tears. "How can you say that! I told you everything that happens in the future. If we can stop this now—"

"Believe me, that is what I intend to do. But I may not survive the attempt. I will not have your blood on my hands."

Siobhan opened her mouth to protest again, but Elaphe held up a hand to stop her. "That is my final word. Good-bye Siobhan. I am very glad I met you. You are quite a remarkable human."

He smiled at her, glanced once over the lake to where the villagers were trying to create some kind of order from the insanity of the night, then he turned and vanished into the darkness.

The way Siobhan saw it, Elaphe knew the type of person she was. Therefore he must have known she would follow. So it was his fault. He couldn't blame her for acting according to her nature.

He probably wants me to help him, she thought as she crept through the now-silent village. A light drizzle had started to fall, dampening the fires and sending a thick pall of smoke into the air. Siobhan shivered. The night was silent, eerily so after the events of the past hours.

Siobhan had watched Elaphe walk along the road leading out of the village. She wanted to wait a while before she followed him. Not too long. Just long enough that he wouldn't know she was behind him, and that when she did eventually catch up with him it would be too late to send her back.

Besides, if she did lose his track, she could simply use the Sight again, like she had done when she needed to find Niamh. She was definitely getting better at controlling it, and she was confident enough to believe she could—at the very least—send one of the tendrils out after Elaphe. Her sense of who he was should be enough to lead her to him.

Siobhan set off after him, walking at a brisk pace so that he didn't get too far ahead. The night passed slowly. The cold bit deep, even through the winter clothes Siobhan was wearing. The chill wind snuck through every tiny hole and opening, blowing across her skin like ice water. No matter how tightly she tried to pull the cloak around her, the wind still got in.

She eventually took to running for fifty paces, then walking for fifty, just to keep her body temperature up.

The night wore on. The drizzle eventually stopped, and the moon appeared briefly between fast-moving clouds. It was by this light that she finally caught sight of Elaphe walking along the road some distance ahead. She breathed a sigh of relief and slowed her pace so as not to get too close.

She judged the passage of time by the distance the moon had moved every time it appeared from behind the clouds. By her reckoning it was sometime around midnight when Elaphe left the road and walked into the woods. Siobhan quickened her pace, worried about losing him among the trees. But she needn't have worried. His footprints were clear in the wet ground.

Siobhan was growing tired, but she couldn't afford to stop. She kept going, yawning and blinking away the exhaustion of the day, telling herself she had to keep moving. For Niamh's sake.

But eventually, sometime close to dawn, even this thought was not enough to keep her going. She had to rest. Her calves ached from walking along the soggy, uneven ground. Her eyes were gritty and dry; the cold wind hadn't stopped the whole night, blowing directly into her face the entire time she walked.

She sat down on an exposed tree root, arranging her cloak beneath her so her leggings didn't get wet, and leaned back against the trunk. She yawned. *How close were Euan and his army? They couldn't be that far,* she reasoned. They had to walk as well, and they were taking a group of humans with them—children included. They couldn't expect them to walk for days on end, surely?

Her eyes drooped. *Maybe just a quick nap,* she told herself. After all, it was too cold to fall into a deep sleep. She'd probably be awake again in ten minutes. But it would be enough to refresh her for the next leg of the trek.

She yawned again, then closed her eyes. *Just ten minutes,* she thought wearily.

Siobhan was being chased. She knew that, but she could not see her pursuers. Winter sunlight filtered down through the dead trees. All around her was blackness. No grass, no green. Everything was dead, burned away. Every step she took raised a puff of ash that spiraled up into the beams of weak light.

She stumbled, then righted herself. She had been here before. She knew that. She remembered being chased by an unseen attacker. She remembered running to the edge of the cliff with nowhere left to go. Trapped.

Not this time.

Siobhan veered away from the path she remembered taking, still running as fast as she could but away from the cliff top.

A loud crack echoed through the still forest—someone stepping on a fallen tree branch. She remembered that as well. Her pursuer was close.

She looked over her shoulder. She could see the puffs of ash slowly settling around her footprints.

And there, in the distance. She caught a glimpse of something darting between the empty husks that had once been trees.

Siobhan refused to give in to the fear that once would have paralyzed her. Instead, she focused on running faster, but it seemed that no matter how fast she ran, the creature always gained ground. There was no way she could escape.

But she kept going anyway. She could hear its breath as it drew closer. Loud, rasping, breathing onto her neck. Siobhan couldn't help it. She cried out in fear as she caught the scent of decaying meat. The coldness spread across her back, painful in its intensity.

The trees started to thin. Siobhan had been veering wildly through the woods as she tried to avoid the cliff top. Maybe there was a town beyond the forest, someone who could help her.

She saw the end of the trees up ahead, a line of black beyond which she could see the clear blue of the sky.

The line grew closer. She could feel her legs turning cold, her back seizing up with the chill. Just a little farther. Nearly there. Her knees ached. The cold reached inside, burrowing deep into her being and slowly draining her life away.

Close. The trees were so close. She could feel herself slowing down, feel the cold reaching up to her heart.

She wasn't going to make it. The tree trunks were not more than twenty paces away.

The cold was spreading. But the cold wasn't just from the creature. It was from the dawning realization that this was exactly the same as before.

She felt something on her shoulder, a blade of ice that shot down through her arm and made it fall useless by her side.

She screamed in rage, furious that the creature had managed to trick her.

A hand clasped over the back of her neck.

But then she jerked forward, and she was through the trees and onto a small sward of brittle grass.

She stumbled to a stop, knowing what she would see.

The sward of grass swept ten paces away and ended at the edge of the cliff. She staggered forward. The drop descended to sharp rocks and crags. There was nowhere left to go.

Except now there was. She wouldn't run anymore. She was tired of it, tired of answering meekly to every order, of living her life afraid of everything. Now there was an option.

Siobhan braced herself and turned around.

She was surprised to find herself facing Euan. He stood a few paces away, looking around in puzzlement. Then he looked at Siobhan, and his eyebrows rose in surprise.

"You?"

But then he vanished. Everything around her vanished, and she realized that someone was shaking her.

Siobhan's eyes snapped open to find Elaphe crouching before her. He looked angry.

"Do you want every predator in the area to know our location?"

Siobhan stared at him, the effects of the vision still fogging her mind.

"You were screaming," explained Elaphe. "I could here you from my camp halfway into the woods."

Siobhan sat up. "Sorry," she said weakly.

"Come with me," he said. "I have a fire going."

Siobhan got up and followed Elaphe deeper into the woods. It was still dark, but after about two hundred paces, she caught sight of the welcoming flicker of flames among the trees. Elaphe led her into a small clearing that was bordered on three sides by thick bushes that shielded the flames from anyone looking from the opposite direction.

"Sit," he said. "Warm yourself."

Siobhan sat as close to the fire as she could get and extended her hands toward the flames. She sighed with pleasure as the heat loosened her numb fingers, working its way slowly up her arms and into her body. Who would have thought a fire could feel so good?

After he had given Siobhan time to warm herself, Elaphe cleared his throat. "Siobhan, I need to ask—what do you think you are doing?"

"Following you."

"That is abundantly clear, thank you. But why?"

"You know why. I want to help."

"Out of the question. You must return to the village."

"No," said Siobhan quietly.

Elaphe looked surprised. "I beg your pardon?"

"I said no. I'm not running anymore. I'm not going back. I want to help. And before you say anything, please understand that the only way you are going to get rid of me is if you tie me up and leave me here, or if you take me back to the village yourself. But even if you do that, I'll just follow you again."

Elaphe stared at her. Finally, he shook his head. "You are a very stubborn girl," he said. "Fine. Do as you wish, but remember this is going to be dangerous."

"It can't be any more dangerous than what I've already been through."

Elaphe smiled. "We'll see. In the meantime, rest. I'll keep watch till the morning."

Siobhan nodded gratefully and lay down on the leaves close to the fire. She fell asleep as soon as she closed her eyes.

Twenty

Siobhan woke to the mouth-watering smell of roasting rabbit. She sat up and looked blearily around the campsite. Elaphe sat by the fire, turning the rabbit on a makeshift spit made from green saplings. When he saw she was awake, he removed the rabbit from the fire and cut it in half, handing Siobhan her share.

Siobhan hadn't realized just how hungry she was until the first of the juices hit her tongue. She devoured every last bite, burning the roof of her mouth in the process.

When they had finished breaking their fast, Elaphe packed up the camp and kicked the fire out.

"Ready?" he asked, as Siobhan licked her fingers.

Siobhan nodded and pushed herself to her feet, wincing at the stiffness in her legs.

The sun hadn't traveled much up the sky before they stumbled across a wide swath of trampled-down grasses and ferns. A large company had passed through the area. Elaphe kneeled down and studied the tracks.

"Looks like they came through here yesterday afternoon. Now it's just a matter of following the path to the end."

They didn't reach the end of the track that day. The path took them out of the forest and into the foothills of the mountains that bordered the loch. The high peaks towered above them, dominating the landscape with their size.

"Surely we're not going to climb those?" asked Siobhan when the clouds parted in the afternoon and she caught a glimpse of the snow-covered peaks.

Elaphe followed her gaze. "I don't think so. The Unhallowed took children and a few of the village elders. They can't expect them to be able to climb a mountain."

They camped that night under an overhang that had been cut into the side of the foothills. Elaphe lit a fire, despite Siobhan's misgivings about being discovered.

"It's either the fire, or we freeze to death during the night," said Elaphe matter-of-factly. "Take your pick."

Siobhan picked the fire.

The next morning the trail was harder to find. The grass and heather that had dominated the ground started to give way to gray, craggy rock. It looked to Siobhan as though the very bones of the earth were heaving out of the ground. Elaphe was still able to follow the trail, but he increased their pace, saying he was worried about the softer ground giving way altogether and the possibility of losing the tracks over the rock.

By midmorning, the mist had descended from the heights, swallowing them up inside a gray shroud. They kept moving, although Siobhan had no idea how Elaphe could see where they were going.

The day wore on, miserable and cold. Siobhan's cloak had absorbed much of the moisture from the air and now lay heavy across her shoulders. She had also developed a sore throat and was convinced she was growing sick. It had to happen sooner or later, she supposed, stuck outside in this weather. She felt a small moment of self-pity. How ironic would it be if Euan won because she died of a severe chill?

The worst thing was there was no way she could get warm now. Even Elaphe would have difficulty lighting a fire in this weather. And that was *if* they were able to find any wood. Siobhan started to worry about what they were going to do to keep from freezing when they had to stop for the night.

Then, sometime late into the afternoon, Elaphe stopped.

"Are we here?" asked Siobhan hopefully.

"No," said Elaphe heavily. "I'm afraid not."

Siobhan shuffled toward the sound of Elaphe's voice until his form emerged from the mist.

"What's wrong?"

"I can't find them," he sighed. "It's what I was afraid of. When I was away these past days, I was attempting to track down Leanan's hiding place. Every time I thought I was getting close, I would end up lost. I thought . . . I thought that now that they have the stone, maybe I could track that instead."

"But you can't?"

"No. They are using magic of some kind to hide from me."

Siobhan stared around at the gray surroundings. Water was dripping somewhere close by. "What are we going to do?"

"I don't know, Siobhan. I really don't know."

Siobhan stood thoughtful for a moment. "Maybe I can help?"

"You? How?"

She quickly told him of the time she used the Sight to find Niamh and how all she needed was a feeling of the person she was chasing, some kind of intimate touch.

"But how will you get that?"

"I've had a vision dream," she explained, "of Euan chasing me through a burned forest. I got it when I first came here, though I didn't know at the time its true nature. It was a warning, Elaphe, a warning of what would occur if Euan triumphs. I had the vision again tonight, but Euan . . . seemed aware of me. He looked confused to be there."

"You pulled him inside your vision?"

"Maybe. But I could try and have the vision again, use it to get a feel for Euan. Then I can use it to track him."

Elaphe hesitated, clearly troubled.

"What other option is there? You taught me how to use the Sight. It is only right it should help us."

Elaphe reluctantly nodded. "You're right. We should at least try."

Elaphe guided her along the rock path until they found an overhang that would shelter Siobhan. She crawled inside and tried to make herself comfortable.

"Don't do anything foolish. Just get what you need and leave. Euan can still hurt you inside a vision."

Siobhan nodded and closed her eyes. She was nervous, filled with fear, but she was so exhausted, she fell asleep in no time at all.

Siobhan opened her eyes. She stood upon the patch of grass that bordered the edge of the cliff. The drop descended to sharp rocks and crags.

Siobhan braced herself and turned around.

Euan still stood there. He stood a few paces away, looking around in puzzlement. Then he looked at Siobhan, and his eyebrows rose in surprise.

"You have the power."

Siobhan walked slowly forward.

"What are you doing?" asked Euan.

Siobhan didn't answer. She kept walking.

Euan was growing nervous. He looked around the burned forest, then settled back on Siobhan. He pulled out a knife.

"Stop moving," he said.

Siobhan ignored him. She had to distract him. "Your time is over, Prince Euan."

"What are you talking about?" he snapped.

"You don't succeed. I know. I've seen it."

"What have you seen? Tell me!"

Siobhan stopped when she stood directly in front of him. He glared at her. She could see the conflict clearly in his eyes. On the one hand, he wanted her dead. On the other, he wanted to know what she had seen.

"Tell me now."

"I'll tell you nothing."

Euan swung the dagger toward her. Siobhan ducked and grabbed hold of his arm, using her Sight to plunge into his mind, the way she had always tried to avoid. Sensations overwhelmed her. Anger, fear, guilt over what he had done to Conal. Suspicion——suspicion that everyone was the enemy, that everyone was out to betray him. Hunger, hunger for power, hunger for his people to live free and long.

And loneliness. He felt lonely, that there was no one for him to turn to. Even Leanan, he thought, was not truly trustworthy.

Siobhan gasped and let go, staggering away from Euan. He stared at her.

"What did you do?" he shouted. "What did you do?"

Then he charged. Siobhan screamed and tried to move away, but the dagger was already moving. She held up a hand to defend herself as she tried to avoid the blade, but she felt it slice across her palm——

Siobhan jerked upright, narrowly missing hitting her head on the rocky roof. Elaphe sat before her.

"Did you get what you needed?"

Siobhan slowly raised her hand. It was bleeding from the shallow cut the knife had made.

"Yes," she said, thinking of the feelings of loneliness and paranoia. "I got what we needed."

Siobhan released her Sight from the door in her mind and let the tendrils make their own way through the mist. All she did was attach her feeling of Euan to them, with the slightest hint that she needed to find him. Then she waited.

"You find it a lot easier now," commented Elaphe.

"I do."

"What changed?"

Siobhan thought about it for a second. "Acceptance. When I accepted the fact that I couldn't control the Sight by force, that the best thing to do was accept it for what it was and work with it, instead of against it, then it got easier."

Elaphe nodded. "That is the same with all forms of magic. Look."

He held up a hand, and a small ball of orange light appeared. It grew in strength, beating like a heart. Light seeped through the mist around them, showing the crags and rock of the mountain.

"You can do this as well. You have mastered the art of controlling without actually controlling. That is what is needed for real magic. You cannot force it. Only accept its existence and allow it into your life. Do you understand?"

"I . . . I think so."

"Try it."

Siobhan looked at him in surprise. "How?"

"You are already working with the Sight. The Sight isn't the talent, Siobhan. The Sight is a symptom—a benefit—of the power you truly hold. That power allows you to do so much, Siobhan. So much you can't possibly imagine. You are very powerful. I've known that from the first time I saw you. Your power will grow with time, and you must always make sure it doesn't control you. Understand? It will be so easy for you to let your power feed your arrogance and control. You must always resist that. Otherwise . . ."

"Otherwise?"

"Otherwise you will end up like Leanan."

"Oh."

"But do not fear. I have every faith in you. Now come, close your eyes."

Siobhan did so.

"Imagine the light in your hands. Imagine it with as much detail as you can: how it will light your surroundings, how it will warm you if that is what you want, how it will affect the others around you."

Siobhan did as instructed. She kept it different from Elaphe's, imagining a cooling, blue light. She imagined how it would light the angles of his face, how it would cast shadows around them on the rocks.

"Open your eyes," instructed Elaphe.

Siobhan did so and blinked at the blue globe gently spinning in her cupped hands. She watched, mesmerized.

"Where does it come from?" she whispered.

"That is difficult. The power is there in the earth. Having talent means having the ability to tap into that power and use it for our own benefit."

"So it is not inside us? It travels through us?"

"Exactly. And if you think of the size and the power of nature, you will understand that there are really no boundaries to how strong you can become in magic. Just as long as you understand that the bigger the spell you try and perfect, the harder it will be to control it by *not* controlling it, if you get my meaning."

Siobhan thought about this. "You mean the stronger

the spell, the lighter the touch I will need to keep a hold on it?"

"Exactly. And that is where the difficulty comes, because a spell such as that will tempt you. You will sense the power and want to touch it, want to embrace it. But you cannot. If you do give in, it will take over your body. The power will snuff you out in an instant."

Siobhan closed her fist, shutting off the light.

"Are you any closer to Euan?" asked Elaphe.

Siobhan felt a moment's surprise. She had forgotten she was even using the Sight. She concentrated, lightly touching each of the tendrils of her mind. One of them held the scent of Euan and was closing in on a location.

"I have him," she said.

"Then let us go."

It took them another hour of walking before Siobhan finally stopped. They stood before a narrow slit in the mountain, barely wide enough for her to slip through.

"Is this it?" asked Elaphe.

"Yes. He's in here."

Elaphe peered inside, then turned to Siobhan.

"Are you ready?"

"As I'll ever be."

"Then let us go."

They stepped through the opening. Tendrils of mist followed them inside, as if trying to grasp hold of them and pull them back to safety. But they soon moved beyond the light, leaving the outside world behind them and entering a world of utter darkness.

"Use what I just taught you," Elaphe whispered. "Conjure a light."

Siobhan did as instructed, holding out her hand and imagining a soft, white light bright enough to illuminate their path.

"Well done," whispered Elaphe.

Siobhan opened her eyes to find the small globe nestling on her fingers. She extended her arm and walked around in a circle. Craggy walls hemmed them in on all sides. The ceiling was about fifteen feet high.

"What is this place?" she whispered.

"I'm not sure," said Elaphe. "I've heard . . ." He trailed into silence.

"You've heard what?"

"Nothing. It doesn't matter."

He started walking again. Siobhan hurried to catch up, not wanting to be left alone in the tunnel.

"What's the plan?" she asked when she drew abreast of him.

"Plan?" asked Elaphe in amusement. "I was hoping you had one."

"Me . . . ?"

"I'm jesting," said Elaphe. "But to answer your question, I don't have a plan. I'm hoping something will occur to me when we reach our destination."

They walked on in silence. The tunnel weaved back and forth, sometimes even doubling back on itself. Siobhan didn't like it. She could feel the weight of the mountain pressing down on her shoulders. What would happen if it collapsed?

Well, said a voice in her head, *you wouldn't know much about it, would you? So why are you worried?*

There weren't many sounds to accompany them along their path. The scuffing of feet in the dirt. Siobhan coughing and sneezing as she inhaled the dust that their passage kicked up. She wanted to speak, to fill the oppressive silence with talk of something, *anything,* but she was afraid that Elaphe was keeping quiet for fear of giving away their position, so she held her tongue.

The tunnel started to slope upward. As it did so it narrowed in on either side so that Elaphe and Siobhan eventually had to walk in single file. A few minutes of this, then Elaphe stopped. Siobhan bumped up against him.

"What's wrong?" she whispered.

He held up a hand for silence. Then he muttered something under his breath, and the light in Siobhan's hand winked out.

But there was still light, coming from up ahead. Elaphe moved forward. Siobhan followed, and she soon found herself standing before a narrow opening that led out onto a ledge.

A cool wind blew against Siobhan's face as she stared around in awe.

It was a vast space, an echoing cavern that wound its way around massive stalactites and stalagmites. But it wasn't just an underground cave. It was an abandoned city.

Dwellings lay half-ruined amid piles of fallen stone, their decaying innards exposed to the dank air. Wide boulevards were strewn with the detritus of decades, toppled spires that once must have soared and twisted up toward the vaulted ceiling. Siobhan gazed around in wonder. The city must have been about ten times the size of Ballach, but she could see it wasn't human built. There was something about the architecture, the way certain walls sloped inward, the way the carved gables on certain roofs hung down halfway to the ground, the elegant shape of spires that served no practical use except to take the breath away. There was something about it all that made the observer instantly aware that what they were looking at hadn't come from a human mind.

And all of it was illuminated by hidden lights. The glow cast around the abandoned city was harsh and white, and in the places where the radiance didn't touch, the shadows were all the darker by contrast.

"What is this place?" she whispered.

Elaphe was silent.

"Elaphe?"

"I think it is an abandoned Fey city."

"But why is it underground?"

"Even the Fey have had their share of defeats, Siobhan. Sometimes, it has been better to retreat instead of fight on and get slaughtered. This must have been one of our safe havens. Maybe a rath that was breached in battle."

"It looks ancient."

"It must be. It's hundreds of years old, maybe thousands. I cannot remember the last time we had to flee underground."

"Are the villagers here?"

In response, Elaphe indicated something in the city with a sharp nod. Siobhan looked, but she couldn't see what it was he was pointing out.

"There. By the marble statue."

Siobhan looked. And she saw it. Or rather, them. Four heavily muscled creatures with the legs of goats. They patrolled up and down a small section of road.

"Satyrs," said Elaphe. Then he pointed to one of the few intact buildings in the city, close to where the Unhallowed kept guard.

"I'd say the villagers are in there."

"Then there's still hope," said Siobhan excitedly.

"Possibly."

"What are we waiting for?"

Elaphe gave her a wry look. "Have you come up with a plan, then?"

"Haven't you?"

Elaphe looked away, but not before Siobhan saw the flicker of sadness pass across his face. "Perhaps," was all he said.

To the left of the ledge was a set of well-worn stairs that zigzagged down the wall into the outskirts of the city. Elaphe looked at them, then turned to the tunnel wall and laid his hands flat against the rock.

"What are you doing?"

"Hush."

Siobhan clamped her mouth shut and watched while Elaphe closed his eyes and laid his forehead against the stone. She could just hear him muttering under his breath.

After a few moments, he straightened up and turned to her. "Let's go."

Elaphe put his foot onto the first step and tested his weight. The top layer crumbled slightly, but the step held.

"Walk where I walk," he said.

Siobhan nodded and followed him down the stairs, keeping one hand trailing against the rough stone to her left. The buildings of the city soon rose up past them as they descended. When this happened Siobhan breathed a small sigh of relief. At least they were hidden from view now. Anyone looking up from the city wouldn't be able to see them.

Or so she thought.

"Stop moving," whispered Elaphe sharply.

Siobhan froze to the spot.

"Very slowly, move up against the wall."

Siobhan sidled to her left, then moved her head gradually to look at Elaphe. He was staring upward at the opposite side of the city. Siobhan followed his gaze to see what it was that had alarmed him so.

It took her a while to make it out. But a movement high up on the opposite wall of the cavern drew her attention. There was a similar set of stairs there, but far more ornate than the ones Elaphe and Siobhan used. They crawled up the wall in the same fashion, but every time they doubled back on themselves to climb up another level, a large landing had been built. Siobhan could see figures on one of these landings. It looked like they were staring out over the city. Had they been spotted? But surely the alarm would have been raised if they had.

There was more movement lower down the other set of stairs. Siobhan shifted her attention and saw the massive, headless creature she had seen the day she arrived. It was leading a line of captured villagers up the steps. When they finally reached the landing, the Fey who had been waiting turned and carried on upward with the group.

"What is that thing?"

"He is called Coliunn Gun Cheann. A very unpleasant creature. There have always been rumors about him. Some say he used to go hunting at night and slaughter the humans' cattle. We could never prove it, though."

"Where are they taking them?" she whispered.

Elaphe looked at her grimly. "I think you know the answer to that, Siobhan."

They waited till the distant figures had disappeared through a large portal that opened off one of the landings. Siobhan hadn't noticed the passageway as it was cloaked in shadow and blended in with the rest of the wall.

Elaphe and Siobhan hurried down the remaining stairs, then crossed a rubble-strewn street, and crouched down behind a broken wall. It was very dark here. The hidden lights that illuminated the center of the city were absent this far out.

Elaphe turned to face Siobhan. "As I see it, we have two goals. One, to retrieve the rathstone. No matter what happens, the Prince cannot be allowed to keep it. And two, rescue the villagers. Agreed?"

Siobhan nodded.

"We have to do them both at the same time. If we don't, our actions will alert the others, and one of the tasks will fail."

He paused to see if Siobhan had anything to add. But what could she say?

"I will go after the stone. I think you'll agree it is the more dangerous of the tasks."

Siobhan wasn't so sure about that. She thought of the four Fey standing guard over the villagers. Elaphe read her thoughts.

"Don't worry. I will create a diversion. Once the guards leave their post it is up to you to get the villagers out and take them back the way we came in."

"What kind of diversion?"

Elaphe smiled. Siobhan saw a flash of white teeth in the darkness. "I'll steal the rathstone. That should do it, don't you think?"

~ Twenty-One ~

SIOBHAN CROUCHED DOWN BEHIND THE MARBLE STATUE OF an old, witchlike woman. The statue towered over her, a large eagle perched on one of the witch's arms, a snake curled around the other. Siobhan was sure it was meant to signify something very important to the Fey, but at this exact moment, it was signifying something very important to Siobhan. It was serving as her cover.

Elaphe was halfway up the stairs already. She could see him only because she'd watched his progress from the very first step. But to a casual observer, he was all but invisible.

Which was something she wished she was. She felt horrendously exposed at the moment. The main street stretched away behind her, empty of life, and about thirty paces ahead, the Fey guards patrolled in front of the building she assumed the villagers were kept in.

Two of the satyrs stood talking while the other two walked aimlessly around. They looked bored, which was good, as it meant they wouldn't be paying much attention.

She looked up again. It took her a while to spot Elaphe.

He was right at the very top of the stairs now, waiting to one side of the tunnel that opened off the landing. After a few moments he ducked around the corner and disappeared.

Siobhan let out a slow breath. Now she had to wait for the diversion. She hoped it wouldn't be too long. She wasn't sure how long her nerves could take the waiting.

A sound from beyond the statue drew her attention. She leaned around the base and saw that the guards had moved to the doors of the building and were pulling them open. Had Elaphe's distraction come already? Had she missed it?

She didn't think so. Then what was going on?

The answer came soon enough. Two of the Fey guards disappeared inside the structure and came out a few moments later leading four villagers—an elderly woman, a young man, Jack . . .

And Niamh.

Siobhan scrambled to her feet to get a better view. Niamh looked scared. Tears fell down her cheeks, and she angrily wiped them away. Jack reached out and took hold of her hand as the two Fey turned them in the direction of the stairs and forced them to start walking.

Siobhan looked to the top of the steps in alarm. She had no idea what Elaphe's plan was or how long it would take. All he'd said was for Siobhan to wait for the sign, then try and get to the villagers. Maddeningly vague, but it was all he could come up with, seeing as he didn't know what he was walking into.

But now the villagers were being separated, and more

importantly, the Fey were taking Niamh away.

And Siobhan thought she knew why. They were leading the villagers away so they could use them in the rite to turn into the Unhallowed.

Siobhan watched the backs of the group as they disappeared along the road. She reached inside her cloak and gripped the iron knife she had taken from the church. She wouldn't stand by and let this happen. She had come here to save Niamh, and that was what she would do.

She would deal with Elaphe's displeasure later.

Siobhan hurried across the road to her right. She climbed over the rubble of a broken wall to get to a small street that ran behind a once-ornate building fronting the main road. She ran to the far wall and looked up. She could see the underside of the stairs as they crawled up into the distance. The prisoners were already on their way up. Siobhan could hear the voices of the Fey filtering down as they ordered the humans to hurry.

Siobhan crept along the wall until she could see down the main street. The two remaining guards were deep in conversation. She hurried to the base of the stairs and peered up. There was no sign of the Fey or the villagers. Siobhan took one last look back over her shoulder, then hurried up the steps, trying to keep to the shadows as much as possible.

Every time the stairs switched back on themselves to climb to the next level, Siobhan would wait by the tunnel opening that led into the cliff wall and listen for any sounds. Only when she was sure no one was there would she move past and resume her climb.

She was worried, though. What if they were going all the way to the top? They might discover Elaphe and ruin his plans.

As they climbed even higher, she decided she had to do something. But what?

Her hand slipped inside her cloak, feeling for the cold iron of her dagger. Could she actually . . . ? Would she be able to kill someone? Even if they *were* Unhallowed?

She swallowed nervously. She didn't know. Nothing in her life had prepared her to make decisions like this. She wasn't equipped.

Siobhan felt a fierce rush of anger toward Father Joe and the other members of the Council. What were they thinking, sending girls like her to do such dangerous jobs? Why weren't they doing it themselves? But no, they were back at Sir James's estate six hundred years in the future, eating five-course meals every night, while Siobhan and the others risked their lives and were forced to make decisions about whether to kill someone or not.

Siobhan shook herself, wiping away tears of frustration. *Get a hold of yourself,* she thought sternly. *It's not like that, and you know it.* They would do it themselves if they could.

She pulled the dagger out and resumed her trek up the uneven stairs. After a while, she heard voices coming from just above her. She looked up. The underside of the stairs were visible about ten paces above her head. She put her back against the wall and moved slowly up to the next landing.

Siobhan peered around the stairs that climbed up past

her head. There was no one here. She realized that the voices were coming from above her on the next landing. She crouched down and edged out from her cover. She got down on her stomach and crawled slowly up the stairs. The old fear returned, the fear that always made her curl up like a whimpering baby, but she clamped her mouth shut and kept moving, despite her worry that at any moment someone would see her and raise the alarm.

But nobody spotted her as she got halfway up the flight of steps, then carefully raised her head so she could see what was happening.

They were there, standing on the landing. The two satyrs were conversing about something, then one of them nodded and disappeared through the opening, his cloven feet loud on the stone. The humans followed after, the remaining Fey taking up the rear.

Siobhan waited to the count of ten, then she raised herself up and quickly climbed the rest of the stairs. She pressed herself up against the wall and peered into the tunnel. Rubble covered the floor, but the fallen debris had been pushed to the side so that a small path was cleared through the fallen debris. At the far end of the tunnel was a door carved into stone. The Fey were standing before it. One of them reached out a hand to push—

And before Siobhan realized what she was doing, she found herself standing in the passage, her dagger held before her in a trembling hand. She wasn't sure how she got there, just that she knew that if Niamh went through that door, she would be lost forever.

"Stop," she called out. Her voice shook. She stood

up straighter so that she wouldn't look as scared as she felt.

Everyone turned in surprise. Niamh's eyes widened in such a comical look of shock that Siobhan almost found herself smiling. The satyr who was guarding the rear turned to face her. He was only a few paces away. The other guard shoved his way past the villagers so he could see what was going on.

Siobhan brandished the dagger again, just so they could see it was iron. "Let them go."

The two satyrs talked to each other in their strange language. The second one laughed and waved his hand, then the satyr who had guarded the rear stepped forward, hands raised to show they were empty.

"What do you intend to do with that?"

"Whatever I have to."

"Is that so? And what have I ever done to you?"

"You've taken my friend."

"Have I? I'm sure there's just some misunderstanding here." He held out his hand. "Hand it over before someone gets hurt."

Siobhan glanced past him to find Niamh. She was reaching down to pick up a good-sized rock from the rubble. Siobhan saw with a surge of happiness that the other villagers were doing the same thing. The second satyr, watching Siobhan facing off against the first, had his back turned to them.

Siobhan hung her head, letting tears spill from her eyes. It wasn't hard. She was so terrified she felt she could cry for hours and hours.

"I'm sorry," she sobbed. "It's just . . . I'm so scared."

The Fey smiled. "Don't worry. Just give me the blade, and we'll sort it out for you." He reached out for the dagger, and Siobhan suddenly thrust it upward, sending the iron blade right through his hand. The point punched out from the middle of his palm, the skin bubbling and sizzling from contact with the metal. He opened his mouth to scream, but then there was a dull, wet sound, and he collapsed to the floor. Siobhan looked up to see Jack standing over him with a large rock held in his hands. The other satyr was also lying on the ground, the young man and Niamh hovering over his body.

"Siobhan!"

Niamh dropped the rock and ran past the others, flying straight into Siobhan's arms, laughing and sobbing at the same time.

"I thought I was dead, Siobhan. I didn't think anyone would come for us."

Siobhan stroked Niamh's hair. "It's all right," she said quietly. "Everything's taken care of."

Niamh leaned back so she could see Siobhan's eyes. "Is it? Have the villagers come to fight? How did you get here, anyway? How did you know?"

Siobhan disentangled herself from Niamh's arms. "Not now, Niamh. Right now you have to get the villagers out of here. How many are here?"

Jack cleared his throat. "Lots. The Fey took prisoners from all the villages around here."

"There's over a hundred, Siobhan."

Siobhan's mind worked furiously. "That's good then.

233

Safety in numbers." She turned and headed back to the tunnel entrance. The others followed her. "See that stairway over on the opposite wall?" She pointed.

"I see it," said Niamh.

"That's how you get out. Elaphe and I came in that way. You have to get to the other villagers and lead them through the tunnels and down the mountain. Get them back to Ballach. The villagers have been rebuilding the crannogs on the loch. That's the only place you will be safe from the Fey."

"Why are you speaking like this?" asked Niamh. "Aren't you coming?"

"I am. But I have to help Elaphe first. He's the one who led me here to help you."

"Another Fey?" The young man spat on the ground. "I'd sooner wait here than listen to anything one of them said. It will be a trap."

"A trap that involves pretending to rescue you and leading you out of the clutches of the enemy?" asked Siobhan scornfully. "Do you honestly believe that?"

The young man didn't respond, but his cheeks colored slightly. Siobhan turned back to Jack.

"There are just two satyr guards down there. Sneak around the outside of the houses that border the street, and overpower them. Here." She handed Niamh her iron dagger. "Use this. The iron is like poison to them."

Niamh took the blade. "Promise me you'll come back to Ballach?"

Siobhan hesitated, but only for a second. "I promise."

Niamh hugged her again. "Be careful," she whispered into her ear.

Siobhan hugged her back. "I will."

Jack and the others were waiting on the landing. "Come on, girl," he said.

Niamh and Siobhan separated. Siobhan gripped her hand tightly in farewell, then Niamh and the others disappeared around the corner.

TWENTY-TWO

SIOBHAN STARED AT THE EMPTY SPACE ON THE LANDING, fighting the urge to run after them. The desire to flee with them back to Ballach was so strong, it took all her willpower to resist it. Instead, she turned around and retraced her steps through the tunnel to investigate the door the Fey were about to use.

It was carved from stone, like everything else around her, but it had been buffed and polished so that it was as smooth as a piece of ice. She ran her hands across it and couldn't feel a single bump or rough spot. Siobhan laid her ear against the stone but couldn't hear anything. No surprise there. The stone was probably quite thick.

There was no obvious method of opening the door, so she continued her exploration of the surface, carefully running her hands all over the stone. Her fingers found a very faint depression in the center. She gently prodded it and was rewarded with a faint click. A second later, the door swung toward her.

Siobhan stopped it from opening more than a crack. She just wanted to look through, to see what lay beyond, as she'd been wondering where all the other

Unhallowed had disappeared to. Back in the forest there had been almost a hundred of them, and if they were using the prisoners for their blood, there must be more than that by now.

She pressed her eye to the crack and looked through, her heart nearly stopping as she saw just how right she was. The door opened onto a small balcony, and the balcony itself looked over an enclosed chamber. All around the walls of the chamber were tiers and tiers of seats.

And they were filled with the Unhallowed. Nixes and goblins, evil-looking daoi, even the horrible, scorpion-like cuideag that had impersonated Sir James for so long.

Siobhan looked on in horror. She couldn't comprehend how many they were, never mind count them. Hundreds, if not thousands, of Fey were all staring downward, watching with rapt attention as something happened below them. Siobhan couldn't see what they were looking at, and there was no way she could sneak out onto the balcony without being seen.

But she could still hear.

"You have a choice," said a loud voice. Siobhan recognized it instantly as Euan's. "The choice is this: You submit to us, let us take your tithe in blood, and you will become our servants. You will become the Half-Born. It will be no worse than what you already are. Do you not serve your laird? Do you not serve your king? This will be no different. Except you will serve us. We will not take more blood than we need. Certainly not enough to kill you, that I promise."

There was a pause. Siobhan could almost see Euan as

he surveyed the humans with that arrogant stare of his. They must be on the ground of the room below.

"If you refuse, then we will assume you are our enemy. And I'm afraid to say we do not keep our enemies alive."

Another pause, while he let those listening absorb the words.

"I will now ask the question. Are you willing to pay the tithe?"

Siobhan heard voices raised in reluctant agreement. She cursed Euan, but what could the trapped humans do? It was either submit or die.

"Excellent," said Euan. "You will not regret your decision. This I promise you. Now, it may be better for you to close your eyes."

Siobhan quickly pulled her head back and closed the door. She had no desire to hear any more.

She retreated back along the tunnel and peered over the edge. She could no longer see the two satyrs. Had Niamh and the others gotten to them already?

A moment later, her question was answered. The door to the building where the humans were held prisoner opened, and Jack came out. He was followed by others, a steady stream of man, woman and child. Jack led them onto the road, and they moved quickly in the direction of the stairs. Siobhan breathed a sigh of relief. At least that was taken care of. They were tough people. They would know how to look after themselves for the journey back to Ballach.

Siobhan hurried up the steps to the top landing. The

opening here was wider than the others, carved into a diamond shape and the borders of the cut decorated with neat etchings of trees and mountains. Beyond was a clear passage lit by guttering torches. There was no rubble here.

Siobhan didn't waste any time. If Euan was waiting on the next batch of villagers, he could come looking when they didn't arrive. She needed to tell Elaphe what had happened and come up with a new plan.

The passage led into another large cavern, although this one wasn't quite as big as the first. The walls on either side were peppered with holes, and Siobhan could see light shining through them. Maybe this was where the Fey slept? But where would Elaphe be? He was looking for the stone, so he wouldn't have bothered to look here. She couldn't imagine Euan and Leanan living in the same manner as their soldiers. He was the Prince, after all.

On the opposite side of the cave was a ramp that sloped upward to another passage cut high up in the wall. Siobhan followed the ramp up and found herself walking through a narrow tunnel that weaved erratically back and forth.

After a few minutes of walking, Siobhan saw an orange light up ahead. It was flickering and growing stronger as she approached. Siobhan slowed her pace, making sure she made no sound. After a few more paces she came to the end of the tunnel. She could see it opened out into a large room of some kind. She stopped at the exit to the tunnel and waited.

A moment later, Elaphe came into view. Siobhan

breathed a small sigh of relief and stepped out of the tunnel. "Elaphe."

He whirled around to face her, his free hand waving through the air in a strange pattern. When he saw it was Siobhan, he clenched his hand into a fist and dropped it to his side.

"Siobhan!" he hissed. "What are you doing here? I told you—"

"You told me to get the villagers out. I did."

Elaphe straightened up and stared at her. "You did?"

"Right now they're climbing the stairs to the tunnel."

Elaphe smiled. "Excellent news. At least Euan will have no more food for his people." The smile vanished. "But I meant for you to go with them, Siobhan."

"I wasn't going to leave you here alone. This is my responsibility too."

Elaphe seemed about to protest, then he clamped his mouth shut again. A strange look flashed across his features, and he quickly turned away from her to resume his search. Siobhan stared at his back, trying to figure out what it was she had seen. Anger? No, it hadn't been anger. Sorrow?

Then she had it. Guilt. He had looked guilty. But why? What did he have to be guilty about?

"I can't find it," he said over his shoulder. "I've looked everywhere."

Siobhan pushed her thoughts aside for the moment and looked around the chamber. It wasn't large. A bed had been placed in a recessed alcove in the wall to her left. Wooden chests were piled up against the wall opposite, and in the center of the room, a large bowl had been placed on a base of stone. Siobhan walked toward it, but Elaphe pulled her back.

"Don't look in there. I don't know what will happen. It is an altar to the Morrigan."

Siobhan looked at Elaphe. "If we aren't supposed to look into it, don't you think that may be the best place for them to hide the rathstone?"

"Yes. As a matter of fact, I did think that, but I wanted to make sure it wasn't anywhere else first. Looking into the bowl is the last thing I wanted to try."

They both stared at the bowl.

"So what do we do?" asked Siobhan.

Elaphe shrugged and smiled. "Grab it and run?"

Siobhan looked around. "Is there another way out?"

Elaphe gestured to a narrow gap in the wall next to the pile of chests. "That leads somewhere. I can smell fresh air coming through it."

"I don't understand," said Siobhan. "You could have been gone by now. What are you waiting for?"

Elaphe looked uncomfortable. "As I said, I wanted to be sure the stone wasn't elsewhere. The Morrigan is not someone you anger lightly."

"Does that matter at this stage?"

Elaphe opened his mouth. Then he shut it again and looked at Siobhan strangely. Finally, he chuckled. "No. No, I don't suppose it does."

Siobhan smiled back and then stepped forward. She

plunged her hand into the water, dimly aware that Elaphe was shouting at her to stop.

But it was too late. Her arm was already submerged in the water. She felt around the bottom of the bowl, and she knocked something with her fingers. It rolled over a few times before she could grab hold of it. The shape was familiar. The rathstone. She had it.

She looked up at Elaphe and smiled, starting to draw her arm out of the water.

Something grabbed her hand from the other side.

She was jerked forward, her arm submerging up to her armpit. She just managed to keep hold of the stone, clenching it in her fist. She grabbed the lip of the bowl with her other hand and stared into the water.

A face stared up at her. A face that constantly changed. One second an old woman, then next a hard-looking warrior, and the next a beautiful lady.

The faces changed, but their expressions never did.

They all glared at Siobhan with an anger so intense, so focused, that it was inhuman. Siobhan thought she could actually feel the heat of their hatred.

Who dares . . . dares . . . dares, said three voices.

A human . . . human . . . human.

A thief . . . thief . . . thief . . .

Siobhan tried to pull her hand out of their grasp. "Let me go!"

Elaphe tried to help, but it was no good. It was as if her arm were trapped in ice. And that was what it felt like as well. The water had turned freezing cold. Steam drifted upward and coiled angrily about her.

"Get me out," she pleaded with Elaphe.

"I'm trying!" He pulled harder, but all that did was hurt her arm. She cried out in pain and Elaphe let go. He looked around, searching for something to help. He ran over to the chests that were piled up next to the exit tunnel, throwing the first one open and rummaging inside.

Then Siobhan heard a noise from the other side of the room and looked up to see Euan and Leanan standing there. Euan smiled.

"I thought it would be you," he said. "Perhaps you can explain the strange dreams I've been having about you. I must admit, they puzzle me greatly."

~ Twenty-Three ~

SIOBHAN TRIED FRANTICALLY TO PULL HER ARM OUT OF THE bowl, but it still wouldn't budge. She looked to Elaphe for help, but the Fey had disappeared. Where had he gone? Surely he wouldn't just abandon her here?

Euan approached her. "This dream I have. I'm in a forest that has been burned to ash, and I'm chasing someone. At first, I don't know who it is, but then I realize it is you." Euan leaned over and peered into the bowl. "After the stone, I see. You really are quite predictable, aren't you?"

Euan grabbed her arm. "I think you will be our next volunteer—"

But Siobhan didn't hear the rest. As soon as Euan touched her skin, she was plunged into darkness.

She looked around, searching for some kind of light, but there was nothing. She was surrounded by a formless void.

"Hello?" she called. "Elaphe? Can you hear me?"

A tiny light winked on in the distance. She couldn't make out its shape, but it grew steadily larger. Then she realized that the light wasn't really getting bigger, but that she was approaching it. She picked up speed, the light brightening, coming closer and closer.

Then she realized what it was. It was an eye, an eye the color of amber.

She tried to stop moving, but it was too late. She surged straight into the eye and out the other side, the light suddenly so bright she had to squint against the glare.

Siobhan waited for the glare to lessen, then looked around.

She was in a forest glade. Trees surrounded her on all sides. Brown and red leaves carpeted the ground, but some of the branches stubbornly held onto their charges. As she watched, a gust of wind blew around her and snatched a final, brittle leaf from its branch. It swirled gently through the air and landed on her foot.

She heard something rustling through the leaves, approaching from outside the clearing. She shrank up against the closest tree, hiding from view. The rustling came closer. She waited, expecting to see a human walk into the glade, but instead her attention was drawn to the ground. A shape was moving beneath the leaves, pushing them aside as it entered the glade. A serpentine head poked up through the blanket, covered in blood.

It was a huge, golden snake. The snake's tongue flicked out, testing the air. It must have sensed something, though, because it quickly turned around.

But not quickly enough.

A massive gray wolf bounded into the clearing, blood-flecked spittle dripping from its jaws. It caught the snake between its teeth and shook its head sharply. The snake hissed and writhed in the wolf's grip, twining a body thicker than Siobhan's waist about the wolf's ribs. The wolf let go and turned its attention to the snake's midsection, snapping as the snake tried to crush the breath from its body.

The wolf managed to get its jaws around the snake's tail. Blood spurted from between its teeth, and the snake released its hold with a hiss of pain. The wolf jerked its head and sent the snake flying through the air. It landed in an untidy pile close to the tree Siobhan hid behind.

The snake writhed and threw itself upright just as the wolf bounded over and tried to grab it again. The snake reared up and then struck straight down, sinking its fangs into the wolf's hindquarters. The wolf howled in pain, snapping at the snake's head. But its scales protected it from the worst of the wolf's bites. It let go of the wolf, venom dripping from its fangs. The wolf backed up, snarling as the snake coiled itself tight, ready to strike. There was a pause, then both creatures launched themselves through the air at the same time . . .

And Siobhan found herself lying on the cold stone of the floor, staring up at the uneven rock of the ceiling. Her arm ached with the cold, but she still clenched her hand around the rathstone.

Leanan's face slid into her vision. "Did you see that?" Leanan grabbed hold of Siobhan and tried to yank her upright. Siobhan pulled away and scrabbled backward until she collided with the stone wall.

"She has the Sight, Euan. Can't you tell? As soon as you touched her she had a vision."

Euan's eyes focused on Siobhan, suddenly interested. "About me?"

"What did you see?" snapped Leanan. "Tell me."

Siobhan looked around the room in despair. Still no sign of Elaphe. *Where was he?* Leanan stepped forward and slapped her across the face. Siobhan cried out in pain and raised her hand to her lip. Her fingers came away red with blood.

"Tell me," demanded Leanan.

"It . . . it was nothing. A fight. A snake and a wolf were fighting in a forest. That is all."

Leanan and Euan exchanged looks. Siobhan could see her words meant something to them. Euan approached her. "This battle. Who won? Who was the victor?"

"I don't know. I woke up before the battle ended."

Leanan turned to Euan. "We must keep her alive. She may have another vision. We may be able to see . . ."

At that moment, Elaphe appeared from the tunnel behind Siobhan and grabbed hold of her, yanking her to her feet. Siobhan shouted in surprise, a shout that quickly turned to a cry of anguish as the sharp movement caused her to drop the stone.

Euan and Leanan turned in surprise as Siobhan lunged forward, grabbing for the stone before it rolled away. Euan and Leanan both lunged for it, too, but Siobhan snatched it up and Elaphe caught her again, pulling her into the tunnel. They ran into the torch-lit darkness. Siobhan heard Euan screaming his rage behind them, then Leanan's voice echoed after them.

"She has the stone! Stop her!"

Elaphe whipped her around to face him. "Run. Understand? Do not falter. You will die otherwise."

Then he shoved Siobhan hard. She ran a few steps, then glanced over her shoulder. Elaphe was leaning against the wall, his two hands pressed hard against the rock. She saw Euan appear in the opening beyond him.

Then dust trickled down from somewhere above, followed immediately by a fist-sized rock. The rock struck Euan's shoulder, and he jerked away with a cry of pain.

Leanan appeared behind him and spotted Elaphe. Her eyes widened when she saw what he was doing, and she grabbed hold of Euan's arm. He tried to shake her off and run into the tunnel, but a rain of stones fell from the ceiling, pulling him up short. Both Euan and Leanan looked up, and then a part of the roof caved in, smashing into the ground at their feet.

"My King! Come away." Leanan pulled Euan. Still he resisted, staring at Siobhan through the curtain of dust, his eyes glinting with hatred. Siobhan heard a deep rumble like distant thunder, then a huge boulder detached itself from the roof and slammed into the ground inches from her feet. She remembered Elaphe's words and turned around and ran.

The rumbling increased in volume behind her, accompanied by the crack and thud of breaking stone. Dust billowed past her back, swirling through the air before her. Torches lit the passage through the tunnel, but the choking dust shrunk the light of each one to a small glowing nimbus of yellow.

Even so, it was enough to judge her path by. But only just. The crack and groan of splintering rock followed her as she ran, increasing in volume till it sounded like some terrible beast about to devour her. A huge section of wall sheared away and slid across her path. She leaped across it, only just avoiding it as it smashed into the opposite wall and exploded into tiny shards. Relief surged through her. If the rock had hit her legs it would have cut them clean off.

The dust increased, choking her and turning

everything into a gray cloud. The torches were spaced farther apart now, so she was finding it hard to avoid running into the walls as she fled through the twisting tunnel. Small rocks fell onto her head and shoulders, peppering her body with every step. She didn't know how much farther she had to go. What if this tunnel was miles long? She'd never make it out.

And what of Elaphe? Was he trapped behind her in the tunnel? Or had he ducked out and sought refuge in the chamber where Euan and Leanan waited? Which fate would be worse?

She was finding it difficult to breathe. With every frightened gasp she inhaled more of the thick dust. She coughed and coughed, finding smaller and smaller amounts of air with each inhalation.

This was it. After all she had been through, she was going to die here alone, suffocating to death in a collapsing tunnel.

But still she kept going. Something in her wouldn't let her give up, some newfound determination that had been growing within her over the past weeks.

And it was worth it. After another few paces, she saw a lighter shade of gray up ahead. She stumbled forward, squinting through the dust. A shape emerged, a sharp gash in the rock that was outlined from the other side by daylight.

The exit. She had made it.

A horrendous *crack* exploded above her. She looked up to see a huge section of the roof detach itself from one side of the tunnel. It fell, swinging down like a trapdoor, and slammed into the ground not two paces in front of Siobhan. Shards of rock spun past her, cutting into her legs. She skidded to a stop, then stumbled back in shock, waving frantically at the fresh clouds of dust.

The light was gone, blocked by the huge rock before her.

"No!" She ran forward and pushed against the stone, but it was twice the size of her and a hundred times heavier. It had blocked off her escape.

She leaned her head against the rock. Tears spilled down her dirty face, falling from her chin and creating tiny craters in the dust at her feet.

As she watched her tears fall, the dust floating in the air moved slightly. It was a moment before the meaning of this sank into her battered mind.

Air was coming from somewhere.

She got down on her knees and moved across to the far wall of the tunnel. Sure enough, when the rock fell from the other side, it hit the wall at an angle. There was space to crawl underneath.

Siobhan wasted no time. She got down on her stomach and crawled through the gap, the light on the other side beckoning her forward. She climbed to her feet and ran toward the gap in the rock, finally stumbling through into a large cave.

Gray daylight shone in through the entrance. Siobhan sobbed with relief and hurried forward, stopping only when she was out of the cave and in the open air. She inhaled deeply, coughing and clearing her lungs of all the dust. Only when she had managed to do that did she take the time to look around.

She was high up on one of the mountains, looking down over the landscape of Scotland. Off to her right she caught a glimpse of what must be Loch Tay. It wove in and out of vision, blocked from her view by the green and brown bumps of the foothills. Straight ahead of her the line of the mountains faded into the distance, gaining height as they went until the peaks finally disappeared into the clouds. Siobhan amended her first impression. She must only be halfway up one of the smaller mountains. A footpath wended its way down through the crags.

Siobhan fell onto her backside, glad to be alive. If only Elaphe were here to share her joy.

Then she heard footsteps behind her and whirled around to find the elder Fey staggering into the light. He blinked up at the sky, then his eyes fell on Siobhan, and he broke into a huge smile.

"Elaphe!" Siobhan surged to her feet and caught the Fey in a fierce hug. "I thought you were dead."

"So did I. It was a close one, I'll admit. The spirits of the stone are a fickle bunch at the best of times."

Siobhan detached herself. "The what?"

"Spirits of the stone. I wasn't quite as idle as you thought when you first entered the chamber. I was communicating with a ciuthach, telling her I might need a favor."

"A favor?"

"The rock fall. Stone wants to fill things, Siobhan.

It doesn't like passages cut through its bones, the wind howling through its body. I simply helped it to fill in the gaps. I did the same in the other tunnel, remember? Important lesson, Siobhan. Always have an escape plan."

Siobhan looked at him in shock. "The other tunnel? But the villagers—"

"Will be fine. I limited the rock fall to the first section of the tunnel. It should be enough to keep Euan trapped for a while."

Siobhan smiled, feeling lighter than she had in a long time. "So we did it."

Elaphe's smile faded. "Yes, we did." He held out his hand.

Siobhan looked at it in puzzlement. "What?"

"The rathstone, Siobhan," Elaphe said gently.

"What? But I thought . . ."

"I could never let you keep it, Siobhan. You know that. How would we open Hallowmere without it?"

"But what about all I told you? About what Euan plans to do?"

"Trust me, I will make sure everyone knows what is happening. But to do that, I need the stone so the raths can come together. Without it, we cannot hold our Gathering."

Siobhan stared up at Elaphe, feeling utterly betrayed by him. "I thought you understood," she whispered.

"I do, Siobhan. Honestly. I will make sure the others realize the danger."

All the hope that Siobhan had dared to feel drained

out of her in an instant. She had served tea in and over-heard enough meetings of the Council to know that unless someone has experienced the danger, truly felt their lives threatened, then words would not convince them. People needed to see to believe.

She had failed. It had all been for nothing.

Handing him the stone, she gazed at Elaphe, wondering how she ever could have trusted him. He was the same as all the others, always looking after their own interests, never looking at the grand scheme.

She turned without saying another word and headed onto the footpath.

"Siobhan," called Elaphe.

But Siobhan didn't respond.

~ Twenty-Four ~

Siobhan sat on the same pebbled shoreline at Ballach that she had shared with Conal all those days ago. *Only days? How could that be?* It seemed like years had passed since those brief, intimate, embarrassing moments.

Everything had changed. Nothing ever stayed the same.

The loch shimmered golden red in the rays of the late afternoon sun. She squinted against the light, looking up at the mountains towering away in the distance, the same mountains she and Elaphe had descended from the previous day. The escaped villagers made it back to Ballach safely. In fact, they had beaten Siobhan and Elaphe by a full day.

She should be happy. She knew that. She had helped save the villagers, Niamh was alive, and the people of Ballach had taken to their task of rebuilding their homes over the water. The other crannogs over the loch had been cleared out. Some already had bridges linking them to this main island.

They would be safe here. For a while, anyway.

But she had failed. There was no avoiding the fact. She was sent here to retrieve the rathstone, and she hadn't been able to accomplish this. She had no idea what to do next.

She heard a crunch on the shingle behind her, and a moment later Niamh sat down next to Siobhan. She picked up a pebble and threw it across the water, a gesture so reminiscent of Conal's that it brought a lump to Siobhan's throat.

"Everyone wants to have a feast tonight. To celebrate our rescue from the Unhallowed."

Siobhan said nothing. Niamh threw her a concerned look.

"Siobhan? Are you all right?"

Siobhan sighed. "I'm fine," she lied. "Just tired."

Niamh seemed to accept her explanation. After all, she had just trekked through the mountains. That would be enough to tire anyone out.

She remembered Elaphe's last words as she stood on the shore in the early hours of the morning, ready to cross over the water onto the first crannog.

"I will talk to the other Fey," he said. "Don't think this is all over. They will know the truth. I will tell them what Euan is, what he becomes."

Siobhan had simply stared at him. She'd heard such things before. So she had simply nodded, defeated, and stepped onto the bridge.

"Siobhan," called Elaphe. "I promise you. This is not over."

Siobhan hadn't responded.

Niamh cleared her throat. "Da wants us to go back home."

Siobhan was confused. "To the manor house?"

"No. Back across the sea to Eire."

"Probably a wise move."

"Why don't you come with us?"

Siobhan looked at Niamh in surprise. "Come with you?"

"Yes. We can find work at another noble's house. There's nothing left for us here."

"I heard that Conal's brother is coming back to take over the estate."

"He is, but it won't be the same." A small shiver ran through Niamh. "After all that's happened here, nothing will ever be the same. It's not home anymore."

Siobhan had to admit, Niamh had a point. The mood of the villagers had changed. Most of them were staying, but it seemed to be more out of defiance rather than anything else. They were a stubborn lot, and anyone trying to intimidate or threaten them raised their hackles.

"It's a nice thought, Niamh, but I'm sure your parents wouldn't want me trailing along after you."

"I've already asked them. They both said yes."

Siobhan hesitated, then quickly looked away from Niamh as she felt the tears building up. They already said yes? No one had ever done something like that for her.

Could it be so easy? Just . . . *go away?* Head over the water to Ireland and start a new life? She'd already failed here. There was nothing more she could do. Didn't she deserve some happiness? Didn't she deserve a complete family? One she wasn't responsible for, one that wasn't mad and cursed, who didn't die off in crazy, horrific ways?

There was a shout from behind them. Niamh stood up. "That's Da. Think about it, Siobhan. I want you to come. We'd be like sisters."

Eomen called for Niamh again, and she hurried back to the shelter.

Siobhan stared over the waters and thought about her life. The sun disappeared behind the mountains, and dusk started to settle over the loch, bringing with it a pale mist that drifted over the water. Siobhan shivered. The sounds of woodcutting and hammering had ceased behind her as everyone prepared for the feast. It would be a sparse layout though. Not many had the courage to venture into the woods to hunt, and Siobhan wasn't sure how much food was left in their stores.

She stood up and stretched, turning around to face the lanterns and torches that lit the crannog. There were so many of them. It was like the villagers were trying to keep the darkness at bay, afraid of what it could bring.

Who could blame them?

Siobhan walked around the shoreline, listening to the water lapping against the beach. She wished Conal were here to share it with her. She had been under no illusions about the two of them. He was a noble, she a serving girl. Nothing could ever happen between them. But he was nice. He didn't treat her like a servant. He spoke to her like she was . . . like she was just a *girl*. And she had really liked that. It had made her feel special.

Siobhan heard Eomen calling for Niamh again. It sounded like it was coming from . . . No, it couldn't be. Frowning, Siobhan turned her head to catch the direction the voice was coming from. She heard it again, softer this time, and sure enough, she was right. The voice was coming from across the bridge. On the land.

Siobhan ran around the island to the bridge. She pulled herself up the ladder and onto the wood, staring across the water. The light was almost gone, but she thought she could just make out two figures on the opposite bank.

Siobhan gritted her teeth in frustration. Why would Niamh leave the safety of the crannog? Especially after what had just happened! She knew better than that.

Siobhan hurried over the bridge, leaving behind the sounds of life and safety. As she drew closer to the opposite bank, the sounds faded even more. The mist thickened, wrapping around her so that it felt as if she were moving through a cloud. She looked behind her, but could see nothing. No light. No people. Nothing.

She turned to the front and carried on walking. As she approached the shore, the mist parted to reveal two figures standing there.

Niamh and Euan.

Euan held onto Niamh's arm. She struggled, but he gave her a sharp shake, and she stopped moving.

Siobhan came to a stop close to the edge of the bridge.

"Let her go."

"I will," said Euan, "if you take her place."

"Siobhan, I'm sorry. It sounded like Da, and when I saw who it was, he said he'd go to Killin and kill everyone if I didn't come across. I didn't know he wanted you."

"It's all right, Niamh. It's not your fault."

"You're right," said Euan. "It's *not* her fault. It's always the innocents, though, isn't that right? Always the blameless ones who suffer the most."

"What do you want?"

"You."

"Siobhan, don't listen to him—"

"If you speak again, I'll snap your neck," said Euan calmly, never once taking his eyes from Siobhan.

"And you'll let her go if I come to you?"

"Of course."

"How can I trust you?"

"Ah, therein lies the conundrum. How *can* you trust me? But you don't really have much choice, do you? If you refuse to do as I say, your little friend here dies."

Siobhan hesitated. She couldn't shout for help. Euan would kill Niamh as soon as look at her. She tried to think of other options, but what else was there to do?

"Come, come, Siobhan. I am not patient at the best of times. Surely you know that by now."

Siobhan stepped forward until her toes were touching the border between bridge and shore. She looked up.

"Let her go."

"Step forward first."

"No. I think I'm the more trustworthy of the two of us. Let her go and I move."

Euan clenched and unclenched his free hand,

frustration pinching his features. "Fine," he snapped, and released his hold on Niamh. She walked forward a few paces, before Euan called out.

"Stop."

Niamh stumbled to a halt, unsure what to do.

"Come along, Siobhan," said Euan. "I kept my word."

Siobhan raised her foot, hesitated for a second, then walked off the bridge and onto the shingle. It shifted beneath her feet.

"Come on, Niamh."

"Both of you walk at the same time," said Euan.

Siobhan locked eyes with Niamh, and they walked toward each other. As they drew together, Siobhan tried to smile. "I would have liked to come with you, Niamh. Tell your parents I said thank you."

Niamh let out a sob and reached out to embrace her.

"No touching," said Euan.

Siobhan glared at him and reached out a hand. Niamh did the same, and they touched fingertips as they passed.

"Good-bye, Niamh," Siobhan whispered.

Their fingers separated, and Niamh disappeared into the mist. Siobhan heard her footsteps on the wooden boards of the bridge.

"Very noble of you," said Euan. "Now come along."

Siobhan stopped. "What do you want me for? I don't have the stone anymore."

"Of course you don't. Why would you?"

"Then what?"

"That little vision you had back in the mountain."

"What about it?" Siobhan asked.

"I want you to tell me the whole thing."

"That's all there is. I didn't see anything else."

Euan sighed and rolled his eyes. "Leanan tells me that visions can be . . . *induced* in those with the Sight," he said, as if he were talking to a five year old.

Siobhan didn't like the sound of that. "How?"

Euan shrugged. "By putting the person under stress."

Siobhan shook her head. "Why is it so important to you?"

"Because the wolf you saw? That was me."

Siobhan stared at him, realization dawning. "Elaphe," she whispered, wondering why she hadn't realized it before.

"That's right. The snake was Elaphe."

~ TWENTY-FIVE ~

THEY RODE DEEP INTO THE NIGHT. SIOBHAN SAT IN FRONT OF Euan, trying hard to stay in the saddle as they galloped through the same forests Conal had taken her through. Euan pushed the horse hard, not caring how he was harming the creature by doing so. After the first few hours, Siobhan noticed blood-flecked foam spraying from the horse's nostrils with every heaving breath.

They soon left the path that she and Conal had taken. Euan steered them through the twisted trees, somehow managing to avoid hitting the trailing branches. Siobhan flinched and ducked, expecting at any moment to be knocked from the saddle, but somehow it never happened.

Siobhan tried to ask Euan where they were going, but the Fey Prince refused to answer. Siobhan eventually gave up, instead concentrating on coming up with some kind of escape plan. She wasn't sure about Euan's theory that forced stress would bring on a vision. Before Elaphe began teaching her how to control the Sight, every time she'd had one, it had been spontaneous and terrifying, even in her sleep. But now that she'd used the vision to find Euan, she knew she had it under control, and she wasn't about to give him the means to win this centuries-long war.

She didn't tell Euan that. She wasn't sure how he would react when he found out her usefulness was at an end. She could take a pretty good guess, though.

It was round about midnight when Euan finally slowed the poor horse to a walk. But it wasn't out of kindness. The Fey Prince was looking for something, something he must have eventually found, because Siobhan heard him give a grunt of satisfaction. He turned the horse onto a small path hidden behind some thick bushes.

He followed the path for another hour before the forest started to thin, and they found themselves walking on grass rather than dead leaves.

The landscape opened up around them. Siobhan looked up and saw the stars glittering like frozen ice. The moon was full and heavy, casting its silver light over the undulating landscape. Water trickled somewhere nearby. Siobhan soon discovered its source when they crested a small rise, and she saw the small vale stretching away on the other side. A small stream gurgled away to either side.

It would have been like a painting if it hadn't been for the all the Unhallowed Fey waiting there.

Siobhan couldn't count how many there were. So many that she feared for anyone who crossed paths with them. All the creatures she had seen back in the underground city were here, but there were more now. Female and male. Nixes and naiads. Strange spiderlike creatures the size of a human head that scampered between campfires.

"Do you know what tonight is?" asked Euan, and Siobhan could hear the satisfaction in his voice as he surveyed his troops.

"No."

"It is the night Hallowmere is to be opened."

"Where?" whispered Siobhan.

"Not far from here. After tonight there will be a change for the better."

"Change for the better? Do you mean . . . do you actually think you are doing the right thing?" Siobhan was incredulous.

"Of course. My parents are taking the wrong path. My people are being overtaken by humans. We have all these Christian missionaries coming here and turning everyone against us. Look at Father Josephus. He is just like the rest of them."

Siobhan laughed. "Can you blame them? Look at what you've become!"

"I have become the future."

"But you were all for working *with* us. You even said so."

"That was one of the plans. Mordroch carried out another. We have many ideas on how to carry our people forward. I mistakenly thought mine was the correct one. No longer, though."

"Why? What changed?"

"I realized that Leanan was right. Humans are devious and traitorous. I was foolish to place my trust in them." He looked at her suddenly, and Siobhan was surprised to see real sorrow there. "I do not take pleasure in this. I do what I must to protect my people. Would you not do the same?"

"I . . . I don't . . . No, I wouldn't."

Euan searched her eyes, then looked away again. "So you say. But you cannot judge me before being placed in my position."

"But look what you've become. That is not life. That is . . . that is *unnatural*."

"It is necessary. No longer will we need to enter Hallowmere. No longer will we be reborn, bereft of our memories, our souls. We are reliant on no one and no thing. We are our own people."

"But at what cost?" Siobhan shouted. "You need to drink human blood to survive. You're nothing but a monster."

"I am not a monster. Every human is given a choice."

"I heard your choice," said Siobhan bitterly. "Submit or die."

Euan leaned forward. She could feel his cold breath on her neck. "That is not the choice I gave Conal."

Siobhan said nothing, though her heart quickened at the mention of his name.

"Do you wish to know the choice I offered him?" Euan paused, but when she said nothing, he carried on anyway. "I told him to submit willingly, otherwise I would kill you."

"No," whispered Siobhan.

"Oh yes. He made the decision rather quickly. I think

he actually liked you." Euan straightened in his saddle. "There's no accounting for taste, I suppose."

"My lord," Leanan called, hurrying toward them. She glared at Siobhan. "I see you were true to your word."

Euan dismounted. "I told you I was going to get her, Leanan. I need to see how the vision finishes. I need to see if I am triumphant over Elaphe."

"You will find out on the morrow."

"I need to know before!" he shouted. "Don't you understand?"

Leanan looked at him coldly. "Obviously not," she said softly. "And I would appreciate it if you didn't speak to me the same way you speak to your pet."

Euan ignored the jibe. "Is everything ready?"

"Your subjects await the order to attack. The Half-Born are ready."

Euan glanced over the river. Siobhan followed his gaze and saw that the humans who had been turned to the Unhallowed's side were sharpening weapons and readying shields.

"They will do as ordered?" asked Euan.

"I think so. I have made the compulsion as strong as possible."

"You're sending the villagers in to attack?" asked Siobhan. "You're not even brave enough to fight yourself?"

Leanan gazed up at her. "Would you like me to cut your tongue out?"

"The villagers fight with iron. It does not affect them as strongly as it does us," said Euan.

"It *does* still affect them," said Leanan, smiling coldly. "But they should be able to kill a few of our enemies before the metal overwhelms them."

"Will they survive?"

Leanan shrugged. "Who knows?" She turned to Euan. "I must go now. Remember. They will arrive with the dawn. You must be ready."

"Of course I'll be ready."

Leanan took out a dagger and cut off a small lock of her hair. "Put this in the bowl. The rest is up to you."

Euan took the hair. Leanan turned away, walked a few paces . . . and *twisted*. It was the only description Siobhan could come up with. It was as if her whole body turned in upon itself, and a moment later a large white owl flapped through the air. Euan watched it go before turning to Siobhan.

"Get down."

Euan led Siobhan and the horse down into the camp. The Unhallowed stared at her with cold eyes, eyes that belonged to corpses more than anything living.

Euan led her to a section of grass that had been trampled flat. A large stone bowl similar to the one back at the mountain had been placed on a flat-topped rock. Euan pushed her to the ground.

"Do not move. If you do I will kill you." He stared at her intently. "Do you believe me?"

"Of course I do. What is another murder to your conscience?"

Before Siobhan could react, Euan slapped her hard in the face. She fell to the grass with a cry of pain, and before she could do anything, he whipped out a knife and straddled her, holding the brass blade against her throat. "Do not test me, child. Death is a release. I could keep you alive for days while I peeled the skin from your body."

Siobhan swallowed in fear, staring up into his dark eyes. He held her gaze for a long time, seemingly waiting for something, and then Siobhan realized what he was doing. He was trying to bring forth a vision by putting her under stress.

"It doesn't work," she said. "I can't control when it comes."

Euan snarled in anger and stood up. He pointed at her. "Do not move," he snapped, and stalked away to speak to his troops.

Siobhan dozed through the chill night. She shivered nonstop, but she was so exhausted by the events of the past few days, her body simply would not function any more without rest. She curled up on herself, dreaming about battles and fighting and piles of dead bodies decaying in the rain.

She awoke with a start. Dim light seeped into the air around her. There was movement in the camp, the tense coiled energy of anticipation. Euan squatted in front of the bowl. Siobhan sat up sleepily. He glanced at her in disgust.

"I should have heeded Leanan. You are useless to me."

Siobhan said nothing. The bowl Euan looked into

was filled with clear water. He looked up at the sky, then placed the lock of hair Leanan had given him into the water. It sank to the bottom as if it were lead.

Nothing happened for a second. Then a ripple ran through the water. The liquid shivered, lapping against the sides of the bowl.

And the next moment, Siobhan could see trees reflected in the water. She looked up, but there was only gray, pre-dawn sky above her. She looked back to the bowl and saw the viewpoint shift to the side. Siobhan saw a tree branch, then two clawed feet reaching out to grip the branch. She also caught the briefest glimpse of white feathers.

That was when Siobhan realized they were looking through the eyes of the owl Leanan had changed into.

The owl looked away from the tree, focusing on a massive clearing up ahead. In the exact center of this clearing was a large hill with a leveled crown.

The owl looked to the horizon, where the barest glimpse of the sun could be seen just edging over the trees. The owl launched itself into the air and flapped her wings hard, gaining height rapidly. Siobhan fought down a wave of vertigo as she watched.

The owl circled above the hill, obviously waiting for something to happen.

A moment later it did. There was a bright flash of gold, almost as if the sun was rising over the hill instead of the far-distant trees. The gold light spilled in a circle out of an empty section of air, then it grew bigger until it was the size of a doorway. The light stretched forward over the top of the hill, stopping only when it touched a large boulder placed in the exact center of the hilltop. Siobhan saw that the boulder had deep indentations carved into it.

A second later there was another flash of light, then another, and another. All the way around the crown of the hill, doorways similar to the first were opening, the light stretching forward from all sides until the boulder was afire with a magical glow.

The owl dipped low, flying slowly around the hill. Siobhan counted thirteen golden arches, each one almost touching the one next to it, all of them bathing the top of the hill in light.

Then the King and Queen stepped through the first portal. They walked solemnly forward and placed something in the indentation on the boulder that faced their arch. A thrill of excitement ran through Siobhan as she realized that it was the rathstone.

The King and Queen stepped back until they stood before their archway. Then a tall, elderly Fey stepped out of the next doorway and placed his stone in the next placeholder.

All the way around the hillock this was repeated, until Fey stood before all the glowing portals except for the last. They all turned expectantly to the final doorway, and an elegant dryad with skin like a freshly grown sapling stepped through and, with great solemnity, placed the final stone atop the boulder.

The owl veered to the side, flying away from the Fey. She dropped lower and Siobhan watched as a section at the very base of the hill shuddered and pulled apart until it looked like the open jaws of some great animal. A cave was revealed, and inside that cave Siobhan could see a pool of silver water, shimmering and bathing the inside of the hill with light the color of the moon.

"Hallowmere," breathed Euan, transfixed by the sight.

The owl flew high again, and Siobhan saw that more Fey were coming through the various doorways. They were all as different from each other as Siobhan was from other humans. Large, small, fat, thin. Female, male, child. Tiny fairies with wings, huge fairies that looked like oak trees. The solemnity of the ceremony had vanished now, and the Fey embraced and greeted one another with happy smiles before venturing down the gentle slope of the hill. Soon a steady stream of creatures was coming through the doorways to gather in the clearing that surrounded the hill.

Siobhan glanced surreptitiously at Euan. The Fey Prince was transfixed, his attention totally focused on the scene unfolding before him.

She looked around. The others were readying their weapons, moving to stand in neat lines facing toward the rising sun. *They will be attacking soon,* thought Siobhan.

She had to do something. She couldn't just sit back while the Fey were slaughtered. At the very least, she needed to warn them.

The horse that they rode during the night was cropping grass not five paces away, forgotten by everyone. Could she . . . ?

And why not? The poor creature should still be able to outrun the Unhallowed. Maybe it would be glad to get its revenge.

Siobhan slowly moved backward on the grass. No one was paying the slightest attention to her. She carefully pushed herself to her feet, turning to grab hold of the horse.

She took the reins, turned back to make sure she was unseen—

And locked eyes with Mordroch as he approached Euan.

He shouted in anger and started to run. Siobhan hauled herself into the saddle.

"Go!" she shouted, slamming her heels into the horse's ribs. The horse leaped forward with a sharp whinny of complaint, ears laid flat against its head. Siobhan looked over her shoulder and saw Euan on his feet and running toward her. She snapped the reins and the horse surged forward, nearly throwing her off the saddle. It bounded down toward the stream and splashed through it without slowing, up the opposite bank and through the midst of the surprised villagers.

As they scattered out of her way, Siobhan's eyes were drawn to the one figure who did not move. He stood and watched her flee with an empty expression on his face.

Conal.

~ Twenty-Six ~

SIOBHAN DIDN'T KNOW WHERE SHE WAS GOING. ALL SHE knew was that the Unhallowed were facing the rising sun, so that was the direction she headed.

She had forced Euan's hand. She knew that. She wasn't sure exactly when he had been going to attack, but he would have no choice but to make his move now. She hoped that this would damage his plans.

She also knew that the hill she saw in the bowl couldn't be far away. Not if Euan expected to get there in a reasonable amount of time.

The forest grew denser again as she traveled, forcing her to slow down or risk the horse tripping over a root and breaking its leg. She found it hard to keep the rising sun directly ahead of her because of the unpredictable undergrowth. She had to veer off-path, heading around clumps of trees and bushes that were too thick to ride through.

She briefly considered getting off the horse and running the rest of the way, but eventually rejected this idea. One or two miles were easy while riding, even if her path was a roundabout one. But having to run that distance was a different story.

After enough time had passed that she honestly feared she would be too late and that Euan and his troops had already attacked the Gathering, Siobhan suddenly found herself in the huge clearing. She wasn't expecting it. One minute she was surrounded by thick fir trees, the next she was blinking in the open air with hundreds of eyes turned toward her in surprise.

Siobhan ignored them all and stood up in her stirrups, searching for Elaphe. She thought she caught a glimpse of him close to the base of the hill. She snapped the reins, intending to plow straight through the gathered Fey, but hands grabbed hold of her and pulled her from the saddle.

"No!" she screamed. "Let me go. I need to speak with Elaphe."

Uncertain faces swirled around her, unsure what to do with such an unprecedented interruption.

"Elaphe!" Siobhan screamed. "Elaphe! Euan is coming! He's going to attack!"

She wasn't sure if he heard her, but the faces of those holding Siobhan grew alarmed at her words. A tall Fey with skin like tree bark and long hair made of tangled roots grabbed her and pushed its way hurriedly through the throngs until a circle finally opened up around her. She saw the King and Queen first, then Iamblicus the priest, then Elaphe as he turned around and looked at her in amazement.

"Siobhan?" he said. "What are you doing here? I said I would talk to them. I gave my word."

"It's not about that—"

"She says that Euan is approaching with an army," interrupted her captor.

Elaphe focused on her, alarmed. "Is this true?"

"Yes. They're not far off. Euan wanted to try and force me to have a vision so he could see who won the fight."

The Queen stepped forward. "Elaphe? What is this? What vision does she speak of?"

"There is no time, my Queen." Elaphe straightened up and turned to those closest to him. "Spread the word," he said. "Euan approaches. Take to your arms. *To arms!*" he shouted.

His call was taken up, and soon Siobhan could hear the words echoed from the farthest edges of the clearing.

"He is using the villagers," she told Elaphe. "They are carrying iron."

Elaphe nodded grimly. "Which direction do they approach from?"

Siobhan pointed toward the line of trees, invisible now as the jostling bodies of the Fey obscured them from view. "That way. They will only be minutes off."

"My King. My Queen. We must gain higher ground." The royal couple nodded, and they hurried toward the hill.

They were only halfway up when the attack came. And it didn't come from where Siobhan had told them it would, but rather from the opposite direction, throwing the defenders into chaos.

Siobhan watched in horror as the villagers surged out of the trees on the other side of the hill, slamming into the backs of the Fey and causing massive casualties with their iron swords. Euan must have changed his plan, knowing that Siobhan would give the Fey all the information she had.

Screaming filled the air, then the clash of metal on metal as the defenders shifted position and turned to face the attackers.

The humans pushed forward their attack, and while the Fey were focused on turning the onslaught, Siobhan saw Euan lead the Unhallowed from the trees off to the right, smashing into the flank of the defenders and driving a wedge deep into their ranks.

The attack was coming from two sides now, and without anyone giving commands, the defenders were unsure where to turn. Siobhan watched in horror as those Fey farther back pressed forward in an attempt to get closer to the fighting, in the process pushing those in front to the ground to be crushed underfoot. Euan wouldn't have to bother fighting if this carried on. The Fey would all be out of action within minutes.

Elaphe grabbed her arm. "Where is Leanan?" he asked, shouting to be heard above the terrible din of battle.

Siobhan looked instinctively to the sky. The owl was still circling, far up in the air. Elaphe followed her gaze, then all the color drained from his face.

"The stones," he whispered. He turned and climbed frantically up the hill. Siobhan wondered what he meant. She looked up and saw the owl veer to the side and fold her wings back, heading into a dive.

Then she understood.

The attack was a diversion. All those lives lost, all the pain and suffering—it was all for one purpose: to distract attention away from the rathstones so Leanan could take them.

Siobhan quickly set off after Elaphe. There was no way she was letting Leanan get them. Not after everything she had been through.

The sounds of battle surrounded her on all sides as she ran, her breath rasping harshly in her ears. She gained the crest of the hill to see Elaphe running toward the boulder on which the stones had been placed. She looked up and shouted out a warning. Leanan was diving straight down, only a few yards above him. Her claws were outstretched, ready to grasp as many of the stones as she could.

Elaphe jerked his head up at Siobhan's shout. When he saw Leanan, he leaped into the air, changing form as he did, so that the huge, golden snake of her vision was now soaring toward the owl.

Leanan spotted the danger and tried to change course, but Elaphe was moving too fast. He fastened his jaws around her body and pulled her out of the air. They landed hard on the ground, close to one of the archways. Elaphe writhed around on the grass, the owl screeching in pain and tearing at his scales with her beak.

Siobhan headed for the stones, but stopped when she heard someone shout Leanan's name somewhere behind her. She turned and saw Euan running up the hill. He jumped over a large stone lying in his path, and as he did so, he changed. One minute it was Euan leaping through the air, the next a huge gray wolf landed on the grass on the other side and carried on running toward her.

"Euan's coming," she screamed, turning back to the fight. She wasn't sure if Elaphe had heard her, but a moment later, he snapped his head to the side, sending the owl hurtling through the closest golden portal. Then he whipped around and slithered quickly to the boulder, rearing up just as Euan bounded over the crest of the hill and barreled past Siobhan, sending her sprawling to the ground.

She saw Elaphe take the stones into his mouth, swallowing them so that Euan could not get hold of the treasure he desired so strongly. As he did so, each portal winked out of existence, the golden light cast by each vanishing suddenly.

Then Euan was on Elaphe as he swallowed the last stone, the wolf's jaws clamping hard over the snake's scales. Blood sprayed out, spattering over the boulder. The snake whipped around and bit the wolf on the leg. Euan released his grip, and Elaphe quickly turned and slithered away, vanishing over the lip of the hill. Euan followed after, barking his rage.

Siobhan scurried forward to see them rolling down the hill into the clearing, writhing and flipping through the air, locked in fierce battle. The section of clearing they rolled into was empty of the battling Fey, the focus of the fighting being kept to the other side of the mound.

The snake and the wolf were flung apart when they rolled into the trunk of a tree. The wolf pushed himself shakily to his feet, staggering slightly. Then it turned to

Elaphe just in time to see the snake's tail vanishing into the trees surrounding the clearing. The wolf howled in anger and gave chase.

Siobhan ran down the hill, squinting against the rays of the rising sun. She sprinted into the forest, pausing to gauge the direction Elaphe and Euan had taken, then ran after them.

As her feet kicked through the red and brown leaves covering the forest floor, she realized with a sick lurch of fear that she was about to see the outcome of her vision for real.

~ Twenty-Seven ~

Siobhan stumbled to a halt, straining to hear the sounds of Elaphe and Euan. Nothing.

She looked around. She was in a small forest glade. Trees surrounded her on all sides. Brown and red leaves carpeted the ground, but some of the branches still held onto their charges. As she watched, a gust of wind eddied around her and snatched a few brittle leaves from their branches. They swirled gently, one of them landing on her foot.

She looked down at the leaf. It was curled up on itself, a desiccated husk. She lifted her eyes and studied her surroundings once again.

This was it. This was the place.

She turned to look directly at a spot outside the clearing, knowing what was going to happen. And sure enough, the sound came a moment later, the sound of something rustling through the leaves. She looked around, spotted the tree she had hidden behind in her vision, and took up her position.

The rustling came closer, and then she saw the shape moving beneath the leaves, pushing them aside as it slid into the clearing.

The golden snake broke cover, tasting the air with his tongue. His head was covered in blood.

Then Euan bounded through the trees, blood-flecked spittle dripping from his jaws. He caught Elaphe between his teeth and shook his head sharply. The snake hissed and writhed in the wolf's grip, twining his large body about the wolf's ribs. Euan let go and turned his attention to the snake's midsection, snapping as Elaphe tried to crush the breath from his body.

The wolf managed to get his jaws around the snake's tail. Blood spurted from between his teeth, and Elaphe released his hold. The wolf jerked his head and sent the snake flying through the air. He landed in an untidy pile close to Siobhan's hiding place.

The snake writhed and threw itself upright just as the wolf ran over and tried to grab him again. Elaphe reared up and then struck straight down, sinking his fangs into the wolf's hindquarters. Euan howled in pain, snapping at the snake's head. But Elaphe's scales protected him from the worst of the wolf's bites. He let go of the wolf, venom dripping from his fangs. Euan backed up, snarling. The snake coiled himself tight, ready to strike. There was a pause, then both creatures launched themselves through the air at the same time . . .

And Conal appeared from out of the trees and stabbed his iron sword straight into Elaphe's underbelly.

Siobhan screamed in horror and ran out from behind the tree. The snake sailed through the air, changing back into the form of Elaphe. He landed heavily on his back and lay still. Siobhan ran over to him, oblivious of everything else.

"Elaphe!" she sobbed. "Elaphe."

She looked at the wound. It was a gaping hole directly over his heart. Blood fell in heavy rivulets into the leaves. She turned her hatred to Conal, who was standing five paces away, watching impassively.

"How could you? How could you do that? He cared about you. He cared for your people! You've killed him!"

Conal blinked, his eyes shifting to look at Euan, who was limping toward them in his natural shape, a satisfied smile on his face. His wounds were terrible to look at. Deep gashes on his ribs and his legs, blood welling from the deep cuts. Siobhan could see the flash of bone through the worst of them. Euan stopped an arm's length from Elaphe, staring down at him dispassionately.

Elaphe coughed. Siobhan could hear the blood rattling in his throat.

"I win," said Euan weakly. "You fought a good fight, old man, but youth will always triumph."

Elaphe coughed again. His chest heaved painfully, and Siobhan realized with amazement that he was laughing.

Euan frowned. "What's so funny?"

"The . . . the only thing youth triumphs . . . triumphs at is *arrogance*."

"Arrogance?" Euan fought to control his anger, then apparently decided it wasn't worth the effort anymore. He turned to Conal. "Kill her," he said, nodding to Siobhan. "Cut her head off."

Elaphe tried to sit up. "No. You . . . you—"

Siobhan looked up at Conal. His gray eyes stared into hers, unblinking. He didn't move. Siobhan saw his hand trembling on his sword, his knuckles white against the skin.

Euan frowned at the Scotsman. "Didn't you hear? I said kill her."

Conal still didn't move. Euan turned to face him fully. "Are you disobeying me? *Kill her!*"

Conal forced his eyes away from Siobhan and locked gazes with Euan. There was a pause, and then Conal spoke, the word sounding like it was being forced from his body with great difficulty. "No," he whispered between clenched teeth.

Euan took a step back, staring at Conal in amazement. "You dare to defy me? You cannot. You are my slave. You are compelled to do my bidding."

Elaphe wheezed again. "Looks like you're not as strong as you thought you were, Euan."

Euan roared with anger and lunged forward, grabbing hold of Conal's sword. His roar turned to a scream of pain as his skin touched the iron, but he didn't let go. Instead, he raised the sword high in the air and brought it down, aiming for Siobhan's head. She didn't even have time to react, so quickly did he move.

She closed her eyes, waiting for the killing blow. But all she heard was a grunt of pain. She opened her eyes to see Conal and Euan wrestling on the ground, the sword thrown a dozen paces away. They traded ferocious blows, Conal seemingly free of whatever curse Leanan had placed him under.

"Siobhan," whispered Elaphe.

Siobhan turned her attention to the Fey.

"You were right. I apologize," Elaphe said. "Euan needs . . . needs to be stopped. It is up to you."

"Shh," said Siobhan through her tears. "You'll be fine. You'll see. You can speak to the others. You can sort this out, Elaphe, I know you can."

Elaphe smiled. "I will be dead soon," he replied. "But I can do one last thing before I go."

Siobhan shook her head, tears flowing freely down her face. "Don't talk like that."

"Listen to me. Euan cannot . . . cannot get the stones. It will be the end of all our lives if he controls Hallowmere." He put his hand to his mouth and coughed. When he brought his hand away again, he held a rathstone. It was covered in his blood.

Siobhan reached out a trembling hand and took the stone. There was a shout of outrage behind her. Siobhan turned to see Euan staring directly at her. He fought free of Conal and started moving in Siobhan's direction, but Conal threw himself at the Fey Prince, and they tumbled to the ground. Euan kicked Conal in the face, turning around and crawling toward her once again. Conal rolled over and grabbed hold of his foot.

Euan turned, catching sight of the iron sword off to his side. He dived toward it and caught it up in his fingers, screaming his fury and agony. He shook free from Conal and pushed himself to his feet, using the sword as a crutch. Conal rose and grabbed hold of Euan's arm, but Euan yanked free and then spun around, swinging the sword in an arc that would have killed Conal in an instant.

Except the blade didn't strike.

Siobhan held her hand outstretched, sending the tendrils of her magic twining around the blade, freezing it in midair.

"I won't let you, Euan. You've hurt enough people."

Euan let go of the sword and let it drop to the ground. Conal looked gratefully at Siobhan and sank painfully to the grass.

Euan raised a badly burned hand and pointed at her. Siobhan could see glimpses of bone through the weeping blisters. He breathed heavily, raising a shaking finger to point at the rathstone.

"That . . . that belongs to me," he said hoarsely. "And I will have what is rightfully mine."

Siobhan heard a terrific crash from the forest beyond the glade. Voices shouted, then others answered from close by. They were shouting Elaphe's name. Siobhan thought she Iamblicus' voice among them, and she remembered seeing him back at the opening of Hallowmere. Elaphe must have invited him to witness the event.

"He's here!" she screamed as loudly as she could. "Elaphe is here! He is wounded."

Euan snarled in rage and ran toward them, falling onto Elaphe and wrapping his bloodied hands around his neck. But the next instant there was a silent explosion of color and Elaphe was thrown back through the air, smacking up against a tree. Siobhan winced and shielded her eyes, watching as Elaphe disappeared in the burst of light. Something shot up into the sky, and she saw that it was the rathstones, all of them flying away through the air, far away from Euan or his followers.

She looked down again and saw Elaphe smiling grimly up at the sky.

"There!" he shouted. He opened his mouth to continue, but fell into a fit of coughing. He struggled to gain control, then raised his voice once again. "I hope you are satisfied Euan! Hallowmere is lost forever, closed to our kind from this point on. The rathstones are scattered through time, hidden away where you will never find them."

He looked into Siobhan's tear-filled eyes. His face twisted briefly with pain, but then he did something that surprised Siobhan.

He winked.

"That's not exactly true," he whispered. "Iamblicus will gather them up and hide them. But we don't have to tell Euan that." He reached up and laid a hand on her shoulder. "Go now. Go to where you are needed the most."

Siobhan started to respond, but at that moment she heard a great rushing in her ears, and her vision started to fade, her surroundings seeping free of color. It was difficult for her to focus, but she saw Iamblicus rush into the clearing. He fell to his kness beside Elaphe, and Siobhan saw the wounded Fey whispering to the priest.

Euan pushed himself to his feet and pointed at Siobhan. "I curse you!" he shouted. "Your family will be plagued with the Sight for untold generations. It will drive you all mad. You will wake up at night trembling in fear of me. Because I will get you, girl. I will hunt you down until the end of days."

As soon as Euan said these words, Siobhan felt something in her mind snap, and the Sight burst out of the hole and attacked her. It was the only way to describe it. It tried to overwhelm her mind, drive her to the depths of madness, destroy her sanity with its power. It was what she had always felt growing up, that the Sight was a separate presence in her mind that was trying to drive her out of her own head. Somehow, Euan's words had released it back to its former state.

But Siobhan was stronger now. No longer was she the whimpering little girl. No longer would she curl up in a ball and try to hide from the world. No.

"NO!" she screamed.

She grabbed hold of the Sight with her mind. Siobhan had once seen a baby octopus wrap its tentacles around a fisherman's arms and refuse to let go. It took the man a long time, but eventually, after much pulling and yanking, the tentacles gave, one after the other.

That was what it felt like to Siobhan. She was pulling the tendrils back, stopping them from wrapping around her mind, from suffocating her with their power.

She managed to gather them all up, but this time, instead of trying to push them back into the hole, she embraced them, pulled them into her heart, her soul. She made the tendrils—the Sight—hers.

She made them part of who she was, and no one would be able to control that but her.

287

She owned her power.

Time had slowed to a crawl around her. The Hallowed Fey started toward Euan, but he crouched onto all fours, twisting, changing into the wolf, before running away into the woods.

The world faded to blackness. The pain in Siobhan's heart was like a fiery red wound that she knew would hurt forever.

Sleep would be no relief from the dreams of death.

Siobhan opened her eyes to bright sunlight. She squinted, the harsh white light of afternoon blinding her. The heat was intense, unnatural in the almost-winter. Perhaps it was a result of the magical battle that had just taken place—she wasn't sure. It bled everything of moisture, sucked her breath from her throat as she tried to breathe.

Siobhan reached up to her face, felt the dampness of her tears drying in the heat. Conal, looking all right but probably forever changed, sat nearby being taken care of by Hallowed Fey that Siobhan didn't recognize. Iamblicus and Father Josephus stood talking animatedly with the King and Queen. Siobhan sat up and opened her clenched fist. The rathstone sat there, Elaphe's blood dark on its surface.

She had succeeded.

But at what cost?

AFTERWORD

Writing a book set in a different time period is always going to be a tough job. And this one was made even more difficult because there didn't seem to be much information to be found on 13th century Scotland. And true as true can be, once I'd finished the book and Stacy was editing it, she came across this great resource detailing the area surrounding Loch Tay. If you are at all interested in the area in which Oracle of the Morrigan takes place, then there are some wonderful maps here:

http://www.nls.uk/pont/specialist/pont18.html

ACKNOWLEDGEMENTS

First off thanks to Tiffany and Stacy, the former for creating such a great world to play in, and the latter for allowing me to join the gang. And secondly, to Caroline, for understanding my moods when things weren't going well, and for offering suggestions that invariably fixed whatever was bothering me in the first place.

—Paul Crilley

Mara's mysterious past comes back to haunt her!

The
Marsh King's
Daughter

*J*N ORDER TO FIND THE RATHSTONE SHE SEEKS, MARA RELIVES her early years in New Orleans training in dark magic with the voodoo queen Marie Laveau—and rediscovers a great mistake she made during that time.

To right this wrong, Mara must travel deep into a rath that resembles ancient Egypt, where her father is worshipped as a god. Will the family reunion be joyful? And will Mara be able to reverse her mistake? The key to Hallowmere could be Mara's—but only if she finds it before her father raises an ancient spirit that could defeat the Council for good.

Want to find out what it's REALLY like to live life with a bunch of suckers?

Sucks to Be Me:

The All—True Confessions of Mina Hamilton, Teen Vampire (Maybe)

Mina Hamilton's parents want her dead. Or, actually, undead. They're vampires, and like it or not, Mina must decide whether to become a vampire herself by her birthday—only a few months away. How's a girl supposed to find the perfect prom date when her mom and dad are breathing down her neck—literally?

Fall 2008